Bewitched

"Do you have any idea who would want to do something like this to your housekeeper, Colonel Driver?"

The officer shook his head. "I don't even know what happened to her, Inspector. All I know is there is a helluva lot of blood all over the first floor bathroom. I don't even know how she died."

The young Lieutenant swallowed hard. "Your housekeeper is dead, Colonel Driver, because someone carved her heart out. And I think it's safe to say that what we're dealing with here is not a typical homicide, Colonel, not by a long shot. What we've got here is something unusual, real unusual."

R. KARL LARGENT

THE WITCH OF SIXKILL

LEISURE BOOKS   NEW YORK CITY

A LEISURE BOOK ®

September 1990

Published by

Dorchester Publishing Co., Inc.
276 Fifth Avenue
New York, NY 10001

Printed in the United States of America.

THE WITCH OF SIXKILL

Now I push back visions, move ahead,
Feet slip on leaves red and brown, bled out,
I carry an armful of late pink roses
to hide the raw earth of my wounds.
There is an end to it, an answer:
One of us must die.

Pat Mills
"The Answer"

Prologue

It was a treacherous stretch of road, potholed and corrugated, tortured by too many Newfoundland winters. It seemed to go on forever, past craggy outcroppings, sheer drop-offs into swirling jetties and dirty plowed mounds of crusted snow. In most places it appeared as though it would be impossible to pass another car even if he encountered one. For the record, he hadn't. As he thought about it, he realized that he hadn't seen any other signs of life since he left the outskirts of Two Ports—at least not anything that walked upright. Who counts trees?

The windshield wipers were working overtime. Big, exquisitely contoured flakes were wet and wind driven. Even though his rear window was covered and the window on the passenger side was almost as bad, it was no problem keeping the old Roadmaster on the road. Big as a tank and twice as heavy, it settled nicely into the ruts that were already hidden by the present snowfall.

He passed a sign. It was a good thing he did, because he needed some reassurance. "Sixkill - 6 Miles."

Son of a bitch! This whole affair was turning out to be a lot more than he had bargained for. Goldstein was probably sitting back in the BOQ laughing. "Look, Charlie, it ain't no big deal. You take Route 10 down to Windless Bay and keep your eyes peeled. About two miles out of town you'll see a road. There'll be a sign for Sixkill. It's an old fishing village, can't be more than thirty or thirty-five people livin' in that Godforsaken dump. But, old buddy, that's where you gotta go to find her."

Now he wondered what else Goldstein hadn't told him. That was always what concerned him, what people didn't tell him. "She's good, Charlie, really good. Believe me, you ain't seen anything like it. She'll dazzle ya. But I gotta warn ya, the lady is one expensive broad."

Charles Everett Frazier reached down and patted his pocket; the wallet was there. There were eight, crisp, new one hundred dollar bills, carefully folded and securely wedged in the tiny compartment behind his I.D. Eight hundred big green ones, Charlie figured, ought to be enough to handle just about anything the lady could conjure up.

Damn that Goldstein; he didn't warn him that the road switched back on itself several times, and he didn't tell him about the incline, either. The old Buick was equal to the task so far, but he had to hope the storm didn't get any worse.

There was a sudden gust of wind. The snow swirled and twisted on the hood of his car, forcing him to drop the lumbering beast down a gear. Pine branches staggered dramatically under the weight of the wet snow, bending to the ground; even the trees had given up. The storm's onslaught was relentless. Charlie grunted and slumped further down in his seat; the band of visibility through the foggy windshield was narrowing rapidly. The day was getting grayer. It was getting harder to tell the difference between earth and sky.

Now he had no choice. The party was tomorrow night, and the next day it was the big silver MATS bird back to the good old States—the States and the separation from active duty. The final and bitter farewell to the Air Force and six years of chicken shit and ugly memories.

Charlie Frazier blinked twice, rubbed his eyes, then finally slowed down. The man was standing right in the middle of the road.

He brought the car to a sliding halt, rolled down the window and squinted into the swirling flakes. "Got a problem?"

The old man stared back at him, his face all but concealed by a heavy slate-gray wool stocking cap pulled down to the ridge of his prominent brow and the thick mackinaw collar turned up to protect him from the wind.

"Which way you going?" Charlie's words were muffled by the snow and howling wind.

The man hesitated, then pointed in the same direction Charlie was headed.

"Well, old man, you're in luck. I'm going on into Sixkill. Crawl in; I'll give you a lift."

The old man hesitated. Finally, halting, half-articulated words began to worm their way out from behind the pulled up collar. "Don't wanta' be troublin' ya none."

Charles Everett Frazier, or Charlie, as he was known to most, didn't say it, but he had already gone to all the trouble he intended to for the old man. If there had been any doubt in his mind about being able to get the Buick rolling again, he wouldn't have stopped in the first place.

"Climb in before we get snowbound," he said impatiently.

The old man labored through the snow and

around the front of the car, working his way slowly back to the door on the passenger's side. To Charlie's way of thinking, the whole process confirmed just how stiff and immobile a man could get and still get around. Finally, the man opened the door, sagged heavily on the seat beside him, laboriously pulled the door shut and began rubbing his gloved hands together to fend off the cold.

"I know it's none of my business, old timer, but what the hell are you doing out here in the middle of this Godforsaken chunk of nowhere in weather like this?"

The old man didn't answer. Instead, he collapsed into a racking series of coughs and hacking sounds that compelled Frazier to look away, wishing he hadn't stopped in the first place. There was no telling what kind of germs the old bastard was carrying. One thing Charlie Frazier didn't need was a rotation back to the States only to get himself confined to a sick bay. When the coughing fit had finally passed, Charlie looked his passenger over. The old man was filthy, and a stale, musty, unpleasant aroma had already begun to permeate the interior of the car.

"It had ta be," the old man rasped. "It be Tuesday. Tuesday be payday."

"Nobody needs money bad enough to haul the old body out in weather like this," Frazier assessed.

The passenger turned slowly in his seat and looked at him. For the first time, Charlie got a real good look at the haunted emptiness in the man's hollow, lifeless eyes, the likes of which Charlie had never seen before, almost totally void of color. It sent a momentary chill racing down his back, an altogether different kind of chill than the one induced by the icy world outside.

Anxious now to get on with it, Charlie gunned the big beast and felt the rear end drift slightly to one side. But, just like Charlie figured it would, it slowly began to inch its way forward, plowing a new set of furrows in the drifted, narrow road.

To Charlie's surprise, he discovered that the old man wasn't a talker. He had figured he would be. Instead, he rode in silence until they reached the outskirts of the tiny village. Only then did he inquire why Charlie was out on such a foul day.

The truth was, Charlie Frazier felt a little foolish, and he knew he would feel even more so if he admitted out loud his real purpose for being out on a day like this. Still, he figured, what the hell, he knew he would never see the old man again, and it was a whole lot easier to be honest with the old-timer than to go to the trouble of making something up. Admissions to complete strangers, in Charlie Frazier's book, were a whole lot easier than admitting something to someone you knew. All too often those were the things that came back to haunt a man.

"Ever hear of the lady they call the Witch of Sixkill?" He asked the question through a half-forced grin. It sounded even more ridiculous than he thought it would.

His passenger nodded. "Jubell," he whispered and immediately began coughing again.

Frazier waited for the spasm to pass. He was hoping for more.

"Then there really is someone called Jubell, the Witch of Sixkill? I thought maybe some of my buddies back at the base might be putting me on." He had a clear mental picture of a hysterical Goldstein, sprawled across his bunk laughing uncontrollably.

"There be a woman called Jubell," the old man acknowledged.

Before Frazier could launch another question, the old man leaned forward apprehensively, staring intently through the narrow unfrosted band at the bottom of the windshield. He was suddenly animated, pointing excitedly to a delapidated old house, sheltered from the raw cold by waist high drifts of snow and heavily coated pine boughs.

"I be gettin' out here."

Frazier eased to a stop and his ancient passenger laboriously hauled his twisted body out of the car and steadied himself in the snow. He had again turned to Frazier, giving the officer a chance to study his gaunt, melancholy face. It was obvious there was more the man wanted to say, but all he managed was a raspy, "You'll find her place at the end of the street."

Frazier watched the heavy car door slam shut, at which point he realized just how alone he was.

Charles Everett Frazier had always considered himself to be a reasonably articulate man, but the village of Sixkill betrayed his inadequacy. It was old, decrepit, weather-beaten, forlorn, isolated and even the word "scary" came to mind. He inched the Buick down the street until he found the last house. In this most isolated of places, the house somehow managed to be even more isolated than the rest.

A weathered, whitewashed and battened affair with a widow's watch, it was a full three stories. It was perched high on an incline so that it held domain over a vast and brooding expanse of the turbulent Atlantic.

Still, there was something else about it. Despite its solitary and ominous location, bereft of trees and surrounded by snow and ice-covered boulders, it managed somehow to appear more inviting than the sorry assortment of structures that seemed to cower in its presence.

Frazier studied the house for a moment and shut the engine off. What the hell, he had come this far. It would be as foolhardy to turn back now as it was to undertake the whole venture in the first place. He took a deep breath, opened his door and stepped out into the icy blast of the storm.

A small sign, carefully lettered in classic Olde English script on a weathered and ice-covered board, was affixed to the gate of the broken picket fence. It said simply, "JUBELL CARON—CONSULTATIONS." In light of what Goldstein had told him about the lady's powers, he had expected something a little more melodramatic. A thin, slightly sardonic smile played with the corners of his mouth.

His second surprise was the sidewalk. Despite the intensity of the snowstorm, the ribbon of flagstones leading up to the great porch was swept clean. He pulled his collar up, braced himself, walked up on the porch and knocked.

In his mind, and again considering what he had been told by the two people who actually purported to have contracted business with the woman, Charlie Frazier was prepared for just about anything—anything, that is, except for what occurred next.

The door was opened by a creature of stunning beauty. She was, Frazier quickly decided, the most beautiful woman he had ever seen.

"I'm . . . I'm Charles Everett Frazier," he blurted, still thrown slightly off balance by the vision that confronted him. "I . . . I have an appointment with Miss Caron."

The woman's enticingly sensuous, crimson-colored lips parted in an inviting smile. "I know who you are, Captain Frazier. I am Jubell Caron, and it's not Miss. It's Mrs. I am a widow."

Without even realizing it, Charlie had crossed over the threshold into the foyer. To his surprise, there were no lights in the room, just candles. The surrounding shadows danced in the glow of a dozen or more flickering flames.

"You seem somewhat taken aback, Captain. A little short of breath maybe. Is something wrong?"

Charlie Frazier, like most young men, had worked long and hard at developing the cherished image of "cool under fire," but his long practiced aplomb had deserted him. His senses were reeling. "You . . . you aren't quite what I expected," he stammered. He was suddenly feeling even more foolish than he had earlier with the old man.

The woman had a musical laugh, an enchanting, inviting sound that happily searched out the darkened corners and instantly filled the room. "Come, come, Captain, don't tell me you were expecting the old snaggle-toothed stereotype from children's books."

Frazier's face was folded in a foolish open-mouthed grin. "I guess I'd better confess I was," he admitted.

The Caron woman's assessment was coolly dispassionate. He had the feeling that her intense gray-green eyes could see through him, into his mind and perhaps even into his very soul. Finally, she turned gracefully and led him into the parlor.

In every sense of the word, it was a world of mind-boggling dimension. It had been heavily draped to shut out the accompanying chill of storms such as the one that raged outside even now. It was, for Charlie, like entering another world. The furniture was exquisite—richly carved mahoganies, accentuated with beaded and brocaded cushions and pillows, as well as velvets and silks and fabrics he couldn't identify. She had drawn him into a world of brooding yet compelling colors. At the far side of the room was a massive, rough stone fireplace. In it, a crackling fire charmed the darkness.

"Well, Captain," she invited, "won't you have a seat?"

Frazier half-stumbled into the first available chair, a high-backed, overstuffed affair with enormous wings. He sank into it, suddenly feeling even more foolish then than he had at any time since he had begun his little adventure.

Jubell Caron continued to appraise him with a look that he would have been tempted to describe as passing amusement. He was uncomfortable with the protracted silence, but it didn't seem to be affecting her one way or the other. He cleared his throat nervously.

"I hardly know where to begin."

The Caron woman continued to smile. She had a lovely smile, radiant and sensuous. It was the most beguiling smile Charlie Frazier had ever encountered. She sat down, leaned gracefully back on the plush velvet love seat and picked up a small bell. The sound it emitted was barely perceptible, but almost instantly a tall angular man of advanced years emerged from the room's shadows. He bowed stiffly. Despite his presence, she kept her eyes fixed on the young officer. Finally, almost as if she were reluctant to do so, she glanced up at the old man.

"We have a guest, Raymond. This is Captain Frazier. Captain Frazier would like a perfect Manhattan. Am I correct, Captain?"

Charlie looked at the woman in amazement. He was tempted to ask the inevitable, but she cut him off with a wave of her hand. "A mere parlor trick, Captain, but it serves to make a point."

Raymond, apprised of their needs, moved in his peculiar halting fashion from the room. Despite the difficulty with which he moved, it was disconcertingly quiet.

"You've driven all this way, Captain, because you heard about the Witch of Sixkill. Am I correct?" While she talked, she took out a jeweled cigarette case, removed a long, pastel cigarette, slipped it into an onyx holder and lit it. As she exhaled she began speaking again. "And you have need of something, something you believe the Witch of Sixkill can provide. Am I correct once again, Captain?"

Before Charlie could answer, Raymond returned with the drinks. The old man served them and slipped unobtrusively back into the shadowy world from which she had summoned him. Frazier bolted his drink in two gulps. The Caron woman picked up the delicate rose stemmed glass of claret, savored the bouquet and sipped it. She was waiting for his response.

"I know a man," he began slowly, "by the name of Goldstein. He told me about you."

"You mean about my services?"

Frazier nodded. He was still uncomfortable. More accurately, he was beginning to feel slightly desperate. He was anxious to get the whole ludicrous thing over with. "My friend told me you might be able to help me."

"And you seek exactly what, Captain?"

Goldstein had coached him. Frazier knew the appropriate response. Even with that, he was having difficulty forcing out his answer. "I seek—revenge."

The woman's exquisite face displayed an intensified radiance. "Excellent, Captain Frazier, excellent! The correct channel to true happiness is the ability to articulate our needs and, of course, to have them fulfilled." She paused long enough to inhale, then extinguish her cigarette. During the process, she was momentarily veiled by a misty cloud of blue gray, sweet-smelling smoke. "The more practical aspects of my service dictate that such needs be fully defined. Let us deal with who and when, Captain Frazier."

The officer fished hurriedly through his pockets until he located the hastily scribbled document containing the four names. "Here are the names of those who have wronged me."

The woman took the piece of paper and refolded it without looking at it. "And what is the nature of their offenses, Captain? Would you care to share that with me?"

Charles Everett Frazier shook his head. "I didn't know I was supposed to," he stammered.

"It is not necessary, Captain Frazier," she said, smiling. "I ask only out of interest. You see, Captain, I find the human condition to be a most curious anomaly. The desire for revenge is a purely human emotion. No other creature harbors so dark a need."

Charlie Frazier, now that he had found the courage to express his desires, was in no mood to dwell on the philosophical aspects of his request. He had come all this distance to buy a service, a service that he was told only the Witch of Sixkill could provide. He was a practical man; now he was interested in the nuts and bolts of the plan. Now he wanted to know how and when she would do it.

Finally, the Caron woman unfolded the piece of paper and looked at it. She studied it momentarily and laid it on the table beside her. "Your desires will be tended to," she assured him.

"When?" he blurted.

"You will know," she said calmly.

"How?"

The woman dismissed his question with a subtle wave of her hand.

"Look, you haven't told me how much this is going to cost me." The dam had broken; the matter was out in the open. They were discussing it now just like any business transaction. He had asked for something, and she had agreed to supply it. Despite the ethereal aspects of his request, there were the practical aspects of the thing to deal with. "How do I know you will do what you say you will do?"

There was a diminishing of her radiant smile. Charlie wondered if he had offended her with his bluntness.

"Mark this date, Captain Frazier," Jubell Caron instructed him. "One year from this date, you will return to this house in Sixkill. Then you will know."

"Can't," he interrupted. "The day after tomorrow I'm rotating back to the States. And when I do, I'm gonna do my damndest to forget I ever spent two years of my life in this Godforsaken place."

The woman smiled knowingly. "You will return, Captain Frazier—it is part of our contract—and you will be happy to do so. You see, then and only then will you be able to judge how well I have served you."

Before Frazier could react to her insistence, she stood up and walked slowly across the room until she was standing directly in front of him. Slowly, she reached out her hand to him.

Her unexpected embrace was hungry and passionate. It was less a union than a devouring.

Their lovemaking was frenzied, void of tenderness, a communion between disciples of darker beings. When it was over, he slept at her side like a cowering dog, fearing an expression of her displeasure.

In the waning hours of the day, she awakened him. "You must go now."

Frazier dressed in the darkness.

The once crackling fire had been reduced to a few smoldering, near lifeless embers of faded orange.

"When will I see you again?" he asked.

She touched her fingers to his lips. "We have a destiny, Captain Frazier . . . remember?"

Without knowing how, he found himself back out in the cold, standing beside the old Buick. To his amazement, the lumbering vehicle had been turned around and was headed back down the village's single street. The snow had stopped and a cold, empty moon flooded the landscape with an eerie yellow-gray light. In the distance he could hear the relentless waves of the north Atlantic crashing against the icebound shore of the nearby coastline.

Slowly a smile encompassed Charlie Frazier's handsome face as he crawled into his car. He put the key in the ignition and the frigid metal beast roared to life without hesitation. As he put it in gear, he realized how good he felt. He turned on the lights, glanced down and noticed something on the seat beside him. It was a cardboard box—a box containing four glass jars.

For Charlie Frazier, it was one of those good news-bad news situations. The good news was obvious; two years of tolerating Newfoundland were behind him. At 0700 Zulu the following morning, MATS flight 656, the regularly scheduled Friday morning NEAC personnel flight to Westover, would be carrying him and two stuffed flight bags back to good old American soil. Seventy-two hours later he would be a civilian again, packing around a little green card that proclaimed him to be an inactive reservist.

The bad news was that there was still the ritualistic ordeal of the Newfie "last night in Saint Johns" to endure. To Charlie Frazier, that meant sitting through a plethora of painfully insincere speeches, the obligatory rounds of final toasts, and one last dance with Cappy Salem. If there was a bright spot in all of this, it was simply knowing that within a matter of hours, he would begin to dispose of the four jars he had carefully positioned on the front seat of his car when he left Sixkill.

He had committed the instructions to memory.

In his room at the BOQ the previous evening, after returning from his encounter with the Caron woman, Frazier had opened the unassuming box. He had studied the cloudy contents of the four jars and speculated far into the night as to just what might be the outcome of his contract with his lover.

Now, he laughed. What if he told Goldstein that he had made love to the so-called Witch of Sixkill? What would Goldstein say? But, even though he wasn't sure how he knew, he did know that it was something he could never tell.

His attention returned to the four glass containers. All in all, they were not very different from the ones he remembered his mother using for her annual canning ritual when he was a boy, except these were perhaps a bit larger. Each was sealed, and in each case the contents of the jars were impossible to determine. Whatever the individual jars contained, the milky gray-green liquid that filled the jars to the brim concealed the identity of the contents.

Also in the box, he had discovered a carefully penned set of instructions about the use of the contents. The rules for the handling of the various jars were spelled out in a series of terse and cryptic statements. He repeated them now, much as a schoolboy repeats important facts and figures before a test.

"DO NOT OPEN THE JARS PRIOR TO PRESENTATION. AN APPROPRIATE CHOICE HAS BEEN MADE FOR EACH OF THE FOUR NAMES ON YOUR LIST. YOU WILL AUTOMATICALLY SELECT THE RIGHT GIFT FOR EACH OF THEM. DO NOT DEVIATE FROM THE PSYCHIC COMMUNICATION. DO NOT FORGET YOUR COMMITMENT TO RETURN PRECISELY ONE YEAR FROM THE DATE OF OUR PACT."

The last instruction made Charlie laugh. But not much more than the entire Sixkill lark. After all, that's what it was—a lark. If it worked, great, and even if it didn't, the whole thing had been one hell of an adventure, a thoroughly unique experience. And to top it all off, the episode between the sheets with the enchanting Witch had been an unexpected bonus.

Charlie Frazier, in his two years in Newfoundland, could boast of quite a few conquests, but Jubell Caron, the so-called Witch of Sixkill, was the prize of the lot. He could think of a whole lot of "with it" ladies back in the States who could learn something from his raven-haired one night stand.

His thoughts shifted from the episode in Sixkill back to the agenda for his last evening in Newfoundland. For an officer with just a few hours to go before his long-awaited rotation, Charlie Frazier still had a number of loose ends to attend to.

First, there was the matter of Cappy. Until the encounter with the Caron woman, she had been the best over the past two years. Cappy Salem, the girl from Cornerbrook, had big tits, a propensity to spread her legs, and was about as gullible as they come. Charlie laughed. The dim-witted little bitch actually believed he was taking her back to the States with him, actually believed he was going to marry her, actually believed he had made and paid for her reservations on the same MATS flight that was carrying him far away from this stifling place.

Charlie's symmetrically handsome face sobered as his thoughts kaleidoscoped to the night he decided to give Cappy Salem a gift she would never forget. Driver had sent him on a 14-day swing through the command's Arctic outposts where he was expected to introduce a new synoptic code. He had done it. In fact, he accomplished the task with a day to spare. The combination of good weather and good luck had put him back in Torbay a day early. Charlie jumped in his car and headed straight for Cappy's place to surprise her, hoping she'd be there. It was Charlie who got the surprise. Cappy was there, all right, but she wasn't waiting for him. Cappy had a young Lieutenant from Command Staff locked between her legs and Charlie caught them in the act. It turned out to be the longest night of Charlie Frazier's life. Sleep didn't come until the early hours of the morning, and when he awoke, he was no longer naive. Something had happened. During the fitful hours of unrewarding sleep, he had undergone a metamorphosis. Hurt had been transformed into bitterness, innocence became stupidity, and getting even became a commitment.

Sure they made up. Sure they slept together again, and there were a lot of others. Charlie changed. Charlie Frazier no longer loved Cappy Salem—he used her. And tonight, when she was expecting something quite different, Cappy Salem was going to get a stupid glass jar full of a cloudy, foul-looking liquid containing he knew not what, and in the process she would be told that he had no intention of marrying her, taking her stateside, or ever seeing her again. If that wasn't revenge, what was?

With that thought, Charlie Frazier felt good. He laid out a fresh set of blues, peeled down to his shorts and walked down the hall of the BOQ to the latrine for a shower. By the time he pulled the curtain, the tiny metal cubicle was choking with steam. The water cascaded down on him and he felt the warmth spread across his knotted shoulders.

There his thoughts turned to Colonel Harry Preston Driver, a man he had once revered, a man once known as one of the Air Force's most respected arctic specialists, and the main reason why Charlie had put in for the Pepperell assignment in the first place. Driver had been the chance of a meteorological lifetime, a chance to work for the master.

Now it was Driver, the son of a bitch, the man who had twice denied him the opportunity to go before the promotion board. Driver, the moralist, had condemned Frazier for his behavior. Driver, the pompous ass, had actually scribbled across his promotion appeal, "Denied because of licentious behavior unbecoming an officer and a gentleman."

Driver had a gift coming if anyone did, and tonight he was going to get one.

Frazier crawled out of the shower, toweled off and walked briskly back up the hall to his room. He walked over to the closet and stared at the box containing the four jars. One for Cappy. One for Colonel Driver. One for Ruthie. And last, but not least, one for his brother, wherever the simpering bastard was hiding these days.

He checked the time—7:10. And since the Witch had assured him that he would arbitrarily know which jar to give which person, Frazier's work was almost done. He rummaged through the few remaining items in his closet until he found the oversized canvas bag his mother had given him, wrapped two of the jars in newspapers and carefully packed them for the journey to the Crystal Club.

After he finished dressing, he went briskly down the back stairs of the BOQ, brushed the residue of the late afternoon snow squall off his car and drove off. The journey on slippery streets would take all of ten or so minutes. It would give him an opportunity to think about the two remaining jars.

One, of course, was for Ruthie. These days he seldom said her name without tagging on the epithet, "that two-timing bitch." His thoughts dwelled for a moment on the then trim young blonde who had married him just three short months after his graduation from officer candidate school. Ruthie hadn't waited long to deal out her own special brand of misery. In the twelfth month of his first tour of arctic duty, she informed him of the separation, and by the time he returned to the States, she had the divorce in her hot little hands. Now she was remarried, and Charlie Frazier had gone to a lot of trouble to locate her. But persistence paid off, and Ruthie, bless her little black cheating heart, was entitled to a gift from Sixkill. Before he stepped on the plane tomorrow morning, the postal service would be doing its best to see that she got it.

That left one.

An ugly, sick smile began to play with the corners of Charlie Frazier's mouth.

Revenge was going to be doubly sweet.

The last one could only be for good old Theodore. He hoped that the Sixkill woman was right, that no matter how he selected the jars, each would be appropriate. Theodore deserved something very, very special.

He ended up parking on a deserted side street almost two blocks from the club. He locked his car, turned up his collar and began trudging through the snow. As he walked through the front door of the Crystal Club, he made his selections. He knew which ones they would get.

PART ONE

Chapter One

It was a sharp, irritating, tinny sound.

Harry Driver rolled over, snaked his hand up and out of the protective cocoon of his covers and slapped at the interloper. The defenseless alarm clock clattered off the nightstand and rattled to the floor. The collision was muffled by the deep pile carpet.

Within a matter of seconds he had blissfully returned to the shadowy world of half-sleep, shutting out for the moment the inevitability of another day.

"Harry." The sound of his name wormed its way up the stairs, down the hall and into his darkened room.

Harry sighed, pushed the covers down from

his face and cocked one eye open. The undeniable chill presaged a rainy, depressing, dismal February morning. The stale taste of the club's bourbon crawled up from somewhere deep inside him and flooded his dry mouth. Ugly reality!

"Harry." This time the voice was a little firmer, but still void of stridency. Flora was never strident.

"I'm up," he grumbled, knowing she couldn't hear him, yet hoping he wouldn't have to repeat himself. Harry hated to repeat himself. Harry mumbled, and he knew it. Still, it infuriated him that he lived in a world that didn't listen. He had considered having a little badge made that he could wear when he was on duty. A badge that would warn the world, "LISTEN CAREFULLY. I'M ABOUT TO MUMBLE."

The truth of the matter was, he wasn't up. He was still flat on his back in the middle of a big, oversized, empty bed—empty because Janet wasn't there anymore.

How did she put it? How did she say it when she stood there, her face flushed, in a fit of feminine rage? He remembered, only pretending not to remember. He remembered the whole ugly scene verbatim. He remembered where she was, how she was dressed, how she looked and every other painful detail.

"You what?" she had shrieked. It was her

reaction to his decision to decline her father's offer of a position with her father's real estate firm in Chicago. Harry didn't want to sell real estate, in Chicago or anywhere else. Most of all, he didn't want to work for Janet's father.

"And that's only half of it," he had continued sheepishly.

Janet had flopped down on the edge of the bed, face colored with outrage, her usually sensuous mouth stupidly agape, elbow cupped in one hand, cigarette in the other. Her carefully shaped eyebrows were knitted in a tight little knot over her undeniably angry eyes. Harry remembered every little thing about that morning.

"Well," the woman hissed, "suppose you just tell me the other half."

"I've decided to extend my tour of duty here at Pepperell." Though he mumbled it, Janet was listening for a change.

It was the reaction that surprised him. He expected the rage, because Janet was very good at rage. He expected recriminations, because she was very good at that as well. Instead, she stood up, walked slowly to the bedroom door and out of the room. He never saw her again. She filed for the divorce when she got back to Chicago. Harry signed the papers, and it was over.

This was all part of Harry Driver's monotonous ritual of waking up. As surely as he would inhale the musty, dank air of the old house overlooking the bay and would reach out in the middle of the night and realize that the bed was still empty, it was equally inevitable that he would start the new day with the same dreary scenario that reminded him where he had been cast in time and space.

For openers, there was Flora to think about. The woman would be scurrying around the kitchen, doing for him what so many women do for so many men, mindlessly yielding to some irrepressible propensity for nesting. The smell of the maple oatmeal permeated the entire room and wafted up and out of the kitchen on the same wings that carried her voice. She never called him until the oatmeal was done—always coffee, oatmeal and crumb cake. Just one more reason, he suspected, why Flora had never married; she had no imagination. He wondered if she made love the same way. Better yet, he should ask, had she ever made love at all? Maybe today would be the day he would ask her.

Harry clawed his way out to the edge of the big bed, dangled his legs momentarily over the edge and stood up. His head was a little fuzzy and his vision a little blurred from too much bourbon. Another goddamn rotation! Everybody was going back to the States, rotating back to something better. California. Florida. Hell, at this point, even a duty station in some forgotten Texas hellhole sounded good. He could handle that, something down by the gulf. He stood staring in the cloudy old mirror, assessing the damage. "You look like a piece of shit, Harry Driver," he mumbled, "and what's more, you feel and act like one." He filled the basin with steaming water, dropped in his razor and launched into the manly ritual of scraping his face. He had considered growing a beard, but this wasn't the morning to start. Removing the stubble actually accomplished little more than to put on review the pasty white, sallow complexion that resulted from the long, rainy and confining Saint John's winter. He smeared the Barbasol around and began tugging the sharp piece of steel over his face. The welcome smell of coffee greeted him and he looked up. Flora, bless her heart, was standing in the doorway with two steaming cups, one of which she handed to him.

Flora Saint Quentin was a Newfie. Driver had once referred to the woman as a light cruiser of uncertain vintage. She had confided once that she grew up in Doll Bay, a small fishing village south of Torbay, that her brother was a priest, her father was a fisherman and that she never recalled being hugged by her mother. For the most part, she was sober faced and, because of her appetite, possessed of portly dimensions. She smiled sometimes, but not very often, at least when Harry was around. He had hired her when Janet had left.

Flora Saint Quentin filled the bill. As MIC of the Eighth Weather Squadron, headquartered high on a hill overlooking Pepperell Air Force Base, Harry Driver had a multitude of responsibilities, mostly military but sometimes social. Flora filled the void created without a woman in the house. She kept the ramshackle old off-base unit squeaky clean, the pantry filled and happily attended to all those irritating and time-consuming little chores that Harry never seemed to get around to after Janet left. To Harry's way of thinking, "colorless" was a good word to describe Flora Saint Quentin. He thought of her as colorless and intellectually dull. Her hair was a mousy brown, tinged here and there with strands of telltale gray. Her eyes didn't fare much better —muddy, without mirth and too often too sad. Harry suspected that the woman knew all of this, because she tried to hide the entire lackluster mishmash behind large round steel-rimmed glasses that tended to give some character to her otherwise featureless face. On occasion, she smiled. It wasn't much of a smile, but it was all she had. She was bestowing it upon him now as she handed him the coffee.

"You got in late," she observed.

Colonel Harry Driver slurped some of the coffee past his sudsy lips, grimaced, set the cup down on the toilet tank and went back to the task of clearing out the stubble. As usual, unless the woman confronted him with a direct question, he saw no reason to give her anything other than one more in his string of inarticulate mumbles.

This was one of Flora's pink chenille mornings as opposed to light blue, sort of a powdery color that he liked a great deal better than the ridiculous pink. He washed away the residue of the shaving, wiped off his face and rinsed out the bowl.

"Fixed your favorite, Colonel," she informed him. "Maple-flavored oatmeal."

Harry wondered if the dull-witted woman had actually deluded herself into thinking he liked it. "Good," he mumbled, brushing past her and walking back into the dimly lit bedroom. He could hear her waddling back down the hall and descending the stairs.

A man in the military, especially one stationed in Newfoundland in the middle of February, doesn't have many uniform choices. So Harry Driver pulled out his blues, affixed the insignia to his lapel, combed his thinning gray-yellow hair and went downstairs.

Flora was ready for him. The table was set, his cup had been refilled and the morning mail stacked neatly beside his place mat.

"You look quite fine this morning, Colonel," Flora offered. It was her way of trying to make conversation. "Did you have a good time last night?"

Driver assumed the question was based on interest rather than prying; after all, she was his housekeeper, nothing more.

The Colonel grunted and shrugged his shoulders. Now in his sixth year of an extended tour of duty at Pepperell, he had picked up lots of Newfie habits; shrugging his shoulders and grunting were some of them. To the people of the island province, it was an entirely acceptable response.

Harry Preston Driver, like so many of his counterparts in the Air Weather Service, was on a fast track to military career oblivion. After 48 summers, 22 in the Air Force, he had the rank, but he was still pulling second-rate duty assignments in out of the way corners of the world. Now it was Newfoundland, the Northeast Air Weather Command and a stint as Commander of the Eighth Weather Squadron, an assignment so small that he could count his detachments on one hand—three in Greenland, one at Goose Bay and one at Torbay. Only now, with world-wide attention focused on the International Geophysical Year, could he even lay claim to being involved with the area's isolated duty stations.

At the moment, in one way or another, his personnel were scattered throughout the Arctic and his days were filled with report accuracy assessments, personnel evaluations and a whole host of other mundane duties that kept him far from his real interest—climatology.

He was not a tall man, nor did he cut a particularly striking figure in his Air Force blues. He was, in fact, the kind of man, who, despite his rank, fails to command respect. Harry Driver was easily lost in a room of four or more. True, he had achieved the lofty status of "full bird," but even that, it was said, was mostly attributable to the fact that he had two things in his favor. His brother was an under-secretary in the Department of Defense, and Harry had fulfilled the tedious function of "time in grade." Harry Driver, as one of his critics said, was always second, a man of dubious credentials.

"By the way, Colonel," Flora asked absently, "was it you who put this disgusting thing on my kitchen counter?"

Driver shifted his bloodshot eyes from the bowl of oatmeal to the woman. She was holding up the eight-inch-high glass jar that he had brought home the previous evening. It was filled with a cloudy gray, milky substance. The jar contained something else—a brownish-red object, ill-defined and decidedly unappealing. He had no idea what was in it.

In deference to the woman's question, he shrugged. "Yep," he admitted. "Charlie Frazier gave it to me. He's rotating back to the States. He said I needed it."

"What is it?"

Harry gave the woman another shrug and returned to his oatmeal.

Flora managed a delicate wrinkle of the nose, a notable achievement in light of the fact that her prominent probiscus more closely resembled the snout of a small pig than that of a woman. "Whatever it is," she assessed, "it's a vile-lookin' thing."

Driver studied it momentarily from his position across the room and through the light of the dismal gray morning, then went back to sorting through his morning mail. He didn't bother to tell the woman that he had very nearly neglected to bring it home.

Flora continued her intense study of the glass container, turning it first to the right, then to the left. Finally she set it down and pointed at the particularly dark object floating in the center of the nearly opaque fluid. Her pudgy finger traced along the curvature of the glass. "See this thing here? What's this supposed to be?"

Harry ignored the question.

"Know what I think? I think it looks lonely, real lonely." All her life Flora had had a way of droning on about something. This was one of those times, and as usual the person she was talking to wasn't listening.

Driver shoved the mail aside and picked up the morning paper. Soon enough she would get the message; he wasn't in the mood for talking. Frazier probably knew that would happen. He had probably already figured out what Driver would do with the useless object. Furthermore, Frazier was probably already on his plane, winging his way back stateside and released from active duty. But most of all, he knew Frazier would be laughing about the hoax he had perpetrated. And what had Driver gotten out of it? Nothing except a pointless glass jar filled with something tasteless, some kind of joke that Flora Saint Quentin was trying to identify while all Harry Driver really got out of it was a continuing line of whining chatter.

"Hey," Harry finally grunted, "if you don't want the damn thing sitting around your kitchen, throw it away."

The woman shifted her attention from the jar to the old electric clock over the sink. "Glory be, Colonel, are you keepin' track of the time?"

Driver checked his watch, folded up his paper and pushed himself away from the table. The maple-flavored oatmeal had been completely ignored, and because the old woman had chattered on endlessly about the jar, the morning mail suffered the same fate. It was only half-opened and the paper went unread.

For the time being, the jar was forgotten. Flora rustled about the kitchen, restacking the Colonel's mail, refolding the paper, locating his briefcase and searching out his earmuffs and umbrella.

Outside, the dreary and unseasonal winter drizzle partially obscured the piles of dirty wet snow. It was a typically gray, Newfoundland winter montage of nothingness, the kind of day that drags on hour after hour with no promise of anything except more of the same. It was the kind of day Flora liked. Colonel Driver was a kind and considerate man. He would not expect her to be out and about on such a day. As a consequence, as soon as she had completed her chores, she would have much of the day to herself.

"Will you be eatin' in tonight?" she asked.

Driver paused, mentally reviewing the tidy little calendar he kept in the forefront of his thoughts. "Thursday," he mused. "I'll stop by the officer's club for a drink. Somebody told me Major Boykin was in town, so I'll try to catch him. Should be home by nine or so. Leave a light on." And with that, he stepped out into the damp grayness of the Saint John morning.

* * *

It was midmorning before Flora finished her chores. The beds were made, the Colonel's parlor dusted and the now wet, clinging snow was cleared from the back stoop so she could take out the trash. Only the breakfast dishes remained, but before she tackled them, there was the ritual of her midmorning cup of coffee. It had to be done in just that sequence, because only then could the percolator be scoured and her last cup washed and put away and the counter wiped off one final time. Then and only then could she tackle the things that benefited her as well as the Colonel. Today it would be a crumb cake. The Colonel liked crumb cake with his coffee almost as much as he liked the maple-flavored oatmeal. Flora wondered if these little gestures in any way revealed how she really felt about the man.

At precisely 10:30 she turned on the small radio sitting on the window sill over the sink. She dialed in the CBC midmorning concert and carefully poured her final cup of coffee. From where she sat she could see patches of the ice-crusted bay through the foggy mist shrouding the world beyond her sanctuary. At last, she was alone with the haunting strains of a Strauss waltz and her fantasies.

It was the New Year's ball. Elegant ladies in delicious, heavily brocaded gowns twirled gracefully, each escorted by handsome, uniformed military partners. Overhead, a three-tiered crystal chandelier sparkled merrily, reflecting the dancing orange and blue flames of countless candles. The strains of the waltz filled the magnificent, opulent hall.

"You have never looked lovelier," Driver whispered huskily in her dainty ear as she twirled disarmingly close to his handsome face.

Flora demurely averted her eyes, knowing his intentions, anticipating the passionate but inevitable encounter. He was gentle, so considerate, so patient, yet at the same time enticingly demanding as a lover. She was enraptured by the way his fingers traced hungrily over her throbbing breasts, manipulating the countless hooks and buttons, slowly eliminating the constraints between their eventual fulfillment. There would be the sweetness of taking him in, the violent passion, the release, and finally, the warm, glowing feeling that they had reached their zenith together.

Flora closed her dreamy eyes and smiled, humming along with the waltz.

It was only a small noise, but it jolted her back to reality.

Her muddy brown eyes slowly scanned the room. The ceaseless wash of the drizzle against the kitchen window clouded her view of the bay, and she suddenly felt very isolated.

Again there was the noise, a scraping sound, nothing more.

Her eyes darted apprehensively from one corner of the room to another. Was the weight of the wet snow on the roof of the old house shifting? Was it something in another room?

She pushed herself away from the featureless gray Formica expanse, senses now alert. If it happened again, she would capture it. The usually cold and drafty old house suddenly seemed unusually warm. The wind shifted, sending a new series of shudders through the old house. The drizzle had intensified; it had evolved into a steady rain. The clouds, what she could see of them, were lower. Long, low, gray, ominous-looking tentacles hung from a fragmented sky, wrapping the rooftop. Flora had to catch her breath.

The noise again!

Her eyes darted nervously about the room. She had blinked, and she had missed it.

It was here with her now, close by, in the kitchen.

The absence of light caused a chill to race the width of her shawled shoulders. She shuddered involuntarily.

The jar had moved.

Or had it?

She studied the murky container carefully, now convinced. The ugly glass jar with its cloudy gray milky fluids obscuring the contents had moved. It had rotated, ever so slightly. The faded label was now twisted to one side. She got up and walked over to it, momentarily distracted by the scene visible through the window.

The warm rain had eroded the snow's stranglehold on the roof of the old house and sheets of gray-white ice plunged by the window, crashing to the ground. It startled her. A shutter banged as the wind swirled and gusted. Despite the chill, Flora Saint Quentin felt small beads of sweat form under the high buttoned collar of her flowered dress. The droplets traced an erratic pattern down the hollow between her hunched shoulders.

The wet snow mass on the roof shifted again, and she knew it was inching its way toward the precipice. The old house creaked and groaned. This time she would be prepared.

Now a noise came from another part of the house.

Shadows grew longer, and the darkness seemed to intensify.

The noise again. A grating sound. Barely perceptible.

This time she saw it.

The jar had moved—actually moved.

She reached out to touch it, and her hand recoiled. Now it was warm to the touch.

Earlier it had been icy cold.

To her surprise, the liquid seemed to be less cloudy. More was revealed. She picked it up, and when she could control the unexplained tremor in her hands, began to rotate it. She tried to calculate the size of the object within. It was a mass, something with no particular shape, rusty-colored, wrinkled, yet bunched. It appeared to be undulating as if it had a life—not a life, but a purpose.

It frightened her, and she set it down.

Now she was certain that it was moving by itself. She stood staring at it, terrified and transfixed.

A glass container no more than eight inches high and no more than that figure in circumference, containing a clump of something that defied her limited descriptive powers, had seduced her into a trance that made it all but impossible to move.

The monotonous rain continued, etching the splotchy windows with bizarre patterns that created monsters in her mind.

The movement from within the jar had become repetitive, a staccato beat, primitive, flexing, enticing. She could actually see it now.

Flora Saint Quentin's trembling hands again reached out for the container. Grasped in her two hands, it seared the flesh and the stench assailed her. Her hands recoiled and she screamed out. She had accomplished nothing. Gradually the pain subsided.

Its movement was now apparent and obvious. Her hands went for the lid, involuntarily twisting, attempting to loosen it. Now it was throbbing. Sweat trickled down her flushed face. She gave it one final twist and the metal lid clattered to the tabletop.

Somehow she found the strength to inch her way back from it.

The mass had begun to move, inching its way up through the murky liquid toward the top of the glass, spilling out the sickening gray-green, foul-smelling fluids, sending it cascading down the side of the jar, forming a putrid pool around the base of the glass.

It continued to gain strength, evolving into something hideous yet hypnotic, pulsating in a labored, primitive fashion, now emitting a faint chorus of whimpering sounds like a small animal. The sound was rapidly becoming guttural.

Flora Saint Quentin, unable to move, began to cry.

The thing, freed of its glass prison, began to move along the surface. It reminded her of something she had seen on television—a wounded heart. There was a large open lesion, a rupture in the mass itself, a broken heart. The tear in the mass separated it. It moved as if it tried to repair itself.

The woman's hand flew to her mouth as she vainly tried to muffle the scream that seemed to be lodged halfway up her fear-frozen throat.

It was impossible, yet she heard the words clearly.

"Help me."

It was a pleading, abstract sound, a sound without substance.

The terrified woman stared back in disbelief. Uncertain words formed in her dry mouth. "What . . . what are you . . . what do you want?" Her body was trembling uncontrollably and the thunderous pounding of her own hammering heart drowned out the fury of the rain assaulting the windows.

The thing was growing stronger. From tiny, all but invisible lesions, minute droplets of thick rich crimson trickled down and mingled in the gray-green liquid pool.

Flora's head was spinning, a wave of nausea engulfing her. She reeled backward, struggling to regain some semblance of equilibrium. She staggered from the room and into the darkened hall on the verge of hysteria. Finally she broke into a run. The fear wrenched its way up and out of her, spewing out in vile green waves until she collapsed in front of the bathroom basin, choking on her own bile.

Just as she closed her eyes, she saw it.

It was at the door!

Pulsing and demanding, yet somehow pleading. Not moving, yet coming closer and closer.

Then, it was on her.

Tearing! Clawing!

Flora Saint Quentin screamed, a shrill sound, terrifying in its primitive simplicity. A desperate plea reduced to its simplest form, became a purposeless gesture in an empty house.

Chapter Two

The two men worked their way methodically up the hall, each careful not to step in the crusted trail of discoloration that traced its way from the kitchen to the first floor bathroom.

They were about as opposite as two men could be. The older was short and stocky, and even though he had been out of the storm for well over an hour, he was still wearing his damp coat and the collar was still turned up.

"Damn near couldn't make it over here," he groused. "The streets are sheer ice." He flicked the ash of his cigarette in the palm of his hand and jammed it down in the recesses of his coat pocket.

His counterpart was his antithesis, tall and ramrod straight with an obvious military bearing. "My orders on something like this are fairly specific," the younger man acknowledged. "This is off-base housing and the victim looks like a local, but the house is leased to a Colonel Harry Preston Driver. He's the Commander of the Eighth Weather Squadron out at the base." His voice was clipped and militarily precise.

Dawkins knew the young officer couldn't be more than 25, or 27, tops. From the look of the fuzz on his youthful face, he wasn't even sure the young man was old enough to shave. Another damn shavetail, he thought to himself. Wonder where the hell the Air Force keeps coming up with them?

The two men worked their way back into the dimly lit kitchen. Each had a job to do, and they knew they had to tolerate each other.

"Is that him?" Dawkins asked.

The young officer approached the man slumped wearily at the kitchen table. "Colonel Driver, this is Inspector Dawkins of the RCMP's special investigation unit." There was the slightest tinge of trepidation in his voice. Whatever the charges, Driver was a senior officer.

Dawkins nodded nonchalantly. A man lacking in social skills, he made no effort to shake the Colonel's hand. Instead, he walked around to the other side of the table, pulled out a chair and dropped into it. "Mind if I ask you a few questions, Colonel Driver? You've probably already been asked a couple of them, but I've got to catch up with the Lieutenant here. He got a head start on me."

Driver nodded numbly. His eyes searched the Inspector's pallid, full-jowled face.

"Why don't you tell me exactly what happened here tonight—where you've been, who you were with, that sort of thing."

The Colonel stared down at his interlocked fingers. When he tried to talk there was an emptiness in his voice. The noncommittal shrug before he began was nothing more than an unfortunate habit. He did care a great deal about what had happened to the Saint Quentin woman. He glanced at his watch as though the gesture might help to clear his mind. "I got home a little after nine. I'd been at the Officer's Club. Had supper there and stayed around afterwards to have a few drinks with a friend."

"And all this can be verified, I suppose?" Dawkins knew he had made it sound as if there was an element of doubt in his mind. It was exactly the way he had intended for it to sound.

Driver's eyes snapped up at the stocky little man with a surprised look on his face. "Of course. What kind of question is that?"

Dawkins' pudgy face was implaccable. He had ugly little needlepoint eyes that pierced rather than assessed. Driver noticed that the man never seemed to blink. He was the kind of man you couldn't stare down, and Driver knew his rank meant nothing to the man. "Nothing personal, Colonel. This is just for the record. Obviously you have to realize that everything you tell us here tonight will be checked and double-checked."

"Surely you don't think I had anything to do with this," Harry stammered.

Dawkins ignored the question. "Why don't you just tell us what happened after you finished your stint at the club?"

Driver blinked, glanced at the young Air Force Lieutenant from the Pepperell Air Provost Office and started over. If anyone was keeping score, the Inspector had won the first round.

"The rain had turned to ice while I was in the Club. I had a helluva time even getting to my car." He hesitated for a moment, wondering just how much detail the Inspector really wanted. "I had to leave my car at the bottom of the hill. I walked up the hill from Third Street and came in the house. There weren't any lights on. I found Flora, er, Miss Saint Quentin, in the bathroom, just like you saw her. I didn't touch a thing. I've been around long enough to know that the first thing you do in a situation like this is get in touch with the O.D.'s office and tell them what happened."

Dawkins turned to the Lieutenant. "Are you the officer of the day?"

The young man shook his head. "Nope. When the O.D. heard what Colonel Driver told him, he called the Provost Office. Lieutenant Colonel Hemmings told me to hustle over here and see what was going on. I arrived just a few minutes ahead of you."

The Inspector nodded and began fumbling around in his pockets until his hand emerged with a battered box of Players. To the Lieutenant's surprise, the cigarette he extracted was already half-smoked. He lit it, took a drag and promptly put it out, stuffing the still promising remains back in the box. The whole ritual had taken less than 30 seconds. While he exhaled, he looked around the room.

"Do you have any idea who would want to do something like this to your housekeeper, Colonel Driver?"

The officer shook his head. "I don't even know what happened to her, Inspector. All I know is there is a helluva lot of blood all over the first floor bathroom. I don't even know how she died."

The young Lieutenant swallowed hard. The

gruesome scene Driver had led him to when he first arrived was still all too vivid in his mind.

Dawkins got up, walked across the room and stood staring out the window at the darkened landscape. It was the same one where Flora Saint Quentin had monitored the progress of the storm earlier in the day. "Your housekeeper is dead, Colonel Driver, because someone carved, and that's exactly the word I want to use, carved her heart out. Brutal and vicious and crude is how I'd describe it." He paused to let the words sink in. "And I think it's safe to say what we're dealing with here is not a typical homicide, Colonel, not by a long shot. What we've got here is something unusual, real unusual." He had managed to get the emphasis on the word "real." "I'd even go so far as to say I've never seen anything quite like it before, and I've seen a lot."

"I . . . I . . . I figured she must have been stabbed," Driver admitted, "when I saw all that blood."

Dawkins hesitated. He was like a man groping his way through a complicated equation, each symbol and word conveying precisely what he wanted it to convey. "Was it Miss or Mrs.?"

Driver looked up at the man absently.

"Was your housekeeper married, single,

divorced, widowed or what, Colonel Driver?"

"Single," Driver muttered. "Divorced? I guess she could have been. She never talked about a family."

The Inspector revolved slowly, turning away from the window to confront him. His eyes locked on the Lieutenant's and then Driver's. "Were you, uh, involved with the lady, Colonel?"

Harry Driver choked back a sardonic little laugh. "Involved? With Flora Saint Quentin? Come on, Inspector, did you get a good look at her? Miss Saint Quentin was a simple-minded woman with simple-minded ways. She had a very specific talent for keeping things orderly; nothing more."

Dawkins' multifaceted face assumed a look of instant puzzlement. He had lit another cigarette, this time taking more than one drag, and he was again putting his ashes in his cupped hand. Now he began to grope around in his coat pocket again and emerged with a crumpled piece of paper. He made a small production out of unfolding it and clearing his throat before he started to read.

"Darling Harry,
    Why must you be away so long? The hours seem like an eternity without you.
                Love, Flora."

Dawkins looked up from the piece of paper at the astonished man's face. "It's dated with today's date."

Driver snapped to his feet and snatched the piece of paper out of the Inspector's hand. He glanced at it hurriedly and handed it back. "That's not even Flora's handwriting."

Dawkins reread the note with a perplexed look on his expressive face. "It's signed 'Flora'. That was the woman's name, wasn't it?"

Harry Driver was suddenly aware that he didn't like the way the Inspector's line of questioning was leading them. His eyes danced uneasily from the Lieutenant to Dawkins and back to the young officer again. "What the hell's going on here?" he snapped.

The Inspector crammed the piece of paper back into his coat pocket without folding it. His face had furrowed into a grim visage that accentuated the wear and tear of the years.

"We've got us a real problem here, Colonel. Somebody murdered your housekeeper. The fact is, they didn't just murder the poor woman—they mutilated her. Flora Saint Quentin's heart was cut out."

The younger officer shifted his stance uneasily.

Harry Driver's mouth fell open. His lower

lip trembled and his hands were shaking. "Heart cut out," he repeated numbly.

Dawkins nodded. "'Course, I'm no judge of such matters, but from the looks of things I'd say that whoever did it had at least a modest amount of surgical talent."

Driver stared back at him.

"Actually," Dawkins droned, "viewing it objectively, it was a rather tidy accomplishment with a minimum amount of trauma to the chest cavity; a certain lack of technique, though, is evident from the excessive bleeding."

Lieutenant Proctor gulped and swallowed hard. An acid taste was swirling around in his mouth. "I'm afraid I'll have to intervene here, Inspector Dawkins. It's my duty to remind you that Colonel Driver is a United States military officer and a U.S. citizen; as such he is entitled to specific counsel before he answers anymore of your questions."

Dawkins' face mirrored his impatience. "So what are you telling me, young fella? You telling me I can't talk to him? You telling me I can't talk to him about a woman who was murdered in his house?"

Proctor's face flushed. "Not at all, sir," he stammered. The momentary bravado submerged as fast as it had surfaced.

"So far, Lieutenant, I haven't charged the

Colonel here with anything. Fact of the matter is, if you'd been listenin' real close to what I've been saying, I haven't even implied anything. Furthermore, when I do start making accusations, it'll be damned well apparent to everyone concerned."

The Inspector continued to glare at the two men for a moment, then drifted over to the Formica counter next to the sink. He picked up a bulky-looking glass container, momentarily inspected the shrouded contents, set it down and ran some tap water over what was left of his latest cigarette.

"You see, Colonel, I find all of this rather perplexing. I mean, what's the motive? You weren't robbed. You've already told the Lieutenant here that you didn't notice anything missing. And, from what I can see, everything appears to be fairly tidy, nothing torn up, nothing obviously disturbed. But we've sure got us a lot of blood, and we've got us a lady in there with her chest carved open and her heart gone. Makes you wonder what kind of person would do something like that, don't it?"

Harry Driver collapsed back into the kitchen chair where he had been sitting when the Inspector had walked in. He was visibly shaken.

Only Proctor seemed to have anything left. He followed the Inspector out of the kitchen and back down the hall to where the body of the dead woman lay. He glanced at his watch and cleared his throat. "Look, Inspector, it's going on two o'clock in the morning. I have to report in to both the O.D. and the A.D. What do you want me to tell them?"

Dawkins lit another cigarette, eased his way around the body, pushed his hat back off his furrowed forehead and sighed. "Tell them," he said wearily, "that I'm holding your Colonel Driver for further questioning."

Proctor was stunned. "But . . ." he started to sputter.

The Inspector inhaled and leaned his weight up against the small wash basin.

"On what ground?" Proctor insisted. "You don't even know what happened here. You don't know how she died. You don't have a murder weapon. You don't have a time of death or a motive. As far as I can see, you haven't got anything but a body and a lot of questions."

Dawkins' face stumbled through the transition from frown to half-smile. He looked at the young officer and reached into his pocket. "You're right, son. I ain't got any of those things, but I sure have got me a parcel full of hunches. And, don't forget, I've got this." He held up the crumpled piece of paper.

* * *

It was late afternoon when Harry Driver was informed that he was free to leave on his own recognizance. Dawkins had detained him, questioned him and finally released him. Proctor, who had been with him through most of the ordeal, drove him back to the old two-story house on Magglin Lane overlooking Conception Bay, inquired if he needed anything and, when informed that he didn't, deposited the officer on the slush-covered sidewalk in front of his house—a house that had now been witness to both the end of his marriage to Janet and the death of Flora Saint Quentin.

Driver walked slowly up to the front door, unlocked it and entered the darkened house. Not the sort of man to avoid the obvious, he headed directly for the first floor bathroom where he had discovered Flora's body less than 19 hours earlier. True to his word, Proctor had taken care of matters. The body had been removed and a cursory inspection indicated that whoever had been assigned to the distasteful task had pretty well removed all evidence of the previous day's violence.

From there he went to the kitchen, opened the door to the freezer, removed some ice cubes, put them in a tall glass and splashed it nearly a third full with bourbon. After adding a dash of water, he sagged disconsolately into the same chair where Flora always had sat and stared out at the churning, wind-whipped bay. The warm, unseasonal rains of the last several days had created a chaotic pattern of ice patches and open water. The whole normally placid scene now looked hostile and foreboding, void of life. The heavy, dark rolling clouds were encroaching again, and it wouldn't be long till they were hit with another onslaught of the unseasonal rains. They would descend upon him and plunge the day still further into a premature darkness.

The bourbon burned its way down his dry throat and slammed into his empty stomach. It had been too long since he had eaten. Now, in the silence, his thoughts turned to the Saint Quentin woman. He had known her all of the five years he had been stationed at Pepperell. She had worked for General Collins when he first met her, and when the stodgy old bachelor and former base commander rotated back to the States, the general gave the woman glowing recommendations. Then, after Janet left, the Saint Quentin woman seemed to be the logical solution, the ideal person to keep the lonely old house from deteriorating into the typical, ill-kept bachelor quarters of his fellow officers. And since there hadn't been a romantic interlude in Harry's life since Janet, it seemed altogether logical to have the woman live in and use the spare bedroom on the first floor.

Looking back, it had all worked out quite nicely. Flora Saint Quentin never had gentleman callers, never mentioned any family and, in actuality, had very few friends except for Anna, whom he didn't know and had never met. Anna was a name—nothing more than a name—and he regretted that. He wondered if anyone had called this person named Anna and informed her of his housekeeper's untimely demise. He wondered how to do it, how to find the woman's last name. Beyond that, he wondered if anyone really cared about what had happened to Flora Saint Quentin.

Harry Driver finished his drink and went in to the dead woman's bedroom. It was neat and tidy. He could have easily believed that she would be returning at any moment, laying down her packages, donning her apron and preparing to fix the evening meal.

Where to start? Where does a woman like Flora Saint Quentin keep the things that are important to her? He went through the drawers of her dresser first and found only those things one would expect to find—lingerie, a few blouses, two sweaters, three pair of hose. Two of the drawers were empty. The closet revealed even less—three dresses, one of which he had seen her wear to church on those infrequent occasions when she attended, a heavy coat, a light coat, and a cardigan that she wore frequently. It had a tear in the right pocket. There were several pairs of shoes, two purses carefully wrapped in a plastic cleaning bag, and a small cardboard box full of inexpensive jewelry. On a shelf he found a Bible, and inside he found her birth certificate. She was 49 years old when she died.

Inside, on the fly leaf of the gilt-edged book was carefully inscribed: "To Flora Saint Quentin, June 13, 1914. Received into the house of our Lord and Savior, Jesus Christ, on this day of your first Holy Communion." It was signed, "Father Conroy."

Slowly and carefully, he put everything back in its place, closed the closet door and glanced around the shadowy room wondering where else to look. He could hear the sound of rain again. The streets were already flooded with a thick, soupy slush, and when the temperature fell again during the long, cold night, the ice would recapture what the warm rains had temporarily set free.

He glanced at the old wrought-iron bed and the flounce that concealed the space underneath it. Janet had kept things there; he wondered if by chance Flora Saint Quentin had developed the same habit.

And there it was—a battered, leatherette stationery box crammed with the trash and treasures of a lifetime of no particular significance. Driver opened it and was astonished. There, carefully nestled on a small pink satin heart-shaped pillow was a stack of letters, primly tied by a pink satin ribbon. Next to it was a brownish, three-by-five spiral notebook.

He picked up the stack of letters, uncertain what he was going to do with them. Did it matter that he pried into her life now that she was dead? Were they left behind to show the world that someone actually did once care about Flora Saint Quentin? Did any of it have meaning or purpose? Driver contemplated the invasion of privacy and finally sagged down on the edge of the bed, yielding to his morbid curiosity. He peeled away the pink satin ribbon and began to read.

Two hours later, the bizarre story of Flora Saint Quentin had taken yet another grotesque twist.

The stack of letters were all written on the same pale pink, slightly scented stationery. They were all written to the quiet, homely woman who said little, asked for less and revealed nothing of her hopes and dreams. Now he knew why. It was all there, gently scrolled by a delicate hand on wafer thin sheets of paper. Each began, "My Darling Flora." Each passionately appealed for her favor. Each professed undying eternal love. Each was signed, "Forever, your loving Harry."

The bundle of letters slipped from his hand and tumbled to the floor.

In the world beyond the rain-streaked windows, darkness had captured what was left of the day. The wind buffeted what was left of the old house, and Harry Driver felt the icy fingers of his destiny clamp down coldly on the back of his neck.

Several minutes later, he picked up the small brown spiral notebook and went to the phone.

A faint, whispery voice answered after the third ring. "Hello?" The salutation was almost too soft to record an impression.

"May I speak to Anna?"

There was a long, almost unbearable silence on the other end.

"Anna, please," Driver repeated. "I'm sorry, but I don't have a last name."

There was another protracted silence, until a man's gruff, impatient voice bridged the emptiness. "Who the hell is this?" the voice demanded.

Driver tried to explain. His housekeeper was dead. He was simply trying to contact the woman's friends. All he had to go on was the name Anna and a telephone number.

There was an impatient tolerance on the other end. Finally the man interrupted him. "Look, buster," he growled, "if you say the old woman is dead, let it go at that."

Harry Driver didn't understand. "But . . ." he started to protest and was cut off again.

"Look, fella, I don't know what's goin' on over there in that cave of kooks, but if it's over, it's over. Some half-baked old woman by the name of Flora has been callin' over here for years. All she wanted to do is tell my wife about her love life. So I told Flossie to let her call her Anna if it made the old woman happy, but to make damn sure she got the money."

"Money?" Driver repeated.

"Sure, the old woman would call up and tell my wife all about how some guy named Harry made love to her and bought her these expensive gifts. So I told her to ask for money, and she did. Flossie would call herself Anna and tell the old dame that one of our kids was sick or we needed food. The old broad always came through. Twenty bucks here, fifty bucks there, and all just for listenin' to this love-starved old bitch talk about her love life. . . ."

Harry Driver didn't have to listen any further. He placed the receiver back in the cradle and listened to the sound of the rain.

Fantasy and reality had become one. He shuddered. It had occurred to him what Inspector Dawkins would have thought if he had been the one to uncover Flora's little leatherette box or read the letters or called Flora's so-called friend, Anna. It was a dead woman's story against his. Hers was fixed; there was no way to refute it. His, they could pick at.

Flora Saint Quentin had built a world in which he was the hunter and she was his prey; he was the passionate lover and she was the object of his desire.

Harry studied the phone for a moment, then walked slowly back into the kitchen. He headed straight for the counter next to the sink and picked up the heavy glass jar. He didn't know why, but there was something compelling about it. Then he noticed it. Where there had once been only one something in the jar, there were now two. He set the jar down and stared at it.

It was close to midnight when Harry Driver, confused and weary, trudged up to his second floor bedroom. The rain had continued its torrential assault on the old house throughout the long evening. Now it seemed as though the old house was more drafty and decidedly more empty than he could ever recall. In his bedroom, he began to systematically replay the bizarre events of the last 30 hours of his life. A series of events had propelled him straight into the middle of a jumbled nightmare. Anticipating conclusions that Dawkins would reach, he had destroyed Flora's letters and burned the little brown spiral notebook. And he had resigned himself to a second and this time more thorough search of the woman's personal effects. Driver rightly reasoned that he could ill afford to have the Inspector find anything else that would perpetuate the woman's fantasies of the nonexistent relationship between the two of them.

And Dawkins, likewise, had not given up. That was evidenced by the fact that the Inspector had already called twice, the second time less than an hour ago. Dawkins had informed him that he would be stopping by in the morning because he had a few more questions. To Harry Driver that meant one thing; he had to complete his search and destroy mission before the Inspector arrived.

He unbuttoned his shirt, took it off and hung it over the knob on the closet door. It was the same thing every night; trousers were placed on a hook inside the closet, and he kicked his discarded shoes under the bed. It hadn't yet registered that there was no longer a Flora to pick up after him.

From there he went into the bathroom, turned on the shower, adjusted it until it was mostly steam and crawled in. When he emerged, she was there, slouched against the frame of the door, holding two cups of coffee.

Flora Saint Quentin looked, from all reference points, like someone who had been dead for several hours. There was a distorting puffiness about her full face and dark brooding circles under her eyes where the no longer coursing blood had coagulated. Her usual fleshy lips were drained of color and slightly parted to reveal yellowed teeth. If she was breathing, he couldn't detect it. There was a musty odor about the woman, an odor of things not alive. Only the splotches of the too red rouge applied to her sallow cheeks gave color to her death mask. It looked to Driver as though the undertaker had been called away from his grim task before the job was completed.

Lastly, and this was the thing that made him recoil, there was a large, gaping hole in the middle of her ample bosom, where her heart had once been.

Driver's breath lodged in his constricted throat and he reeled backward, the towel dropping from his hand, revealing his nakedness.

Flora appraised him, her dead eyes slowly scanning him. "I've been waiting for you to come home," she said softly. Her voice was somehow fragmented, something apart from what he was witnessing.

Driver tried to respond, but his words never materialized.

"You're later than usual, Colonel, but I knew if I waited patiently that eventually you would come home to me."

He was on the verge of panic when he pushed his way past the woman and ran down the hall to his bedroom. His heart was pounding furiously. He tried to slam the door but she was already there, methodically, almost sensually removing her clothes. First came the tattered old brown sweater. She laid it over the foot of the bed, then began unbuttoning her blouse. It fell to the floor, revealing the bloodstained remnants of her undergarments.

Driver tried vainly to cough out a protest but the sounds were inaudible.

She was smiling. "You know all my secrets now, Harry. I've been watching you. The moment you got home you went straight to my room and began going through my things. You wanted to find a way to reach out to me, didn't you, Harry?"

Harry Driver tried to back away from the specter.

Flora's blunt, stubby fingers began to work with the buttons at the waistband of her skirt. She loosened it and it too fell to the floor. Her half slip was soiled and wrinkled, more gray than the delicate feminine colors that Janet wore.

"I saw the look on your face while you re-read the letters you wrote me. You were reliving your passions, weren't you, Harry? You were remembering how it was with us. You were so passionate, so tender, so gentle. You were a good lover, Harry. You knew I had never been with a man, and you were so patient with me, teaching me what I needed to know to please you. I love you so very much, Harry, and I know how very much you love me."

Harry Driver continued to back away from the woman until he had pinned himself in the corner against the far wall. His mouth was dry and he stared back at the woman, too stunned, too caught up in his terror now to move.

Flora Saint Quentin peeled away the last garment and stood before him in a grotesque and mocking feminine nakedness. Only now could Driver see the full impact of the savage assault that had been inflicted upon the woman. The fatal wound had ravaged her chest and a bizarre geometric pattern of crusted blood trailed away from the orgasm of death.

"I want you, Harry. Oh God, how I want you."

Her trembling hands reached out for his, and he took them.

"Make love to me, Harry. Make love to me with the same gentle tenderness you always have."

She led him over to the bed. He sat down on the edge and she stood in front of him, beginning the slow process of her preparations. He felt her blunted fingers working over him. As she pushed him back on the bed, he felt his arms slowly and involuntarily reach out to encircle her brutish neck.

"I can pleasure you, Harry. You know I can. I've done it so many times before; it's no different now." He was aware that her voice had grown husky with her mounting passion.

Driver tenderly forced her legs apart and pulled her down on top of him. He realized that his eyes had already closed in anticipation.

"Harry," she pleaded, "now! Promise me that we will always be lovers."

He felt the first surge and opened his eyes, looking up into the face of his dead lover.

There was a peel of guttural thunder.

The knife glinted in the sudden orange illumination of a bolt of lightning. It was plunging toward his chest.

For Harry Preston Driver there was one terrifying, fear-filled moment when the world stopped, one solitary moment when sight and sound and sensation froze in the vast spacelessness of time. Then there was pain, excruciating pain.

Even that quickly ceased.

Inspector Lawrence Dawkins arrived, as he said he would, at midmorning, expecting to launch his second round of questions and expecting Driver to mumble protests about having already answered the same questions or any of a hundred variations Dawkins had tried on him. Instead, there was no answer to his knock, and because the Colonel's car was still parked where it had obviously been parked through the long, stormy night, Dawkins decided to take the risk. The door was unlocked, and he went in without hesitation. Only once before in his 27 years as an investigator for the RCMP had he found it necessary to use the small lie that "the door was standing open." He knew then, as he knew would be the case now, that his supervisors wouldn't believe him. But, he reasoned, they also knew that he was first and foremost a man with only one purpose—to do his job.

"Driver?" he called into the darkened house.

There was no response. If anything, there was an eerie, almost stifling silence about the place.

He heard footsteps on the porch, turned and saw the imposing figure of Lieutenant Proctor standing in the doorway.

"Just got here," he said defensively. "I rang the bell and knocked so hard the neighbors could have heard. Driver didn't answer. I think he's still here, though."

Proctor glanced back down at the Colonel's new teal blue and white Ford Victoria. During the night a cold front had moved through and the rain had slowly changed to ice and finally a thin blanket of clean white snow. It was a brighter world than they had seen for days. He looked back at the Inspector.

"The door was standing open," Dawkins repeated sheepishly.

Proctor stepped around him and called out, "Colonel Driver, are you here?" There was nothing timid about the young officer's effort. He glanced back at Dawkins. "Maybe somebody came by and picked him up."

The Inspector graced the young officer with a benign smile. "Colonel Driver lives on a hill overlooking the bay. It's a long way down that hill, a very slippery hill under that fresh blanket of snow. Hardly the kind of weather a man goes traipsing about in. Added to that, my young friend, is the more obvious fact that there are no tracks either up or down that hill made by anyone other than you or I."

Proctor didn't appear to be overly impressed. He was assigned to the legal side of the Air Provost Marshal's office; logic and deduction weren't his game. That was left up to the investigative team from the military police. "Colonel Driver," he shouted again, "are you in there?"

Dawkins started first, meandering aimlessly from one first floor room to the next, and finally into the bathroom where Flora Saint Quentin had died. Proctor's people had done a good job. There was no trace of the violent scene that had confronted them some 36 hours earlier.

Moments later, Proctor entered the room. He glanced hurriedly around. "I was almost afraid of what I'd find in there," he admitted. "Thank you for taking care of the details, Inspector."

Dawkins gave him a quizzical look.

"I mean for having someone come in and clean things up."

Dawkins' craggy face furrowed into a scowl. "I didn't," he admitted matter-of-factly. "Do you suppose . . ."

". . . the Colonel had to clean it up himself?" Proctor finished.

There was an uncomfortable silence while the two men considered the possibility. They went into the kitchen, then gravitated to the stairway leading to the second floor. "Might as well," Dawkins muttered. "It's the only thing left."

Ever the officer and gentleman, Proctor announced his intentions with another shout. "Colonel Driver, it's me, Lieutenant Proctor. Inspector Dawkins is with me. We're coming up."

The scene in the master bedroom defied description. Harry Preston Driver was sprawled out in the middle of the big bed on his back. Pooled around him was a congealed crimson testimony to the fact that he had once lived. A large, cavernous hole had been excavated in his hairy chest. The rib cage had been savagely separated and his heart carved out. Harry Driver's face was eternally fixed in a horrified mask of life's final terror. His body was ivory white, drained of color and grotesquely rigid.

"Holy shit," Proctor muttered. He reeled backward, using the wall for support.

Dawkins managed two or three halting steps forward, then stopped.

The noon hour had come and gone before either Proctor or Dawkins had time to stop and reflect on what they had been witness to. The coroner had come as well as the Saint John's police, a police photographer, the military police investigation squad from Fort Pepperell, and finally, a representative from the Bayside Funeral Home, who deftly removed Driver's body.

Dawkins breathed a heavy sigh. "How about a cup of coffee, Lieutenant?"

The young man nodded. "I could sure use one."

The Inspector led them into the kitchen and put an old copper tea kettle over the gas burner, took out two nondescript cups and set them on the counter next to the glass jar. "Might as well use up Driver's stuff," he said sardonically. "Doesn't appear he'll be needing it any longer."

Proctor felt a cold uneven chill tiptoe across his broad shoulders. He had every intention of drinking his coffee and getting the hell out of there. He had had enough of Dawkins and Driver and the drafty old house to last him for a lifetime. Besides, he rationalized, there were things to be done, loose ends, reports to write and file. The military paperwork alone was going to be a bitch, and that was before he even started to consider how it all had to be tied into provincial requirements. Besides, he was in no particular mood to sit and speculate about the hows, whens and whys of what had transpired in the old house. All of that, he figured, could be done later.

"Well, Lieutenant, how do you figure it?"

Proctor shrugged. "Just a few hours ago I think you were convinced Driver had killed Flora Saint Quentin. What happened to that theory?"

Dawkins noisily sucked the scalding coffee out of his too full cup and studied the young man. "I still could be right about that part of it."

"Maybe, maybe not. But the larger question is, who killed Harry Driver?"

"Lots of possibilities—someone who wanted to revenge the murder of Flora Saint

Quentin, someone who wanted to get even with the Colonel for something we don't even know about, maybe even someone fixin' to rob the place."

Proctor's mouth curled into an impatient snarl. "Come on, Inspector, the way Driver was spread-eagled out on that bed, he was expecting something all right, and it sure as hell wasn't a robbery."

Dawkins nodded, slurped more coffee and mentally began sketching in his file cards for future reference. What did they have? A homely woman, about whom little was known, mindlessly spending her monotonous string of days in a mundane world of insignificance. She had been brutally murdered, her heart carved out of her body. Why the heart? Why not the brain? Why not some other organ? It all meant something, he supposed, to the addled mind of the frenzied creature who had committed the crime. Then, only a few hours later, the whole bizarre scenario had been repeated. The same smouldering question resurfaced—why the heart?

Perhaps, Dawkins thought, it bothered him even more because he saw haunting similarities in his own often pointless, often lonely existence. Except for the outcome, how were they any different from him?

He set his cup down and ambled back over

to the counter. There he studied the glass jar full of nearly opaque fluid and the cloudy object lurking within. "What the hell do you suppose this thing is?" he grunted. "Damn thing looks like a high school student's biology project."

"Maybe, but who for? Driver didn't have any kids," Proctor sighed.

Dawkins held the jar at eye level. The cloudy contents sloshed back and forth against the backdrop of sunlight glistening off of fresh fallen snow and streaming in through the window. "Wonder what the hell those things are in there? Must be growing. It's a hell of a lot heavier than it was the other day."

"Maybe the old gal was culturing something," Proctor muttered. He didn't care what was in the jar. At the moment that was the least of his concerns. The old house was beginning to unnerve him; all he really cared about now was getting the whole sordid mess wrapped up and forgetting about it.

Dawkins, however, was preoccupied with the contents of the cumbersome jar. His probing eyes were squinted into narrow slits.

Lawrence Dawkins was tempted to tell the young officer that his work was his life, that he was intrigued with the amorphous-looking object because the ugly reality of the situation was that he had nothing better to do. Instead, he offered the officer a way out. "Look, Lieutenant, if you have something to do, I can wrap this up here."

Proctor saw the opening and took it. "Matter of fact, Inspector, I do. I've got to get back to the base—paperwork, that sort of thing."

The old man could read between the lines and recognize the impatience of youth. And, even though he didn't feel like it, he forced a tired smile. "I'll stop by your office when I'm through here," he assured the young man.

Proctor left, still buttoning his coat. Dawkins watched him turn up his collar against the chill as he went down the sidewalk.

Alone now, the weary Inspector continued to rotate the jar against the room's inadequate light. To his surprise, it had grown warm to the touch. Finally he decided to do what he had known he would do all along. He pried off the lid just as the jar slipped from his hands and toppled sideways, spilling the contents along with the foul-smelling liquid all over the surface of the counter.

It wasn't one object, but three, varied in size and color from a faded, almost feminine pink to a beligerent red. Each was moving, beating in a labored, unsynchronized, primitive fashion, each emitting a chorus of childlike whimpering sounds. There was something primordial about them, something incredibly urgent, something electric and beckoning. One possessed a large repaired tear in it. The second was small and lonely-looking. The third was a vivid thing, apart from the others. It managed somehow to beat more vibrantly than the others, and as he watched and listened, the sounds seemed to be evolving into something more frightening. Even in the raspy hoarseness of the sound, he recognized their unthinkable invitation.

Lawrence Dawkins recoiled and staggered backward, no longer fascinated. Now he was terrified.

The objects, and he knew what they were now, started to slither toward him. It was a kind of choreographed madness—an insane, incomprehensible summons into their world.

The man sagged to his knees, clutching his throat, his heart hammering. The pain, for one brief moment, was excruciating; there came the tearing of flesh, the severing of life, and finally the oneness with them.

Lawrence Chester Marquard Dawkins, Inspector rank, Royal Canadian Mounted Police, was no longer alone. In his heart, he had joined them.

PART TWO

Chapter Three

Cappy Salem leaned forward and snuffed out her cigarette. With that accomplished, she picked up a paper napkin and delicately dabbed at the corners of her swollen eyes. What the hell, she thought, this yo-yo is too drunk to even notice. She signaled the bartender with a circular motion and reached across the table to pinch her date on the cheek. He would, if he was like most of them —and there was no reason at this point to think he wasn't—interpret her little gesture as an overture. To a pragmatic survivalist like Cappy Salem, the gesture had a much more significant meaning; she was simply testing the guy's level of numbness. Just how far gone was this Yankee yahoo? She needed to know.

The waitress, a friend of Cappy's, swooped in with two fresh glasses. Hers was tea; his contained a cheap facsimile of the bourbon he had started the evening with. Now he was too far gone to know the difference. He reached out with an unsteady hand, captured the glass cylinder, arched it unevenly toward his slack mouth and gulped down the contents. Then Harvey Klinger, Airman Second Class, United States Air Force, on his way back to the States with a stopover in Saint John's, plopped his glass down, grinned foolishly, wiped off his mouth with the back of his hand and waited for applause.

"My God, Harvey," the young lady cooed, "I don't think I've ever seen anyone handle their liquor any better than you."

The slavish compliment made his day. It was his turn to make the circular motion. "Hey," he managed, "barkeep! Over here. Another round." He fumbled into his hip pocket, took out his new wallet and fished out another 20.

None of this was lost on Cappy Salem. She couldn't and didn't miss the fact that there were plenty more where that one came from.

"So, Airman," she said huskily, "how long you been in Saint Johns?"

Harvey blinked sheepishly and held up his pudgy hand. It took a second or two to untangle them but he was finally able to spread his fingers so the lady could count them. "'Bout . . . 'bout four hours," he slurred.

"Four hours." Cappy giggled. "You're a real newcomer, huh? First time out of the States?"

Harvey had to think about that one for a moment before he responded. "Naw," he belched, "I . . . I been up at Thule the last . . . last twelve months. I . . . I'm on . . . on my way back to the States."

"No girls to spend your money on up there, I hear," she said, winking.

"Girl behind every tree," he said giggling, "but you . . . you know what the problem with . . . with that is?"

Cappy Salem had heard the tired joke countless times but she played the game anyway. She shook her head, another practiced gesture that made her long brown-black hair shimmer around her almond-shaped face.

"No . . . no . . . ," Harvey Klinger was breaking up, ". . . there's no damn trees."

Cappy howled. Harvey joined her, repeatedly slapping his flabby palm against his even flabbier thigh.

"So . . . so tell me, what's . . . what's yer name?"

Cappy, listening carefully to the man, noted with some concern that her mark suddenly sounded just a little less intoxicated than she wanted him to. That bothered her; she hadn't fully formulated her plan yet. "Why?" she teased. Cappy was an acknowledged master of the tease.

"'Cause . . . 'cause I like you." He closed his eyes momentarily, then reopened them and tried to focus. It worked; there was only one of her again.

Cappy's tired face collapsed easily. The fatigue was beginning to show. Every guy rotating down from the command's isolated duty stations to the north processed through the local base and caught his MATS flight back to the States from there. Harvey or Harold or Homer or whatever his name was was just one more in an endless parade of girl-starved, gawky, homesick hillbillies that the U.S. Air Force marched through the base east of town.

The best Cappy could hope for most of the time was a couple of drinks, a $20 bill if she made her story sad enough—sick mother, mounting medical bills—and a fast and usually final farewell. Only once had one of them attempted to reestablish contact, but she had ignored him, mostly because she would have been no better off than she was before.

"My name is Cynthia. Cynthia Irene Salem. But everybody around here calls me Cappy."

She watched him tumble the name around in his mouth. His orientation was coming and going. When he finally managed to blurt it out, it had a decidedly southern drawl to it. "Cappee!"

"So, where you from, Airman?" A standard question, part of the routine. She had had to think a minute, since this was only her third night back and she was out of practice. She had been so focused on Charlie for the last several months that her routine was a bit rusty.

"Loo-e-ville . . . Loo-e-ville, Kain-tuck-ee." Despite the slur, he managed to convey the name of his hometown with a certain boozy pride.

Kentucky, Arkansas, Utah—they were nothing more than names. She supposed it was close to New York or Los Angeles. If it wasn't, it should be. They were the only places she ever read about. She smiled, fixed and vacant. What the hell did it matter anyway? Frazier, God damn him, was off the hook. Her chances of getting to the States were shot. She'd let her ticket out of Saint Johns get away from her, and now she had to live with that fact. She refixed the smile, catching a glimpse of herself in the smoky mirror behind him. What the hell, a smile was about all the hillbilly could handle.

"How come . . . a . . . pretty girl like you ain't married?" His words came out bloated and funny sounding, hanging together by the thinnest of coherent threads.

Cappy had a whole book full of snappy answers, but this wasn't a snappy answers night, nor was Homer or Harold the kind of guy who could field them. She reached across the table, over a too full ashtray and curled her fingers around his latest drink. She bolted three or four gulps and gratefully felt the pale tea-colored liquid collide with the back of her throat. There was a quick rush and she pushed another insincere smile center stage. As a rule, Cappy didn't drink. Control was the name of the game. If she drank, she wasn't in control; it was as simple as that. The answer she was going to give him wasn't the one that hurt. It was the ugly version, close to the truth, but painless.

She slipped one of his cigarettes out of the pack of Marlboros, lit it, took a drag and snuffed it out.

"You know what tonight was supposed to be?" she asked.

Harvey Klinger stared back at the lady. He knew he had had too much to drink. He knew his words were coming out slurred. He knew, but at the moment he didn't care. He had finally figured out a way to get out of that hellhole called Thule, and that was enough of a reason to party. If she wanted to tell him why tonight was supposed to be a special night in her life, he was predisposed to listen. "What?" he stammered.

"Tonight's the night I was supposed to get married."

"Marr . . . married?"

Cappy took another swig of his drink and nodded. Despite her resolve not to tell anyone, the painful version was coming out. She reached down beside her chair and produced a simulated brown leather purse. She unzipped it and fished around the cluttered contents until she was able to produce the flight folders for two airline tickets. "These," she sobbed, "are fucking useless. Know what they are?"

Harvey shook his bloated head.

"Two tickets . . . two goddamn airline tickets from Boston to Las Vegas. The lying little bastard told me we were going to get married at the Golden Chapel and catch the midnight show at Circus Circus." The bravado had quickly faded from her voice, deteriorating to a pathetic, little girl whimper.

Harvey blinked. "He . . . he didn't marry you?"

"Married, hah!" Cappy raised her arm to make another circling motion, but the waitress was already there. Harvey dutifully fished out another 20 and slapped it on the table. "Know what he did?" Cappy continued.

Harvey shook his head again and refocused

his bloodshot eyes. As far as he was concerned, the nice lady was far too pretty to have troubles like this.

"We was givin' the bastard a going away party, right here at the Crystal Club. We had the place all decorated with balloons and streamers and stuff. The band was playin' our song when Charlie grabs me by the arm and hustles me out the door. Know what he tells me? He tells me he ain't goin' through with it; he ain't goin' through with it because he caught me and that greaseball in the act."

Harvey's flaccid face was filled with a bourbon-induced compassion. He was shaking his head in dismay.

"Know what that bastard did?" Cappy hissed.

The Airman continued his astounding display of verbal economy by continuing to shake his head.

"He pinched me, hard, right here." She pointed to her breast. It was the start of her act. Honesty was giving way to the ever-pressing need to capitalize on the situation. "Know what I did? I cried." Cappy managed to throw in a couple of theatrical sobs. She had Harvey pegged as someone who would be a sucker for a few tears.

He was. He leaned across the cluttered table and clumsily took her hand. She immediately recorded the fact that his hands were wet and soft, not like the hard hands of most the men she had picked up.

"Why . . . why . . . didn't you go after him?"

All Cappy had to do now was set the hook. "Because of my mother; she isn't well. She had such high hopes for me. It would have killed her if she knew Charlie ran off without . . ." she threw in a few more sobs, ". . . without marrying me."

Cappy's story had lost all semblance of logic but Harvey didn't seem to notice. She was, plain and simple, a woman in distress, and in Loo-e-ville, where he was brought up, men didn't treat ladies like that.

"I've got a job. It isn't much, but it's a job. I thought Charlie would help me; he knew how sick my mother was. He promised me he would take her to Arizona where the climate would be good for her health."

There was a funny little furrow in Harvey's ponderously thick brow, like just maybe he had heard of Arizona before.

Now Cappy was on a roll. The lines were coming back to her. She found the routine easier to slip back into. Her routine was a masterpiece, interspersed with just the right number of carefully rehearsed sobs, expressions of dismay and tears of disappointment.

Harvey reached out again and captured her trembling hand. His flabby face mirrored his compassion. "Jeez," he slobbered, "I . . . I didn't realize . . . realize you was in so much trouble."

Cappy straightened up in her chair and put the back of her hand to her forehead. It was act two, scene one. She batted her eyes and inclined her head forward, tilted at an angle. This was the scene without dialogue.

"You okay, Cappy?" Harvey questioned.

"Yes," she said demurely, "I . . . I don't know what came over me. It's just that suddenly I feel a little shaky."

"Is . . . is there anything . . . I . . . I can do?"

"I hate to ask, but . . ."

"Anything," Harvey blurted. He was beginning to feel a sensation in his fingers again. The numbness was fading.

Cappy forced a smile, slid her hand back across the table, entangled her fingers in his and squeezed. She didn't tell him, of course, but it felt as though she had a fistful of uncooked sausages. "You're very sweet," she cooed.

The rest of the scene played out just like it had so many times in the past, just like Cappy knew it would. In the taxi she used the old "I don't want to trouble you, but if you could just see that I got home safely, I'd be indebted because a girl can't be too careful" routine.

Then she feigned sleep, her head on his shoulder.

Underneath it all, Cappy was smiling. Not bad. She hadn't lost her touch. Actually, it had been easy. Harvey was a piece of cake. She laid her hand on his thigh, a casual gesture in her sleep of course, and felt the tremor in his leg. Too easy. A wallet full of twenties. Getting even. That's what it's all about. Fuck you, Charles Everett Frazier, wherever you are.

Harvey Klinger was the kind who had to be coached. He handled the more obvious parts of his role with a minimum of direction; he assisted her out of the cab, walking her up the two flights of creaking wooden stairs to the cold water apartment on Front Street. He even managed the lock on the door and the part where he had to assist her over to the big, flowered, overstuffed couch. Cappy promptly sagged into it, the practiced look of faintness lost for the most part in the room's long shadows.

Harvey stood in the middle of the cluttered room, mouth slack, hands crammed in his pockets. He had the next line, but he didn't know his part.

Cappy took matters into her own hands. "Want something to drink?" As she made the offer, a funny thought rippled across her calculating mind. What if this stiff really didn't know what to do? What if she had actually uncovered a first timer? She stifled the urge to laugh. What the hell, she thought, why not? Everybody had to start somewhere. It might be fun. Then she had a second thought; what if he were soft all over? Maybe his hands weren't the only things that were spongy. This time she did laugh, out loud.

"Yeah, I do," he stammered, ". . . do you?"

"Maybe I'd feel better if I did have something to drink," she admitted. "A little gin, maybe; second shelf, in the cabinet over the sink."

Harvey located the gin, hunted up two glasses, managed to get them filled and, following Cappy's instructions, added some lime juice. When he came out of the kitchen, she playfully patted the couch beside her, and he sat down.

"You're so sweet, Harry. This sure can't be any fun for you. First night back in civilization and your date up and gets sick on you."

Harvey started to tell her his name, but she leaned forward impulsively and kissed him on the cheek. His skin was as smooth as hers, nothing even faintly resembled a beard. On balance, he looked more flustered than appreciative of the overture.

"Harvey, I have to ask you something."

He had the drink tightly clenched between

his two hands, staring at it, purposely avoiding her eyes. Cappy had the sinking feeling that the carefully engineered effects of the Crystal's bourbon were starting to dissipate.

"Well, before I do, drink up."

A sheepish smile recaptured his vacant face as he bolted the entire glass to please her. Then he caught his breath and looked at her for some tangible sign of approval.

"Have you ever had a girl before?"

Harvey hesitated, then nodded his head. He twirled the empty glass between the palms of his pudgy hands. "Sure . . . sure I have," he lied, ". . . lots of 'em."

Cappy leaned her head back and laughed, pausing just long enough to finish off a good part of her own drink. She was still laughing when she felt him stiffen and stand up.

"Hey, where you going?"

Harvey's pudgy, childish face suddenly appeared older and harder. Despite his unimposing stature, he managed to convey both his hurt and anger without words. "Maybe . . . maybe I . . . I am drunk. Maybe . . . maybe I shouldn't . . . be here. I was just . . . tryin' to help you. You . . . you got no cause to make fun of a guy."

Cappy had pushed herself upright, all too alert to the fact that the funny little man with the billfold full of twenties was starting to slip away from her. All her pretenses at poor health were instantly discarded as survival and greed took over.

"Hey, Loo-e-ville," she giggled, "lighten up. If you haven't been with a woman before, it's no big deal. Look at it like this—everybody has to start somewhere. All it means is you've got something to look forward to."

Harvey, shoulders slumped, walked aimlessly through the still darkened apartment, pausing from time to time to inspect first one thing then another. He was in the kitchen refilling his glass when his eyes fell on a bulky glass jar. He picked it up and held it in front of the small flickering light over the old electric stove, peering intently into the murky contents. When he felt the woman walk up behind him, he set it down and turned around to face her.

Cappy's nimble fingers worked their way up to the wings of his shirt collar and she toyed with them. "Look," she said huskily, "I'm sorry I was insensitive. I'm a girl on the rebound. I'm not exactly what you would call 'in control' these days."

The Airman's face had already softened. When Cappy realized she hadn't completely lost her advantage, she stood close enough for him to feel the heat of her body. It had worked many times before, and she knew it would work now. Her hands slipped from the collar, down the slope of his shoulders and locked behind him, pulling him to her. When she tried to kiss him with her own lips invitingly parted, there was no reaction. Though his whole response was clumsy, Cappy wasn't through. She leaned back, making sure he was completely aware of the contact between their two bodies.

Harvey's mouth tried to form words, but the effort spilled out in a halting fashion. This bozo knew nothing. For a fleeting moment she was filled with disgust, hating herself for what she had become and hating him for being what he was—another stupid damn American Airman.

Cappy's hands fell away from his waist and began to work the brass-plated buckle on his belt. The stay bar was wedged tightly against the heavily webbed fabric. It was a struggle, her fingers suddenly clumsy and unequal to the task. And to top it all off, he was no help.

"I want you to take me to bed," she whispered in his ear. "Make love to me, make me forget about Charlie, make me forget about my sick mother, about all the bills and all the rest of my problems."

Harvey followed her like a puppy. He stumbled into the darkened room, groped his way to the edge of the bed, sat down and let Cappy begin to undress him. She took off his dark blue tie and light blue shirt and hung them on the ladder-backed, cane-bottomed chair next to the bed. She conquered the buckle, pulled off his pants, creased them and hung them over the shirt. By then, Harvey had sufficient grasp of the end objective to remove his own shoes and socks. He dropped them to the floor with an unnecessarily loud thud.

"Now, sweetie," Cappy instructed, "you crawl under the covers. Give little Cappy a minute or two and she'll be right with you."

Harvey didn't budge. He sat in the darkness, staring stupidly back at the woman as she began to unbutton her blouse. With it off and laid over the same chair, she began to undo her bra. It fell to the floor, the part of the show that Charlie had liked intensely. Harvey gave no reaction.

Cappy sighed, walked into the bathroom and turned on the light. It was the first semblance of light in the otherwise darkened arena. The unreal yellow white crept back into the bedroom and she could see him sitting there, pasty white, with repulsive rings of fat bulging out like a bloated donut around the top of his shorts. His shoulders sloped, his chest was narrow and his breasts sagged like those of an old woman. He was blinking like a fat, lazy lizard in the unkind light.

She slowly went about the rest of her preparations, stepping out of her skirt, hanging it on the back of the bathroom door, and finally taking off her panties. She applied fresh lipstick, used the deodorant and brushed her teeth. But she had saved the most important thing for last. It was the one thing she couldn't leave to chance. Harvey hadn't played the game before, at least not often enough that she could trust him to know the rules. She snapped open his billfold and rifled through the hefty wad of $20 bills. When the count soared past the $500 mark, she knew she had made the right choice.

There were $750 in total. She leafed to the halfway mark in the wad of bills, took them and stuffed the rest back in his billfold. Her half was bunched into a tight little roll and tucked behind a stack of towels in a small cabinet under the sink. With the billfold carefully concealed in a towel, she primped one final time, touched her fingers to her hair, dabbed at the corner of her mouth and went back into the darkened bedroom.

Harvey was slumped back across the bed, the folds of skin around his pudgy little eyes creased into a sick grin of anticipation. His mouth was open, and he was snoring.

Cappy carefully placed the billfold beside the chair so that it would look as though it had simply slipped out of his pocket. Then she bent over, kissed him on his flabby, white hairless chest and again on the inside of his thigh, just above the knee. In both cases, she was careful to leave more than a lip print; she smeared the crimson red blotches for added effect. The final kiss was full and hard on his mouth. Then she walked around the foot of the bed, pulled back the covers and crawled in. She was careful not to awaken him, but the longer she laid there, the more unlikely that seemed.

In the final minutes before the blessing of sleep enfolded her, Cappy sighed in relief. Another day of survival was how she looked at it. Mission accomplished. She had a handful of $20 bills stashed in her bathroom behind the towels. Not bad! The Air Force was a bunch of dumb asses, paying these stooges their rotation pay in twenties. It was easy, too easy. Good choice, this Harvey Klinger. She had walked into the Crystal Club, looked over the slim pickings and plucked him out. Good choice! Well done! She had the money and hadn't lifted a finger—or a leg. She smiled to herself, rolled over and curled up into a tight little ball. Then, as they always did, her thoughts turned to Charlie Frazier, and she began to cry.

Chapter Four

It was a tapping sound, perhaps something louder than that. Still, it was there, distant, starting then stopping.

Beyond that she was aware of a murky gray light that had poked its unwelcome way into the darkened room. Cappy pushed the covers away from her face and took inventory. There were important things to remember—his name, what they had done, where they had been. She mentally ticked off the things she knew. Klinger. First name Harry or Harold or—that's it, Harvey. She locked in on it. Loo-e-ville. A mental image started to come into focus. He was a greenhorn, a little short fat guy with spaces between his teeth and rings of fat around the middle. The image fixed. Now, after a brief moment of rehearsal, she would get rid of the little creep.

The tapping noise came again, off somewhere.

She pushed herself into a sitting position, feigned a demure yawn and looked over at the other side of the bed. It was empty.

Her eyes darted to the chair. His uniform was gone. She smiled to herself. Maybe Harvey Klinger knew more than she gave him credit for. Maybe he had already pulled out. If he had, it would rank as one of the easiest nights she had put in since and maybe including the time she spent with Charlie. It was certainly one of the most profitable.

She swung her long pale white legs over the edge of the bed and stood up, momentarily catching a reassuring glimpse of herself in the full-length mirror. Cappy was pleased with what she saw. She went to the closet, pulled out the maroon velvet floor-length robe that Charlie had given her the previous Christmas and headed for the kitchen.

She wasn't expecting to find him there, but it was suddenly clear that she had celebrated the ease with which Harvey Klinger had been dispatched prematurely.

He turned to face her when she walked into the room but avoided looking directly at her. The apology came out in a muted monotone.

"I don't know what to say. . . ." What there was to his voice slowly trailed off into nothingness.

Cappy suddenly realized that in addition to being surprised that Harvey hadn't disappeared into the early predawn gray of the Saint John's morning, she was even more angered by his presence. She did a quick assessment of the situation and decided on the appropriate dialogue. She huffed and brushed past him, heading for the sink. Step one was to make it painfully apparent that she was upset.

Harvey watched her out of the corner of his eye. "You're angry. I guess I must have gotten out of line last night."

The stage was set. Cappy wheeled, one hand perched on her hip, the other holding the half-full glass percolator pot. "Yes, Mr. Klinger," she snapped, "you do have reason to apologize. You did get out of line. In fact, you were just awful."

Harvey's indolent blue-gray eyes masked his true feelings. "I'm really sorry. I guess I must have had too much to drink."

Cappy was determined to play out the scene. First came the moist eyes, then a little tremble to the lips and a slight tremor in the hands, followed by the hopeless sag of her young body against the old cast-iron sink. "I didn't feel good, and you knew I had too much to drink. I never drink that much. I thought I could trust you. Oh, you were just fine, a real gentleman . . . until you got up here to my apartment. Then . . . then you turned into something disgusting." There were three carefully placed sobs and just the right amount of tears. "Why is it that you men think just because you've spent a few months at one of those isolated Arctic duty sites you can come marching through here and treat a lady like a damned animal?"

Harvey stared back at her, appropriately contrite. He looked ashamedly down at his feet, his pasty white face slightly flushed with embarrassment.

Suddenly it occurred to Cappy that he had been up for a while, roaming aimlessly about her stark little apartment. She hadn't heard him poking around in anything, but what if he had been? What if he discovered some of the money she had taken out of his wallet? What if he knew? The thought both frightened her and refueled her anger.

"What the hell have you been up to, anyway?" she snarled. "You don't have any right to go snooping around my apartment, especially not after the way you acted."

The Airman looked past her at the counter. "I . . . I heard a noise," he said. "I didn't know what it was, but you were sleepin' so soundly, I decided to let you sleep and check it out."

"A noise? What kind of noise?"

Harvey was hesitant. He shrugged. "I don't know . . . a noise, like somebody peckin' at a window."

It had been a tapping noise that had awakened Cappy. She looked at him hard, trying to read him. "Well?"

"Well what?" he asked. The expression on his too fat face mirrored his confusion.

"Was it somebody tapping at the window?" Cappy knew that could well be the case. Rosemary had done that before, crawling across the narrow expanse of shed roof that bridged the short distance between the two old houses. Rosemary's husband would lock her out on the roof and her only refuge from the cold would be the sanctuary of Cappy's apartment.

Harvey shook his head. He did it in such a fashion that Cappy could tell he was holding something back.

"Look, dammit, did you find the noise or not?"

He moved uneasily around her toward the counter, ignored her question, bent over and peered into the glass jar. "I know you'll think I'm crazy, but I swear the sound was coming from this jar."

Cappy broke into a derisive laugh. "For Christ's sake, dumbo, you take the cake. A couple of watered down shots of cheap bourbon and ten hours later you're still half-stoned.''

"I . . . I didn't turn on any lights. I came in here in the dark. The closer I got to it, the surer I was.''

Cappy grabbed the jar, scooted it along the counter top and picked it up. The semi-opaque, reddish-gray liquid sloshed back and forth. "Know what this is?" she snarled.

Harvey shook his unfortunate head.

"It's a joke. It's a sick goddamn joke!''

Harvey's face still had a look of puzzlement. She shook the jar violently. "This sorry piece of shit is what I got, all I got, for two years of screwin' Charlie Frazier. It's his idea of a joke, a goddamn glass jar of dirty water!''

Harvey stared at the woman as she raged on.

"You know what that prick did? He hauled me out of a room full of his friends, tells me I ain't goin' back to the States with him, that there ain't gonna be no wedding, shoves me into a damned taxi and tells me to go peddle my ass elsewhere. Then he hands me this jar.''

Harvey looked away. The woman was right; Americans had no right to act like they did.

"Not only that, Mr. damned Airman, you know what I'm going to do with it?''

Before Harvey could conjure up anything resembling a response, Cappy's fit of anger had blossomed into full rage. She slammed the jar to the floor and it shattered. The thick, reddish-gray liquid splattered over the worn linoleum flooring and a foul-smelling stench instantly permeated the room.

In the middle of the jagged shards of glass was a bulky, near shapeless object. As the two of them stood staring at it, it began to move, uncoiling and slowly becoming something identifiable.

Harvey's usually slack-jawed appearance was accentuated now by a mouth agape to the point of looking like it had come unhinged.

"My God," Cappy sputtered, "what is it?"

"It . . . it looks like a hand," he stuttered.

"The damn thing moved," she insisted. "I saw it move."

Harvey cautiously bent over to study the curious object. "It can't be moving," he assured her. "It ain't attached to anything. I mean, it ain't moving 'cause it's alive or nothin' like that."

"Damn it," she snapped, "I saw it move."

Harvey picked up a fork off the counter, bent over and began probing at the withered appendage. "I saw somethin' like this one time when we put an old hound dog to sleep and cut it up in biology class. Even after it was dead you could touch certain parts of the brain and get its legs to move. 'Course that was before we cut him up so everyone in the class had a part to work with."

Between Harvey's description of his class project and the disgusting thing lying in the middle of her kitchen floor, Cappy was certain she was going to be sick.

Harvey was caught up in the details of his explanation. "The way the teacher told us, muscles and nerves and stuff like that all got memories, so probably that hand is just movin' like that because it's been all crammed up inside the jar. I guess it's just sorta takin' its natural form." He looked at her, pleased he had been able to offer what sounded like a perfectly plausible explanation for the phenomenon.

"I don't give a damn what's making it move," Cappy snarled. "Get rid of it. It's disgusting."

"What do ya want me to do with it?"

"Who cares? Just get rid of it." She side-stepped around the grotesque thing, opened a cabinet drawer and pulled out a paper sack. "Here, put it in this, then put it in the garbage."

As much as he didn't want to, Harvey complied with the lady's wishes. With the sack in one hand, he reached out with his thumb and index finger to pick it up.

The reaction was instantaneous. Like a mad dog lashing out with bared fangs, the fingers of the severed hand clamped around his own and there was the sickening sound of tiny bones shattering. Harvey's soft spongy fingers split open like rotting pieces of meat, spewing out a crimson mixture of blood, tissue and chunks of flesh.

Just as quickly, it was over.

Harvey reeled backward, still too much in a state of shock to scream. He slumped against the wall, stupidly inspecting what was left of his right hand. In a matter of a few short seconds, the thing had reduced his hand to a throbbing, mangled and shapeless mass of pulpy flesh. It dangled uselessly from his wrist.

Cappy stared at him, tears of terror streaming down her face. "My God!"

Harvey slid to the floor, cradling his crushed hand in his remaining good one. He was sobbing. Cappy was bending over him, choking in her fear.

"We've . . . we've got to get you to a hospital."

Klinger looked up at her with his pathetic pain-filled eyes, and for the first time since she had met him, she was seeing something in his twisted face. He was shaking his head.

"We . . . we can't," he finally managed.

"What do you mean, we can't? For Christ's sake, Harvey, look at the way you're bleeding."

"We can't," he repeated. "You'll have to put a tourniquet on it."

"That's stupid. You need help."

"Get something," he ordered. His voice was harsh and panic-stricken.

She stared at him momentarily then raced out of the kitchen, down the hall to the bathroom. Within seconds she was back, frantically wrapping his mutilated hand in a large soiled towel. "I . . . I don't think this will do it," she stammered.

"Do the best you can," he said sternly.

Cappy struggled with the profusion of blood, but she was losing ground. A torrential stream pumped from the severed artery in his wrist, bathing him in a sticky pool of his own blood. He leaned his head back against the wall.

"Look," Cappy fumed, "I don't know what it is with you, but you're hurt, hurt real bad. If I don't get you to the hospital and quick, you're as good as kissing your trip back to the States off for good."

"Can't go back anyway," he admitted weakly.

"What do you mean, you can't go back? This is your big day, fly boy; rotation day, remember?" She had stopped fussing with the blood-soaked towel to glare at him.

"Can't go back," he repeated.

Cappy peeled back the towel and probed at the tangled mess of shattered bone and cartilage. His hand had actually been pulverized, twisted and mutilated into something unrecognizable. Near tears, she got up and went to the phone. Regardless of what he said, she was going to call for help. She picked up the receiver. It was dead. She went to the window and stared down into the icy, deserted streets. It was a world of white on white, barren, ice-coated and hostile. Covered with a thick coating of ice, the broken telephone line was dangling from the pole outside of Rosemary's apartment. She slammed the receiver down and headed for the door leading out to the second floor landing. She twisted the knob and heard it click, but it wouldn't open. Then she saw the nails. Nails had been hammered through the door and into the casing from the inside. She raced back into the kitchen and glared down at the little fat man.

"What the hell's goin' on here?"

Harvey stared back at her, his eyes glazed.

"That pounding sound was you, wasn't it?"

He continued to stare at her, his fat, round face void of expression.

"For Christ's sake, Harvey, you're gonna bleed to death. We gotta get you outta here."

"We can't," he said stubbornly.

"Why the hell not?" she screamed.

"Because . . . because they're looking for me."

"Who's looking for you?"

"The military . . . the military police. I killed a man."

Cappy felt the jolt in the pit of her stomach. She stepped back, reeling, her senses deserting her. "You killed a man?" she repeated in disbelief.

"I . . . I had to . . . to get out of there. This guy Klinger was rotating back to the States. He had his papers, he had his pay, he had everything. He was pulling his last shift as a runway observer. I had to get out of there. I cut his throat and buried him under a pile of snow near the observation tower. I took his papers and everything. When his number came up for a MATS flight to Pepperell, I got on. Nobody double-checked anything." Harvey hesitated as though he was playing the scene over in his mind. "By now they probably found his body and figured out what happened. By now they're looking for me."

"If you're not Harvey Klinger, then who the hell are you?" she demanded.

The man who called himself Harvey Klinger, the man with the mutilated hand, looked up at her with his empty eyes. "Does it really matter?"

Stunned, Cappy took a step toward him again. He had started to shiver. If she couldn't somehow get the blood stopped, he was going to go into shock.

She was so focused on him that she failed to notice that the severed hand had started to pulsate again and move, inching its way toward her. By the time Cappy realized what was happening, it was too late. She screamed and bolted, but it had already wrapped its cold, strong fingers around her ankle. She could only watch in horror as the skin above and below the hand's death grip began to discolor—first a hot pink blush, then darker, turning a vivid blue-black. The skin began splitting, tearing open. Blood vessels bloated and ruptured. She heard the bones compress, begin to splinter and finally shatter, exploding like tiny rifle shots as they ripped through her tormented flesh. The scream which had taken what seemed like an eternity to well up in her constricted chest now bolted through the wall of silence, ricocheting off the walls of the tiny room. She jerked violently, staggering backwards and falling halfway into the hall. That final, desperate lunge had loosened the hand's grip, and she began to crawl.

She clawed her way across the stretch of cold linoleum. Her hand coiled around one of the chrome-legged, plastic-padded chairs, and with surprising strength, strength she never knew she had, she knocked the object sideways, toppling it and creating a momentary barrier between her and her assailant.

Between hysterical sobs, she screamed

across the expanse of the tiny room at the man who claimed he wasn't Klinger.

The hand was stymied. She knew it was impossible, but it was almost as if it was confused by the temporary obstacle she had thrown into its path.

Cappy's eyes darted about the room, probing the shadows for a weapon, something, anything she could use to defend herself. "Hey! Can you hear me?"

The dulled eyes of the fat Airman fluttered open, momentarily establishing contact with her and reality. Somehow he managed to convey that he could indeed hear her.

"You've got to get out of there," she panted. "If you can get through the kitchen door, I can shut it and bolt it."

His first effort was nearly imperceptible. With the blood still gushing from his shattered hand, he initiated the laborious effort. He slumped over on his side, like a snake, inching his way along the floor. He was no more than four feet from the door that would give him sanctuary from the hideous thing.

The hand continued to grope after him, gaining ground, seemingly sensing its way along the trail of blood left behind by the wounded man.

Harvey Klinger, or whatever his name was, never made it. The severed hand caught up with him just inches short of his goal. Slowly, with a horrifying single-mindedness, it began inching its way to the fallen man's face. Slowly, methodically, it encompassed the Airman's round, fear-filled face and began to squeeze.

Cappy closed her eyes, but the sickening image burned its way into her mind. She heard the same terrifying sounds over again —the splintering and collapsing of things once solid and rigid and made of bone. The man was screaming. To Cappy it sounded like the shrill screams of the old women in her village when they learned that their men had gone to sea, never to return again.

Suddenly there was an ominous and deadly silence.

Cappy opened her eyes.

Whoever he was, he lay there, ashen and still, a grotesque, fat, rag doll of a man with a head that had been pulverized into a shapeless mass, crushed like something overripe and rotten. The blood-stained stringy brown hair was crusted over with a thick purplish gelatinous substance that seeped from the gaping fissures, tracing crazy quilt patterns back and forth across what was left of the man's mutilated head.

Pain was searing its way up her leg. She staggered from the room, her stomach revolting. She slammed the door shut and threw the dead bolt.

* * *

Seven hours passed.

The grotesque thing that crawled from the bottle was gaining on her.

She had been forced into one retreat after another. This was her last refuge, her final sanctuary.

Doors splintered under its onslaught.

Cappy was down to her final, desperate act; the door leading from the hallway into her bedroom was closed and locked. She had stacked everything against it that she could move; first there was the dresser, then the hope chest was wedged against that for whatever additional safety it would offer.

She could hear it, relentlessly clawing its way up the hall.

The hysteria had passed, and so had the tears. She was motivated now, not only by her survival instinct, but by the thing's destruction.

She had a plan, a simple plan.

The pain in her leg had subsided, giving way to a maddening numbness. It was discolored and bloated. A crusted ring of blood served as the demarcation line between shattered and still intact bone. Her ankle bent grotesquely to one side, and her foot flopped uselessly like something that had been separated from its senses.

The thing was outside her door now, and

she heard the first almost childlike scratches at the surface.

It was now or never. She managed to shove the bulky hope chest to one side, picked up the colorful biscuit tin her grandmother had given her and crawled on top of the dresser. She opened the tin and pulled out a large pair of sewing scissors, determinedly curling her fingers through the looped handles.

The thing—the hand, the sick joke, Frazier's farewell gift—continued to claw at the door, and then it stopped.

Cappy waited.

Minutes, perhaps an eternity, passed.

Suddenly the door was exploding, wood splintering, sending her reeling as the chest toppled, plunging her to the floor. As shock waves of pain bolted up her tortured leg, she screamed out, giving vent once more to the terrifying hysteria that had engulfed her.

The hand was inching its way into the room toward her.

Cappy began a stabbing motion, a frenzied, vicious, final effort to ward off her assailant. Twice she hit it with glancing blows, near misses that gouged out small chunks of rotting flesh.

Each time the thing recoiled.

Each time it renewed its attack.

She lunged again, plunging the fire-hardened steel blades down in a savage arch. A direct hit, a fatal kind of final blow, ripped through the withered appendage, crushing the network of tiny bones, shredding the rotting tendons and muscles, and pinning the horrible thing to the floor like a giant spike.

For Cappy, there was a moment, a single brief void in space and time, when everything stopped. Out of all of that evolved one long, terrible, loud scream.

It was over!

The excruciating pain in her mangled leg stemmed the hysterical urge to rejoice in her victory. She crawled across the floor until her trembling hands grasped the leg of the bed. Hand over hand, she pulled herself up until she could crawl out on the cool expanse of the white cotton sheets.

The room was painted in long, gray, somber shadows, empty and silent. There was only the sound of her own still hammering heart.

She curled up in the middle of her bed, sobbing, tortured beyond endurance. First she'd rest, then get help. Her eyes were heavy. Her labored breathing was interspersed with racking sobs.

She slept fitfully.

When she awoke, it was on her, covering her face. It was too late. The sound she heard was the most terrifying sound of all—the hollow, empty echo of death.

Chapter Five

The rangy, gaunt officer with the burned-out eyes held out the clipboard for the man to sign. His companion was a man of average height, weight and looks, with only his stamina to separate him from the others.

He stepped aside, waiting for the two men from the crime lab to depart, taking with them their proliferation of detecting gimmicks and gadgets.

Peter Machino locked his hands behind his back and began to prowl through the depressing little apartment again. He noted with some degree of thankfulness that the sickening stench of death had started to dissipate. He knew, equally as well, that it would never entirely go away. Anyone who knew what death smelled like and the long neglected residue of that final act would always be able to tell.

For a moment he had forgotten about the woman, but she was still there, sitting patiently in the overstuffed chair, knees pressed primly together, purse poised on her lap. She was an incredibly plain woman; small and slightly hunched, she held her head to one side as though at one time or another she had suffered a neck injury. Her hair, a dull and nondescript brown, was combed unimaginatively to one side, and her face showed not a trace of makeup. Her eyes were swollen, but that was to be expected. If Machino could believe her story, Cappy Salem was one of the few people in the world who had been nice to the woman.

Peter understood that. When the people who befriend you die, you cry; it's as simple as that. There are all too few of them, and they are gone all too soon.

He scooted the cheap, pine rocking chair across the threadbare rug, maneuvering into a position so that he could sit and talk to the woman.

"I know all this has been very painful for you, Mrs. Markle. It is *Mrs*. Markle, isn't it?"

Her voice was as anemic as her demeanor. "Yes, Mrs. Markle, Rosemary Markle. Me and the husband live right over there." She pointed through the kitchen window, across the expanse of shed roof to a dingy-looking window on the other side.

"You knew the Salem woman well?"

The woman hunched her already too narrow shoulders in a noncommital shrug. "We wasn't exactly what you would call close friends. But she was a real nice lady, a lady that was kind to me."

"In what way, Mrs. Markle?" Machino's voice was gentle and nonthreatening.

Rosemary Markle hesitated. She had never told anyone about Fred. Only Cappy knew about that, and even she wouldn't have known if she hadn't discovered the Markle woman huddled on the shed roof, without a coat, shivering, the victim of her husband's grim determination to punish her.

"Mr. Markle scolds me sometimes," she admitted. "Cappy, saw me sittin' out there on the roof. She was kind enough to bring me in out of the cold."

"So is that how you discovered all of this? Trying to get in out of the cold? Let me ask it this way—was Mr. Markle punishing you when you looked in the window?"

The woman nodded.

"Tell me what you saw, Mrs. Markle."

"Well," she hesitated, "I'd been out there for a while, and I had to go to the bathroom. I knew Fred wouldn't let me in, so I came over and tapped on Cappy's window. It was all frosted over and I had to scrape it away so I could see in."

"Tell me what you saw."

"Like I told the other man, the only thing what I could see was a mess. There was broken glass all over the floor, chairs were tipped over, and it looked like someone had spilled something. It wasn't like Cappy to leave something like that. I knew she wasn't no angel, but she was a tidy one, the kind of person who cleans up a mess when she makes it."

"After seeing all that, what did you do?"

"I tapped on the window again, maybe a little harder than the first time, but I was tryin' to get her to come to the window."

"Then what?"

"Well, I crawled back across the shed roof and pounded on my own window, but it weren't no use. I could tell from lookin' in. I knew Fred had gone down to the pub."

"He would go off and leave you locked out on the top of the roof?" Machino asked. This was neither the time nor place, nor was Rosemary Markle the one to ask, but he couldn't understand why women let men do things like that to them.

Rosemary Markle nodded quietly.

"Then what?"

"I was scared. I had the feelin' somethin' bad was wrong. I crawled back across the roof and looked into the window again. I know I'll have to pay for the damage I did, but I knew I had to get into her apartment. I knew somethin' was wrong . . . real wrong."

"How did you get in?"

"That was the easy part. I saw them do it in a movie once, when a house was burnin' and some little children were trapped inside. I wrapped my apron around my hands and used my arms like a club. I was surprised at how easy it broke, just like in the movie."

Machino leaned back in his chair, a wry smile playing with the corners of his mouth. The woman wasn't quite as committed to self-destruction as he had first thought.

"I know you've been through all of this before, Mrs. Markle, but I wonder if you'd mind walking me through it one more time?"

She stared timidly back at the patient man, not wanting to but knowing she had to, because he was the law and he was asking her to.

"Like I said, I broke most of the window. The moment I did I could smell the terrible smell. It was like . . . like spoiled food. I made myself crawl through the window. Everything was rancid. I never smelled anything like it before."

"And where did you find the body of the man?"

"It was over there, inside the door to the kitchen."

"And you knew he was dead the moment you saw him?"

The Markle woman didn't hesitate. "Oh, yes sir, I knew it right away. He was all funny colored and bloated up. And, his head, it . . ." Her voice faded away, and Machino understood the nightmare she was reliving.

"What about your friend, Miss Salem?"

Rosemary Markle's eyes began to cloud up. A single tear traced its way down her hollow cheek and dropped off onto her purse.

"For some reason, I knew I was supposed to go in her bedroom. I just knew somethin' would be terrible wrong. I could feel it. You know what I mean?"

Machino stayed after it. "Try to describe what you saw."

"She was layin' there in the middle of that big bed of hers. She was wearin' her pretty morning robe, but I could see her body was all broken up. There was this awful red crusty stuff all over her, all over the bed. She looked worse than that poor man layin' by the kitchen door."

Peter Machino cleared his throat. He put away his notepad and stood up. He felt compassion for the poor woman. He didn't know what he felt for the victims; he had never met them. Little or nothing had surfaced about the man. He was obviously an Airman from Pepperell, or at least assigned somewhere in the command. They knew only that he was somewhere in his early twenties and that was really about all the RCMP forensic team had been able to establish beyond the cause of death. There was no identification, no billfold, nothing. No one at the base had reported anyone missing. They had been able to get fingerprints off of only one hand, and there was even some confusion about them. At the moment, the dead man was a John Doe in the Saint Johns city morgue—and nothing more. And unless Peter Machino could uncover a whole lot more than he already knew, that was the way it was likely to remain.

A great deal more was known about the woman. She was Cynthia Irene Salem, 23 years old, from a small fishing village near Cornerbrook. She was unemployed and had lived at her current address for the last two years. Of particular interest to Machino was the fact that the young woman had no visible means of support. That fact, coupled with her choices in clothing and jewelry, could lead him to only one conclusion, a conclusion he wasn't about to share with the distraught Mrs. Markle.

Machino heaved a heavy sigh. What the hell!

Cappy Salem wasn't the first, and she wouldn't be the last. As long as that damn air base was out there, and probably even if it wasn't, there would be Cappy Salems.

"I guess that's all the questions I have, Mrs. Markle."

He helped the frail woman gather up her packages and escorted her to the door. She was crying softly when he tipped his hat and closed the door behind her.

Rosemary Markle, still sobbing softly to herself, walked down the steps, traversed the snow-covered sidewalk to the house adjacent to the one where her friend Cappy had lived, and climbed the scarred old stairs to her second floor flat. She knew exactly what to expect. Fred would be angry. She was late preparing his dinner. Fred Markle expected dinner to be ready and on the table when he arrived home promptly every night at six. Now it was a quarter till seven and she hadn't even started the evening meal.

She opened the door cautiously, making as little noise as possible. She hung her worn linen coat on a hanger on the back of the door and waited for his verbal onslaught.

The balding, heavy-set man looked up from his newspaper. She had seen that look all too many times before. "Where the hell you been?" he grunted. "You're late!"

"The . . . the police," she stammered. "They had more questions."

Fred Markle snorted. "That's what you get for hangin' around with a damn slut like that."

Rosemary Markle knew her role in these episodes. It was one of silence, of forebearance, of restraint. She was not expected to respond to his outbursts but was expected to stand there and endure. And for that, she was grateful. His abuse, as bad as it was, was usually verbal, not like what had happened to her friend next door.

"Damn it," he snarled, "how long you gonna stand there? How long before you get yer skinny butt out in that kitchen and start fixin' me some dinner?"

The woman was relieved. She picked up her packages and went to the kitchen, turned on the gas burner under the heavy metal pot of potato soup and began setting the table. Within a matter of minutes, the repast was ready and she called him.

Fred Markle was a man of enormous proportions. He towered well over the six foot mark and his ponderous bulk topped the scale at or near the 300 pound mark. He moved with great difficulty, suffering from a litany of maladies that he complained about constantly. When he sat down at the table, the chair offered a noticeable chorus of creaks and other sounds of protest.

He ate mindlessly, spooning in the thick soup in an unending aerobic of hand to mouth motions.

His wife, who by her own admission found it necessary to recite a lengthy prayer of grace before commencing, was just starting to take in her first spoonful when her husband asked for more.

The woman got up, went to the stove, refilled his bowl and set it in front of him. As she did, her face lightened.

"Oh, I just remembered. I brought you something." She scurried back into the kitchen and reappeared with a brown paper bag. She opened it, pulled out a shoe box and set it next to his bowl of soup. "I hope you like it."

Fred Markle was a man completely lacking in the social graces. Being that way, he snatched the lid off the box and peered in at his new possession.

It was his last act.

The severed hand closed around his massive face, stifling the guttural screams at their source. Bones shattered, skin ripped open, things Rosemary Markle couldn't describe erupted from his splitting skull. It lasted no more than a few seconds. When it was over, he toppled like a great giant oak, pitching his ponderous weight to the floor and writhing in a pool of black, red and green fluids.

That few seconds was all it took.

Rosemary Markle got up from the table, took her coat from the hook on the back of the door, picked up her purse and walked slowly down the narrow flight of steps to the street below.

Outside, in the gently falling snow, she walked briskly to the corner where a taxi waited. She crawled in and sat in the middle of the back seat, her heart still pounding. When she was convinced it was safe to do so, she opened her purse, took out the bulky wallet, and began counting out the $20 bills.

PART THREE

Chapter Six

With a name like Bartholomew, Bartholomew Clements Miller was more than just glad someone early on in his years had the foresight to hang the tag "Bart" on him. Now, as he scanned the stack of mail, he found that with the exception of junk mail and solicitations, most of his friends, at least the ones who could write, had the good sense to use the more abbreviated form of his name.

Along with the daily dump by the local postal service were two packages. One, quite obviously, was from Deta Fredrickson, Malcolm's secretary over at the Chamber in Port Isabel. It was probably the new promotional kit being sent out to compete for the free-spending Yankee snowbirds who in recent years had started to make South Padre a viable alternative to Florida for the holidays. The second package was slightly more intriguing; it was addressed to Ruthie. And it was anybody's guess where she might be. He shook the cardboard box a couple of times, decided the contents were still intact and wondered what to do with it since there was no return address on it. He walked out of the stale-smelling old building for the marginal comfort of the midmorning south Texas October sun.

It was too late. Moxie spotted him the moment he stepped out of the shadows.

"Boss Bart!" the wiry little Mexican yelled across the expanse of sun-parched and cracked macadam. "Everybody been looking for you."

Bartholomew was trapped. He sighed, opened the door of his pickup, threw his mail on the threadbare seat, shut the door again and waited.

Moxie was headed straight for him, occasionally disappearing in the maze of tourists' cars still dotting the parking lot. Moxie wasn't easy to keep track of; he was all of five feet four in height and not much wider in any feature of his emaciated anatomy than a wooden pencil. His crop of jet black hair and razor-thin moustache were the highlights of a weathered face that looked for all the world like a piece of oiled antique leather stretched loosely over a human skull.

Moxie was a fixed part of Bart's life and had been ever since the day Bartholomew had taken over his father's tavern. That was three days after the old man had died. Bart was singularly convinced that the old man, who had always had a flair for dramatics, had made one of those impassioned deathbed speeches that asked Moxie to make sure he took care of Bartholomew, to use his father's favorite expression, "come hell or high water." Whatever the case, Moxie always managed to be around. For the most part, that was good—Bartholomew could depend on him—but not now. He had other things on his mind.

"What is it?" he sighed.

"You see the weather report?"

Bartholomew nodded. "Yup, less than an hour ago."

Moxie looked disappointed. Somehow it seemed that a hurricane sitting less than 200 miles off the south Texas coast deserved more of a response than a mere nod of the head and a subdued "yup."

"Gladys Ann is worried about it," Moxie dutifully reported.

Bartholomew, because he was six foot four and a bit too tall for most of his world, was prone to slouching. He had never given it much thought, but Ruthie had once told him she was convinced he did it to accommodate the Moxies of the universe, who spent their time looking up into his swarthy face, trying to interpret his wants and desires. Bartholomew had learned long ago that he had been blessed with the kind of personality that made people want to do things for him. He supposed his nudging sense of humor didn't hurt matters either.

He was doing it again, slumping back against the door of his truck. "Come on, Moxie, how long have you known that woman?"

It was equally obvious the intended humor in the question had escaped the little Mexican. Moxie looked up at the man he called Boss Bart with a questioning expression on his face. Nevertheless, he dutifully did a couple of quick calculations and responded. "Almost ten year." Moxie had a curious habit of talking in the singular.

"Well then," Bartholomew chided, "if you've known her that long, then you know her well enough to know that Gladys Ann gets excited about a lot of things that aren't really worth getting excited about. Right?"

"But," Moxie sputtered, "the weather bureau people say by late tonight we could have a big problem."

Bartholomew nodded patiently. Moxie was

always well-intentioned. The little man was doing nothing more than conveying Gladys Ann's pre-storm paranoia. It went with the territory. "Look, Moxie, you go back to the Gull House and tell G.A. that I'll be there by noon. If the weather reports aren't any different by then, we'll discuss what we should do. Okay?" Bartholomew always called Gladys Ann "G.A." when he was trying to avoid lengthy conversations.

Moxie Avilla, among his other habits, had a tendency to nod his head like a chicken when Bartholomew was giving him instructions. He was doing it now.

To Moxie's way of thinking, Boss Bart, who owned the Gull House and frequently assisted Sheriff Gleason by serving as a deputy during the off-season, ought to be the one who was most concerned about the impending storm. The Gull House sat out on the point, one of the island's few high places, and if a storm did hit, the Gull House was bound to get a healthy dose of foul weather. Instead, there he was, this tall, open-faced man, the only son of his old friend Lucius, giving him a list of chores that were nothing more than a thinly veiled plot to get rid of him.

Moxie nodded and, because he was dutiful and Bart was boss, set about the task of getting his chores accomplished.

After sending his shadow packing, Bart

Miller climbed into his pickup, turned on the ignition and then the radio. Unconsciously he began tweeking the dial looking for the Coast Guard maritime station. After patiently sifting through a series of squeeks and squeels, he located it. Out of habit, he glanced at his watch. It was 10:07.

The monotone voice droned on about the forecast at Galveston and when it turned to Corpus Christi, he began to listen.

"HURRICANE ERNESTINE IS NOW LOCATED ONE HUNDRED AND SEVENTY-FIVE MILES OFF PORT ISABEL. THE STORM IS MOVING IN A WEST NORTH-WESTERLY DIRECTION AT APPROXIMATELY TWENTY-FIVE KNOTS. THE HURRICANE ADVISORY CENTER IN MIAMI ADVISES THAT SURFACE WINDS ARE GUSTING TO NINETY-FIVE KNOTS AND THAT THE STORM IS TRACKING ON A COURSE THAT WOULD HIT THE SOUTH TEXAS COAST AT APPROXIMATELY TWENTY HUNDRED HOURS THIS EVENING."

The voice then launched into a detailed report of swell sizes, safe harbor locations for tourists and enforced small craft warnings. Bart began spinning the dial again. He picked up a radio station in Brownsville, where a baritone voice somberly waded through the same verbiage he had just heard on the maritime forecast. Maybe, he admitted to himself, Gladys Ann had reason for concern.

He leaned out the window of his truck and studied the hazy sky overhead, then turned his attention to the eastern horizon. It was beginning to look like Red Gleason had picked a poor time to take a day off. In the short time since he had walked out of the post office, had his brief exchange with Moxie and listened to the forecast, the sky to the east had begun to sour. At the moment it was only a thin veil of wispiness, but beyond and further east the clouds were darkening and thickening.

Bartholomew grunted and headed for Morgan's place on the beach. Even if there was going to be a major blow, there wasn't anything he could do about it, and besides, he had more to worry about than the safety of the Gull House.

Less than five minutes later he had turned off the paved comfort of the highway and was plowing his way through the fine brown South Padre sand. It was a good 300 yards back to the old man's place.

When he arrived, Morgan was down on the beach, laboriously tugging his 18-footer out of the now encroaching tide. Bartholomew crawled out of his truck and noted with some dismay that the wind already had started to pick up. Since South Padre wasn't the kind of place where a man stood on formality, he headed straight for the sandy strip of beach.

Pasquel Morgan looked up apprehensively when he saw the tall, tanned law officer approaching. "I can tell by the look on your face this ain't a social call, right?"

As usual, Bartholomew didn't have long to assess the situation. He had wanted to approach the old man as Bart Miller, owner of the Gull House, and not Deputy Miller, Red Gleason's sometime surrogate. But Pasquel had already rightly read the situation. Under the circumstances, there was probably no other way to read it.

"Mornin', Pasquel," he drawled. Ruthie had told him once that when he put on Gleason's badge, his voice took on an affected drawl. He wasn't sure he agreed with Ruthie about that or the dozen other things they were fighting about toward the end.

The old man had stiffened. Once or twice his eyes darted down into his skiff, and Bart suspected that the man had something hidden in there he didn't want Bart to see.

Pasquel's eyes darted out to the gulf again before he turned his attention to the deputy. "It's gettin' choppy," he assessed. "Think there'll be a blow?"

Miller breathed a sigh of relief. At least the old man hadn't gone off half-cocked. In situations like this, a man has to figure for a minute or two that it could go either way. He moved cautiously around so that what was left of the hazy streaks of sunshine fragmenting down through holes in the cloud deck would be in Pasquel's eyes and not his. His thumbs were hooked in his belt, a long way from the ponderous and preposterous-looking Colt revolver that was strapped to his hip.

For the record, Bart Miller hated guns, had hated them since he was a kid. He had even gone so far as to tell Red he wouldn't carry one. But, and there's always a "but," he had changed his mind the night Clyde Mercer got his head blown off trying to break up a fight at the Chino Club. Guns, Bart figured, caused more problems than they solved, but after seeing Clyde Mercer in the morgue at Brownsville, he had decided to carry one whenever Red called him to duty.

Pasquel was studying him through squinted eyes. "Well, if you don't want to talk about the storm, what do you want to talk about?"

There was too much on his mind and too much to do to play games with the old man. Besides, if he had learned anything from Red Gleason in the years he had been serving as a special deputy, it was, especially in situations like this, to get straight to the point.

"You know I gotta ask, Pasquel. Did you do it?"

The old man jammed his hands down in his pockets and turned his back on Miller. He stared out at the ominous cauldron of clouds boiling up out of the sea to the east. It was several minutes before he responded. When he did, it was with a quiet defiance that Bart had never heard in the old man's voice before.

"He had it comin', ya know." Then, as if he suddenly remembered they were talking about another human being, he asked, "How is he?"

"Dead," Miller heard himself say. It all sounded too matter-of-fact, like he was calling balls and strikes in a softball game down at Burson Park. "I got a call from the Brownsville police chief early this morning. He died after he got out of surgery."

"Pretty tough to dig one of them slugs out of the brain," Pasquel acknowledged. "I usually hit what I'm aimin' at."

Miller nodded. Ernie Laws, Red's night deputy, had given him the gruesome details which were probably somewhat embellished, because Laws liked that sort of thing. "What happened?"

The old man wearily lowered himself down on the gunnel of his beached skiff. "You know what I'm gonna tell ya," Pasquel began. "That it wasn't my fault, and it wasn't. I was mindin' my own business, havin' a drink. The place was crowded. All of a sudden this little wetback starts jawin' at me, callin' me names, tellin' me an old fart like me should crawl out in the alley and do my drinkin' there."

"And you shot him because he wanted your barstool?" Miller's voice had a ring of incredulity to it. It was just one more reason to solidify his conviction of "no gun, no problem."

"I get tired of gettin' pushed around," Pasquel muttered. "Them young fellers think just because I'm an old man, they can do any damn thing they wanta. But, I'll tell you somethin', they learned somethin' last night."

There didn't seem to be much for Bart to say. Pasquel had been around; he knew the game and the score. The old man had to know someone would come for him, no matter how it turned out. Finally, Bartholomew did what he had to do. "You're gonna have to come with me, Pasquel. I've got a warrant. I'll have to take you over to Port Isabel."

Pasquel Morgan looked up at him. There was the haunted, disappointed look of passing years in his aging eyes. "You gonna give me time to button up this old place afore the storm hits? Iffin' I beat this rap, I wouldn't wanta come back out here and find my things scattered all over the damn island."

Bartholomew detested the old man for making the request. The longer he was delayed, the longer it would be before he could address his own problems. But he had known Pasquel Morgan for 20 years, and the old-timer had pumped down as much whiskey at the Gull House as he had anywhere on the island. "Make it snappy," he said brusquely. "I got other matters to tend to."

"Give me an hour," Pasquel pleaded.

Bart glanced at his watch and up at the thickening clouds. He was starting to see some build-up. "I'll give you forty-five minutes, and I'll be back to get you." He paused for a moment, looking into the old man's eyes. "And, Pasquel, don't let me down. When I come back to get you, you'd better be here, and you'd better be ready."

The old man twisted his parched lips into what had long served him as a smile. "For Christ's sake, Bart, look at me. I'm seventy-six years old, and I got a wooden leg and a birthmark that covers damn near half of this old face. Where the hell you figure somebody like me's gonna hide? How far you figure I'd get?"

Miller affectionately patted the old man on the shoulder. "Forty-five minutes, Pasquel, that's all." He turned and headed back up the beach knowing that Gleason would give him hell for trusting the old man. As he was crawling back into the cab of his truck, he heard the first distant peal of thunder out over the gulf. Out of the corner of his eye he caught a brief glimpse of lightning. He was pulling back onto the blacktop just as the first drops of rain splattered against his dusty windshield.

From Morgan's place he headed over to the Coast Road, behind the new condos being built by an investment group from Dallas and around the parking lot of the new Sheraton. Official business, for the moment, had been taken care of. He had help, if he needed it, with the Gull House, and that left Linda. Linda was new to South Padre, and Ernestine, if she did slam into the little resort island community, would be her first official tropical storm. And if you were about to meet your first hurricane face to face, it was no time to be alone.

Linda Cavitt had hit town two months ago, fresh from Chicago and, from what everyone said, a nasty, highly publicized divorce. She was the new banquet manager at the Sheraton, the summer season had just ended, and she had taken some much needed time off to get her personal life in order.

Bartholomew had met Linda at Red Gleason's sixtieth birthday party at the Gull House. Gladys Ann had introduced them, and nature had taken its course. They hit it off immediately. Bartholomew Miller, the man with the wife who had disappeared, and Linda Elaine Cavitt, the woman still reeling from a broken marriage, spent what precious little spare time they had together.

Like most places on the beach, her two bedroom bungalow was built on massive steel beams that jutted out of the sandy earth and suspended the living quarters over a parking area underneath. He pulled in and parked beside her car, raced up the back steps and ended up knocking twice before she answered.

When she opened the door, her eyes were swollen; she had been crying. "Damn," she muttered through a half-smile, "I didn't want you to see me like this."

"Are you all right?"

"Just feeling a little sorry for myself," she admitted. It was a level of honesty she hadn't attained with anyone on South Padre except Bart Miller.

Bartholomew glanced around the room. Unpacked cartons and a collection of odd boxes still cluttered the living room. She kept excusing the mess, telling him she just hadn't found time to tackle it. "And," she had confided once, "there are things in some of those cartons I'm not sure I'm ready to face just yet."

She led him through the house into the kitchen, poured him a cup of coffee, and they sat down next to each other at the small breakfast bar with the big view of the gulf.

"So, Mr. Lawman," she said, glancing at the Colt strapped to his hip and at the same time wiping away a tear, "tell Mama what you've been up to this morning."

"Been listening to the radio?"

She shook her head. Her short blonde hair was barely ruffled by the gesture. "Why, should I be?"

"Have you ever been through a hurricane?"

"Damn," she said, grinning, "don't tell me there's something else I've been missing."

Bartholomew squinted out at the gulf and set his cup down. "Actually, there's two ways of getting through one. You can hightail it out of here, look for some nice, safe, dry place and wait out the storm, or you can have yourself a hurricane party and ride the storm out here."

"I've got a better idea," she said. "Why don't you and I get a bottle of wine, a couple of candles and go crawl between the covers until the storm passes?"

The suggestion brought a smile to Bartholomew's face. "Gotta admit, that's a helluva lot better than either of my alternatives."

Linda got up and began searching through the cabinets above her stove. "The first thing I've got to do is find the candles."

"On the contrary, the first thing we've got to do is get your windows boarded up. If we don't, your stuff will be spread all over the island and you won't have a window left in the house."

"Boarded up with what?"

"Moxie should be here any minute with the plywood. I counted from memory, then I sent him down to the lumberyard. In the meantime, fill up several containers with drinking water, just in case the blow hits full force and fouls our water supply."

"You're serious, aren't you?"

Miller nodded. "Never hurts to be prepared. Most of the time all we get out of these things is one helluva soaking and some strong winds. A little inconvenient, maybe, but no serious damage. But, if she comes ashore full force, it gets real nasty in a hurry."

Much of the smile had faded from Linda Cavitt's symmetrical face. She had quit rummaging through the cabinets, instead moving to the windows to look out at the water. "It does look threatening," she admitted.

Bartholomew stood up and gently pulled her to him. Then he folded his arms around her waist. The gesture brought the smiles back to both their faces. "I wish I could stay here and help you, but with Red out of town, I've got a bunch of things I have to take care of. Moxie will board up your windows. You start gathering anything that's loose. Make sure everything is shut off and unplugged, then pull your circuit breakers. When Moxie's

156

through he's supposed to take you back to the Gull House. I'll get everything taken care of and meet you there."

"What's so all-fired important that you have to leave now?" The question turned her pretty face into a little girl pout.

He saw no harm in telling her. If she had been out and about this morning she would have heard the gossip anyway. It was causing as much talk as the storm brooding off the coast. "Pasquel Morgan shot and killed a Mexican kid last night at Las Chinkas. I've got orders to take him to Port Isabel and book him."

Linda looked back at him, a look of disbelief etched into her face. "You've got to be kidding. Pasquel Morgan? He couldn't shoot anyone."

Bartholomew shook his head. "I wish I was, but there were several witnesses." He released her, kissed her playfully on the forehead and started for the door. She caught up with him halfway across the room, turned him around and kissed him, full and hard on the lips.

"Be careful," she said huskily. "I've just about got you trained. You're getting to be pretty good in the bedroom. Linda baby doesn't want to have to start over with somebody new."

"Tell me," he said, feigning a look of bewilderment, "are all women from Chicago pre-occupied with sex?"

"What difference does it make? You've got your hands full with just one." She grinned, spun him around and began working him toward the door.

He was just crawling in his truck when Moxie arrived. The back of his ancient yellow Ford was loaded down with sheets of plywood. Bartholomew barked out a few instructions, rolled up his window and backed out. He didn't want to waste anymore time. He had checked his watch, and Pasquel Morgan had already used up 40 of his minutes. Plus, just in case the old boy was planning something, Bart didn't want to give him anymore of a head start than he already had.

The first few sparse drops he had noticed on the way to Linda's had turned into a series of blustery off and on showers. The intensity varied several times in the short drive back to Morgan's place. The lightning, only a now and then thing 30 minutes ago, had become almost continuous. There was an occasional rumble of thunder overhead and more frequently out over the gulf. He turned on the radio again. This time he could barely hear the voice through the barrage of static.

"THE HURRICANE CENTER IS NOW LOCATED ONE HUNDRED AND FORTY

MILES OFF THE COAST OF PORT ISABEL.
ADVISORY REPORTS FROM THE CORPUS
CHRISTI WEATHER BUREAU ARE RE-
PORTING WINDS AT TWENTY-FIVE
KNOTS WITH PEAK GUSTS TO THIRTY-
FIVE KNOTS IN A SQUALL LINE PRE-
CEDING . . ."

He snapped off the radio and watched the
windshield wipers plow determinedly back
and forth in a fruitless effort to provide a field
of vision. He had been through one too many
storms already. He knew from experience
that unless the old girl veered off at the last
minute and headed north, what they were
getting now was only the first surge. It would
pass. There would be a temporary lull and
then another squall line. The second one
would be more intense than the first. The
pattern was destined to be repeated again and
again until the storm itself hit, and when it
did, there would be hell to pay on South
Padre.

He pulled off the blacktop and worked his
way up Morgan's long, twisting, tree-
shrouded lane toward the old man's house. A
sudden strong gust of wind buffeted his truck,
and a loud peal of thunder rattled the windows. He jerked the truck to a stop, jumped
out and raced toward the house. He threw
open the door and jumped in, turning in the
same motion to slam it against the rain.

"Damn," he complained without looking back, "I hope you got the old girl boarded up. The way the rain's comin' down, you and I are gonna have a bitch of a time just gettin' over to the mainland."

"You ain't goin' nowhere," an unfamiliar, snarling, Mexican voice informed him.

Bartholomew wheeled.

Two men stood across the room staring at him. Their kind needed no introduction. They were the type that spelled trouble. Their intention was as apparent as the malevolent look on their glowering faces. Both had guns, little short-barreled ugly-looking things, the kind pounded out in countless back alley shops all across Mexico.

One was big and beefy with a fat face and a full bushy mustache. The other looked enough like Moxie to be his twin brother. He was the leader, the meaner looking of the two.

"What the hell's goin' on here?" Miller sputtered.

The little one smiled; it was sinister and sardonic. The big one's face was stupidly flaccid.

"Where's Pasquel?" Bartholomew demanded.

"Don't worry about Señor Morgan." The smaller of the two grinned. "We already took care of him."

The big one, almost as tall as Bartholomew

and easily outweighing him by 50 pounds, took a lumbering step sideways so Miller could see into the old man's bedroom. Pasquel Morgan was sprawled out in the middle of a dirty, braided, oval rug. He was lying face down in a pool of something that looked like thick, black-red syrup that had started to wend its way across the floor to what the old man called his living room.

Bartholomew, ignoring the brace of snub-nosed revolvers, bolted past the two men into the bedroom, rolled Pasquel Morgan over on his back and sucked in his breath. The hole began in the old man's lower abdomen, traversed the length of his body and ended up just under the chin. He had been gutted and laid open for all the world to inspect and speculate on how the inner parts of an old man actually worked. Bartholomew felt his stomach do a slow roll and the air stop halfway down to his lungs.

He started to look up and felt the cold, hard steel muzzle of one of the short barrels press against the base of his skull.

"Keep your head down, gringo," the short one ordered.

"That old man killed Acota." The other voice, wet, slurred and slobbering, came at him from the background. "Acota was our friend, man."

"Yeah, man, tit for tat. We killed him because he killed our amigo, because we knew gringos didn't care."

The fat one wasn't through. "We saw you here earlier. You was talking to him and you left. You knew he killed Acota, and you didn't do nothing about it. That just proves you gringos don't give a damn. Just another Mex, right?"

"I was coming back to get him," Miller tried to explain.

He felt the blunted piece of steel press a little further into his hairline. The little one was getting nervous. "I warn you, man, don't look up."

"You going to kill him now?" the fat one asked.

Bartholomew heard the man holding the gun to his head shuffle his feet nervously. "No, man, we don't have to kill him. He don't know what we look like."

"But he saw us when he came in."

Bartholomew already had them pegged.

The little one was the kind who was always sure of himself. "I don't think so," he said cockily. "I think all the gringo saw was the guns. Didn't you see his eyes, man? Big fuckin' eyes. Scared eyes!"

"But he'll come after us . . ."

There was a quality in the mean one's voice that betrayed his contempt for his fat friend's muddled thinking. "Use your head, man. If we kill a gringo cop we could be in big trouble. All we gotta do is get back across the border. Metamoras is big, man. No gringo's gonna go in there looking for us."

Bartholomew's fevered mind had started flashing up one useless set of signals after another. He could bolt sideways, roll over, draw the Colt and start firing—but by the time all that transpired, the snub-nose would have been unloaded in him point-blank. He thought about swinging his elbow up and back, catching the little creep in the crotch, bringing him down like a sack of potatoes. But what if he missed? They both had guns. He could . . .

He never got the chance to develop another alternative. Suddenly his world exploded. He could feel himself sinking; no, he was plunging head first down a long, dark shaft. It was the darkest world he had ever seen. Kaleidoscopic images mixed with whirling sounds. And finally, time stopped.

Chapter Seven

Looks like maybe our boy's starting to come around," Freeman observed.

Bartholomew could hear the sound of moving feet, of chairs scuffing, of people in the room. Beyond that there was the hammering sound of rain pelting the roof. He reached up and touched his hand to the round, egg-sized protrusion at the base of his skull. There was something soft and spongy feeling about it, and his hand fell away.

"It's a bandage." Linda's voice came through the fog, the first truly welcome sound he'd heard.

He opened his mouth to say something, but the whole apparatus felt stiff and unmanageable. Finally, when the words did force their way out, they were distorted and detached. "Where . . . where . . . am I?"

"Bartholomew, my boy, you're right where you were when you nearly bought the farm," Freeman informed him.

"How'd you . . . you find me?"

"We started working backwards," Linda said. "Moxie and I finished boarding up the house, then we went to the Gull House like you told us to. We waited there for over an hour, and when you didn't show up, I called the sheriff's office in Port Isabel. They said you and Morgan hadn't showed up yet."

Moxie's voice creeped in from somewhere back in the shadows of the room. "I call the bridge authority, Boss Bart, and they say they ain't seen you either. I tell Linda that mean you still gotta be somewhere on the island. We think it be a good idea to start at Morgan's place and start tracking you from there."

"You'd have been proud of us," Linda concluded.

"When we find you, Linda Lady think you were dead, Boss Bart. Me, too."

"Yeah, but the little lady here is the one that had the presence of mind to call me," Freeman grunted. Bartholomew didn't know why, but the old doctor and Moxie had carried on a running feud for years.

"Dr. Freeman came right over," Linda added.

"Yeah," Freeman grunted, "I was over tendin' to you when I should've been hauling my old butt off this island." He glowered at Bartholomew. "You know we're gonna be in a heap of trouble when this damn storm hits, don't you?"

Linda bent down so he could see her face. "You might as well get all the bad news at once. The electricity went out about an hour ago; we lost the phones earlier."

Bartholomew Miller tried to raise his head, felt a stabbing pain spring up his back and slam into the recesses of his brain and let out an unmanly yelp. He felt his head sink back into the folds of the pillow.

"Damn it, Bart, lay still," Freeman snapped. "I didn't come here prepared for brain surgery, didn't have the right stuff. Whoever played football with your head laid it open from stem to stern. If there wasn't a lady present I'd tell you how screwed up your head really is."

"The radio says the bridge is out or we'd have taken you to Brownsville by now," Linda said.

"The bridge is out?" Bartholomew groaned.

"You got it—the bridge, the lights, the

phones, everything." Freeman had an unpleasant way of summing things up and giving it the ring of authority.

Linda's head moved out of his field of vision and he heard her ask the doctor what their next move was. He had gotten to know the woman intimately enough to recognize that her voice sounded frightened, something she would never admit. She was a fighter.

"I had Moxie back Bart's truck up to the front door. It's got a cap on it. We're going to use some of Morgan's bed clothes to form a kind of mattress. Then I had him take one of the pieces of plywood off the window at the back of the house; that'll serve as a makeshift gurney so we can carry him out and put him in the bed of the truck. Since we can't get off the island, I think the next safest place would be the Gull House. Moxie tells me Gladys Ann has a generator and enough fuel to ride out the storm. I figure we'd better move him as soon as he thinks he can handle it. When we run out of candles here, it's darkness for the duration."

Bartholomew listened to the plan. He felt surprisingly clearheaded for someone with a hole in his head. All kinds of questions were beginning to rush through his mind. What time was it? Where was the storm now? How many were stranded on the island? Had

Gleason made it back? If not, was he in charge? And if he was, how the hell was he going to get anything accomplished? He had tried to move twice now, and each time it had hurt like hell.

"Well, you heard the plan, big boy. Feel up to it?" Freeman wasn't the kind to pamper his patients, especially not the ones the size of Bart Miller.

"Is it risky?" Linda asked.

"Hell yes, it's risky," Freeman snapped. "I need some needle and thread. At the moment, the only thing that's holding your boy's head together is a couple of adhesive butterfly clamps."

"Then we're not going to risk it," Linda said adamantly.

"Neither can we risk sitting here on the beach in the dark in this old house. The storm could turn this old dump into a bunch of broken sticks in a matter of minutes. Besides, if those clamps let go, I'm gonna need a hell of a lot more than what I got in that black bag of mine."

It was left to Moxie to resolve the dispute. He had a way of reducing all situations to their simplest elements. "I drive you." He looked at Linda. "You ride in the back with Doctor and Boss Bart. Then I take Doctor to his place and get what he need."

Freeman looked at Linda. "Well?"

"We don't have any choice, do we?"

"Let's get with it," Freeman groused.

The procession of the soggy entourage to the Gull House came off with a minimum of hitches. Over Linda's frequent admonitions to "be careful," Bartholomew made it to the bed of the pickup. The diminutive Moxie propped him up on one side and the rotund Freeman held him up on the other. The cap over the bed of the truck kept the area reasonably dry, and the trio decided at the last minute to prop the battered lawman in the corner next to the cab. If anything was going to take an unexpected jolt, Freeman figured Bartholomew's spine had a better chance of surviving than the back of his skull.

Perhaps out of respect, but she suspected more out of a feeling of helplessness, Linda decided at the last minute to cover up Pasquel Morgan's mutilated body with a tattered flannel sheet she found in the old man's hall closet. If there was going to be anymore paying of final respects beyond that, it would have to wait till another time.

Getting out of the old house on the beach proved to be decidedly easier than getting Bart's battered six foot four inch frame up the steps to the Gull House. Even Gladys Ann had to lend a hand. With Moxie and Freeman occupying the same stations as before, the old woman and Linda got behind and performed a kind of push-steady-push operation. By the time the quartet maneuvered the man onto the second floor porch and through the entrance of the Gull House, they were soaked. Safely out of Ernestine's driving rains and howling winds, each of them dropped into the nearest chairs.

The Gull House had been built on a strip of sand and rock known as Monitor Point. In its day, and that day had long since passed, it was the first place that the tourists flocked to when they hit the island. But now the developers had changed the tiny island with its pristine beaches and shifting dunes from a quiet, well-kept secret for a handful of wealthy Texans into a winter mecca for sun-starved midwesterners. The advent of the high rises, the building of the resort hotels, a main drag that was now replete with fast food houses, T-shirt shops and go-go joints had changed what used to be something the locals cherished into something they didn't. All of which had the effect of taking the Gull House full cycle; it had once again become the watering hole for the locals. All this suited Gladys Ann just fine, but it kept Bartholomew walking the thin line of solvency.

The respite was brief. Freeman, taking Linda along primarily for moral support but ostensibly to hold the flashlight while he searched through the medical supplies, headed out for his clinic. Bartholomew's battered head needed stitches. It was clearly a concern with the old man as to just how long they could expect the overtaxed adhesive to hold the man's head together. The more Bartholomew moved around, the greater the risk.

Gladys Ann, not to be outdone, had a list of chores for Moxie that would have staggered a mere mortal, but the little man, soaked to the bone and managing to look even smaller and wiry than usual, leaped to the task. With Moxie dispatched, the old woman turned out all but one light, the one by the cash register at the back of the bar, checked the temperature in the generator-cooled refrigerator and began mopping up puddles of water.

Bartholomew watched her and smiled. The Gull House was creaking and groaning under the onslaught of the storm, sounding like it was ready to give up the ghost and cave in at any moment, and Gladys Ann was mopping. Well, he mused, if it did, and if anybody ever bothered to check, they'd be impressed with the fact that the old place had a clean floor right up to the end.

Gladys Ann had placed a small portable radio next to him on the table. That way he could get the bad news in both massive and repeated doses. She had tuned it into a

Brownsville station that was making the most of the storm with a blaring rock and roll hurricane party. With the exception of an infrequent commercial and public service announcement, the disc jockey played one blaring song after another and gleefully informed his listeners that "Ernestine was now situated some forty-five miles off of Port Isabel," and "she hadn't moved any closer to land in the last two hours, which means, gang, that good old Fuzzy Benson is gonna be with you throughout this long, ugly night, playing your favorites on your Hurricane Music Station, good old KTZZ."

Bartholomew winced.

"Gladys Ann, shut that damn thing off!" he ordered.

The old woman shuffled across the dimly lit room and slumped into a chair across the table from him. In typical G.A. fashion, she had to glare the person down before she said her piece.

Bartholomew looked down at the floor. It was a learned response, and the best way of shortening the glare interval.

"Don't ya want to know about the storm?" she hissed.

Gladys Ann Davidson was the kind of woman Bartholomew's father called "long in the ugly tooth." All of which meant that she had accumulated a few years and had a raspish mouth to match. Bartholomew knew for a fact that the woman was somewhere on the far side of 65, because he had seen her squirreling away her social security checks for years. But Gladys had stopped counting the years, and so had everybody else. Bartholomew always figured Gladys Ann could get away with it because there weren't too many around who could still remember when she first arrived on the scene. His father had told him that G.A., as the old man called her, had simply showed up one day, panhandling and mooching her way to her sister's house in Metamoras. The old boy took a liking to her, and she had been a part of the Gull House ever since, a stretch of time that now dated back more than 30 years.

Bartholomew, returning home after his stint in the army, had heard all kinds of stories about her, some of which intrigued him, all of which he discounted through the process of rationalization after his father died. Gladys Ann stayed on, and whatever the real truth about her checkered past was, she had become the house mother and the heart and soul of the Gull House. It was her passion, her obsession, her lover. He was convinced that in Gladys Ann's mind the Gull House was actually hers and he was just a part of the unfortunate legacy.

She reached around behind her and

scooted a stack of damp looking objects across the table at him. "Here," she grumbled, "if you're gonna sit there and feel sorry for yourself, go through this stack of bills. Linda said they was a'layin' on the seat of that sorry thing you call a truck."

Bartholomew looked at his chore and winced. Here he was, with the back of his head split open, one hell of a throbbing headache, listening to the advance of a storm that could reduce to rubble his one earthly possession that amounted to anything, and the old woman was insisting he go through a stack of bills.

He shrugged, ignoring the obvious, and began inspecting the two packages. The one from the Chamber was expected, the one with Ruthie's name on it wasn't. He inspected the second one a little closer, noted the postmark and started to smile. It had been mailed from Saint Johns, Newfoundland, in February, and it was now October. Whatever it was, it stood a darn good chance, after all that time, of being either broken or spoiled or both. A closer look revealed another curious fact; there was no return address. He shook the package and heard what he would have described as a sloshing sound. The effort sent a pain rippling through the base of his skull, and he set the package back on the table.

Further speculation about the tardy package was curtailed by the frenzied sound of footsteps racing up the wooden steps leading to the bar area. When the door opened, a bedraggled looking pair slipped through the door and hurriedly bolted it against the fury of the storm.

"Got it," Linda said triumphantly.

Freeman looked a little less pleased with their accomplishment. He set his black medical bag on the table next to the packages and headed for the bar. Gladys Ann knew exactly what to do. She set a glass on the bar and a bottle of Jack Daniels next to it. Freeman finished off one and poured another before he began his report.

"We took a couple of extra minutes to check out what's happening. It's worse than any of us thought. The iron bridge has collapsed, and there's a big chunk of road missing out of the causeway. No way over, no way back. The only lights I saw on the whole damn island are over at that new Sheraton. They've evacuated everybody but a security crew, and they're getting what little power they've got from an emergency generator."

Gladys Ann had stopped polishing glasses long enough to listen. "You sayin' we're the only ones on the island besides them folks over at the hotel?"

Freeman shrugged. "There's probably a

couple of others scattered here and there around the island, but there's no way to be sure with everything boarded up."

Linda situated herself in a chair next to Bart. "How are you holding up?"

The deputy forced another puffy-faced smile. "Better," he admitted, "but not good enough to sit and listen to an all-night rock and roll hurricane celebration."

Linda managed her own smile, half-veiled by a quizzical expression.

"Private joke," Bartholomew muttered.

The door slammed and Moxie emerged from the storeroom on the lower level. Under the circumstances, he wasn't quite sure who he was supposed to be filing the damage report with. "Water is comin' in everywhere down there," he announced. "Everything gonna be ruined."

"If you can lift it, stack it on a shelf somewhere," Gladys Ann ordered.

Moxie shrugged his shoulders, glanced at Bartholomew to see if there was a counter-command, and when he didn't get one, turned and dejectedly trudged back down the stairs. The door slammed behind him.

Linda Cavitt busied herself with the dials on the radio. "This still work?"

Bartholomew nodded and immediately regretted it.

"THE LATEST ADVISORY FROM THE MI-AMI HURRICANE CENTER ADVISES THAT HURRICANE ERNESTINE IS STALLED SOME THIRTY-FIVE MILES OFF THE SOUTH TEXAS COAST. SUR-FACE WINDS IN PORT ISABEL AT THE SEVEN O'CLOCK OBSERVATION WERE REPORTED AT SEVENTY KNOTS WITH PEAK GUSTS IN EXCESS OF EIGHTY KNOTS. FURTHER REPORTS INDI-CATE . . ."

The room went silent except for the cease-less fury of the storm hammering the old structure. Linda had clicked it off. "Better save the batteries," she said dejectedly. "Looks like it's going to be a long night."

She turned her attention from the radio to the two packages. "Ruth Miller," she read aloud, catching herself when it was too late. She looked at Bartholomew with an apology on her face. "Sorry," she said, "I wasn't prying."

The owner of the Gull House shrugged. "That's all right, it's reality. She used to exist."

"That's an odd way of putting it." Linda scowled. "Even if she isn't here now, she still exists somewhere. Don't you have any idea where she went?" Linda had lowered her voice so that neither Freeman nor the old woman could overhear her.

The deputy leaned back in his chair, being

careful not to induce any more pain. "It's just that it seems strange for someone to send her a package here. It's obviously from someone who hasn't been in contact with her for a long time, or they'd know."

Linda turned the package around and read the postmark. "Did she have friends in Newfoundland?"

Bartholomew raised his eyebrows. "Who knows? If she did, she never talked about them. Besides, what difference does it make? Look how long it took to get here. Whatever it is, it's probably all busted up after floating around the postal system for seven or eight months."

It was Linda's turn. She slid the candle across the table so she could see his face. "Tell me about her."

"Are you serious?" His question was nearly drowned out by a sudden rush of wind that sent a shudder through the old tavern.

She nodded. "Real serious. You and I have gotten rather intimate in the last several weeks. You know a lot about me, a lot more than I know about you. Maybe it's time you share some of what's going on inside that head and heart of yours."

Few people were that direct with Bartholomew Miller. He had a reputation for being a private person, a singular man, all too often unapproachable. He had been that way long before Ruthie had faded from the Gull House scene. He realized how uncomfortable he was with the woman's request. He tried another shrug but it didn't work.

"Talk to me, Bart. Let me inside."

"She was married when I met her. Her husband was in the Air Force. We met at a party. It was instant chemistry. One thing led to another and before long she was staying at my place. Six months after we met, she filed for divorce. Two years after that my father died. He'd been sick for a long time. When we'd come down to see him, Ruthie and I slept together. I told my father we had gotten secretly married. That pleased him because he wanted grandchildren in the worst way."

"Were you?"

Bartholomew hesitated and glanced at Gladys Ann. Then he shook his head. "No," he said softly, "we were never married."

"Who all knows that?"

Miller looked around the room again. "Funny thing about that—nobody ever asked. Everybody just assumed. Before long she was actually signing her name Ruthie Miller. At the time I thought it was cute. It was only after things started to go sour that it didn't seem like such a good idea."

"What do you mean, 'sour'?"

"Life on South Padre and running the Gull House weren't exactly Ruthie's formula for unbridled excitement. It wasn't long before she got bored with the whole shooting match —this tavern, the island, the lifestyle. You name it, Ruthie was bored with it."

"So what happened?"

"About that time some of the developers started showing up and buying parcels of property. Some guy from Fort Worth approached me about selling the Gull House. Ruthie was all for it. She wanted me to sell out, take the money and run off with her."

Linda took a sip of her drink and winked at him. "Didn't like that idea, huh? That's too bad. I was thinking about asking you to sell this place and run off with me."

Bartholomew made another feeble pass at a smile. It worked better this time. He cocked his swollen head curiously to one side. He recognized the ugly sound; the shingles were starting to peel off the roof. The same thing had happened the last time they had a big blow.

"When I told her I couldn't do it because it had been my dad's place and because I felt an obligation to Gladys Ann and Moxie, she got real upset. From then on, the situation deteriorated. The day before she disappeared she told me she'd been to a lawyer. She said she thought I'd better cooperate because she was pretty sure she could walk away with half of everything the way common law marriages work in Texas."

"And you have no idea why she picked then to leave?"

Miller gave a subtle shake of his head and followed it with a grimace. "None. But I'll tell you this; Ruthie was a strange one—educated, ambitious, but most of all, greedy. I guess she found herself a better deal."

"Kinda sudden, don't you think?"

"That's Ruthie—impulsive."

"And you haven't heard from her since?"

"That's Ruthie, too. When it's over, it's over."

"Do you miss her?"

"Did," he admitted, "for a while. You gotta understand that she was the kind who sucked up all the air in the room. When people like that get out of the picture, you're gonna notice them not being there. But I eventually got used to the peace and quiet. Ruthie had running feuds with everybody, including Moxie and Gladys Ann. They knew what she wanted me to do. I guess they were happy to see her go."

Linda was herself an impulsive lady. As a reward for coming out of his shell, she leaned forward and kissed him gently on his swollen lips. Then she leaned back in her chair again. "I can't help but wonder what the lady would think if she could see you now."

Bartholomew forced another half-grin. "I'll tell you one thing. She'd be a helluva lot more interested in what's in this package than she would my welfare."

"Of course she would." Linda laughed. "You should know by now women can't stand not knowing what's in a package. It drives them right up the wall."

"Is that a roundabout way of telling me that even you are curious about what's in that package?"

"Certainly I'm curious. What if it's something really valuable, like somebody paying off an old debt?"

"Well, what Ruthie doesn't know won't hurt her," Bart drawled.

"Are you serious?" Linda giggled.

"Sure. Go ahead . . . open it."

Linda slid the package over next to the flickering candle and began to systematically peel off the soiled brown paper wrapping. The cardboard box inside was equally battered and had the word "Ruthie" scrawled along the side with a black crayon.

She tore open the box, reached in, extracted a handful of shredded newspapers and pulled out a large, cumbersome jar. She set it on the table and sagged back in her chair, looking disappointed. "Well, so much for my theory on something valuable," she sighed.

"What is it?" Bartholomew blinked. "From here it looks like it could be a jar of pickles or something."

The pair was joined by a curious Gladys Ann and an even more curious Dr. Freeman. Like Bartholomew, neither of them appeared to be overly impressed with the contents of the package.

"Well, one thing for sure," the old woman complained, "it ain't pickles. At least it ain't any pickles I'd want to eat, floatin' around in stuff that color."

Freeman maneuvered himself around the leering old woman and bent over the table to study the jar. He began to rotate the cylinder slowly, studying it against the feeble light of the candle. "Hell, can't make out a damn thing," he groused.

Gladys Ann wasn't the kind to speculate. She nudged the doctor aside, grabbed the jar and twisted the lid. It opened far more easily than she had anticipated and almost instantly, the room was filled with a nauseating odor.

"For God's sake," Linda complained, "put the lid back on that thing. It smells awful."

Freeman stepped forward. "Nonsense, that ain't the way to find out what's in it." He scooped the jar up, carried it across the room to the sink behind the bar and there, under the illumination of the room's single light, held it up for inspection. "Still can't tell anything," he muttered.

"Look, Doc, if you're so damned curious

about it, dump it out in the sink," Bartholomew chided.

"The old fool oughten' to be messin' around with that silly jar," Gladys Ann groused. "He'd be doin' somethin' far more valuable if he'd get yer head sewed up."

Linda was standing up now. She didn't need a radio to tell her the storm had intensified. The Gull House was actually shaking under the constant buffeting of the winds. The tiny light behind the bar flickered off and on, and the thunder was continuous. She took several halting steps toward the jar, still curious.

Freeman wasn't the least bit hesitant. When he twisted the top off for the second time, the metal lid clattered noisily into the stainless steel sink. Even across the room Bartholomew could smell the foul stench. He saw the old man tip the jar and heard the contents plop unceremoniously into the bottom of the sink. Freeman looked up and then back at them, his round, fat face twisting into a mask of surprise and disgust.

"Well, what is it?" Gladys Ann grunted. She was curious enough that she had gone over to the bar and was standing on her toes, peering over the edge.

Freeman's voice had lost some of its authority. "You got any idea who sent this to Ruthie?"

Linda was standing beside the old woman, and she answered for him. "It was post-marked from someplace in Newfoundland."

"Damn it, Roy," the old woman complained, "you still ain't told us what it is."

Freeman turned around, picked up a soiled towel and spread it out on the surface of the bar. Then he reached back in the sink, lifted the object out and put the hideous thing on display.

Linda recoiled, her hand flying involuntarily to her open mouth.

Gladys Ann stood her ground, staring defiantly back at the grotesque-looking thing. "Now, that's what I call ugly," she hissed. "What the hell is it?"

"Damn it, Gladys Ann, ain't you ever seen a brain before?"

Linda turned away. The greenish-blue pulpy mess was nothing more than a mound of revolting contours and convolutions. Laced through the object was a delicate network of tiny blue blood vessels.

"Whose brain? What kind of brain?" Gladys Ann probed.

Bartholomew tried to force himself forward in his chair, but the rush of blood to his own head and the accompanying surge of pain forced him back.

Freeman took a sharp wooden pencil out of his shirt pocket and began to poke unscientifically at the object. "Well," he speculated, "from the size and mass, I'd say it was a man's brain."

"Just 'cause it's bigger don't mean men are any smarter than women," Gladys Ann challenged.

Freeman forced a crooked half-smile. "No," he agreed, "it simply means they're usually bigger in total mass."

Linda was starting to regain part of her composure. She forced herself to look at the grotesque object again. When she did, what she saw was terrifying. The pulpy object, the awful thing that had been imprisoned in the glass jar, had moved.

She managed to stifle the scream, but the tears streaming down her face betrayed her terror.

Linda was vaguely aware of a shuffling sound somewhere in the darkened room. She had been sleeping fitfully, her small, tired body curled up on the bench seat of a booth. When she was awake, and that seemed to be all too frequently, she was aware that the storm was continuing to hammer the helpless old building. It was an unending symphony of groaning timbers and things dying in the violence called Ernestine. On more than one occasion, she tried the radio, but the batteries were too weak now. The signal was garbled.

Disappointed and still not knowing, she had shut it off and slipped uneasily back into her nightmare world.

All this followed a tense 20 minutes when Freeman had sutured up the wound in the back of Bartholomew's tortured head. Linda had tried to assist the old medic while Gladys Ann held the flashlight. They had even had to pause while Gladys Ann changed batteries, using the last in the display rack near the Gull House cash register. Then, in the glow of the revitalized beam, Freeman had carefully bandaged the deputy and administered a double dose of painkiller. Bartholomew Miller had been in a deep sleep ever since.

During that time, Moxie had come up from the lower level. The little man, soaked and exhausted, reported total devastation; the side walls of the first level storeroom had started to buckle and the flooring was now buried under eight inches of swirling water. He had done what he could, moving whatever possible to already overburdened shelves. And, only minutes after giving his report, the little man had collapsed into a deep sleep.

Linda opened one eye and saw the shadowed image moving through the darkness. It was carrying a candle.

"Doc," she called out softly, "is that you?"

The old man made a shushing sound. "I'm just checking on our patient. I was laying there and thought I heard something, thought maybe he might be stirring around."

Linda watched apprehensively as the image bent over and silently took Bartholomew's wrist. He nodded off the pulsebeat, and she could almost hear the old man counting to himself.

"How is he?"

"Pulse is strong, but a little erratic. He'll settle down; all he needs is time. All things considered, Bart's a pretty healthy boy." She watched as he laid the man's hand back down on the makeshift bed and walk over to where she had been sleeping. "I'd sell my soul right now for a steaming hot cup of black coffee," he admitted.

"The stove in the kitchen is gas fired," she heard herself saying. "Moxie told me he shut off the gas because it was too dangerous."

"What about the hotplate?"

Linda felt a smile curl involuntarily onto her haggard face. "What can it hurt? Surely we can fire up the generator long enough to make some coffee."

"Why not?" Doc said. She could hear the pleasure in his voice. He turned and threaded his way across the darkened room, through the swinging doors and into the kitchen. She could hear the generator sputter, cough and finally face up to its mundane chore. The small 40-watt bulb behind the bar flickered to life, and she plugged in the hotplate. Almost instantly there was a pale orange glow in the darkness. She picked up two heavy green mugs, searched through the supplies till she found a jar of instant coffee and thought about the wisdom of making enough for Moxie and Gladys Ann as well. In the same instant she decided not to, figuring they needed their sleep worse than they needed coffee. She didn't know what time it was, but there was still a long time to go until the storm abated.

Freeman was lumbering back through the darkness, around the end of the bar and coming toward her, when she looked up. What she saw sent a chill racing across her shoulders.

"Doc, what's wrong?" she stammered.

Freeman stopped and looked at her, his face twisting into a quizzical frown. "Wrong with what?"

She walked slowly toward him and reached out her hand. "Your face," she said uneasily, "there's something wrong with it."

She could hear the old man laugh. "Always has been; always knew I wouldn't win any Tyrone Power look-alike contests."

Linda's fingers traced hesitantly through the accentuated pattern of wrinkles and folds. "You . . . you look like you've aged!"

"Hell yes, I've aged," the old man groused

back at her. "This damn island would age anybody, between the damned tourists and the . . ."

The woman didn't wait for him to finish. She reached up, grabbed the man by the shoulders and spun him around so he was facing the smoky glass mirror illuminated by the single flickering light behind the bar. "Look," she insisted.

It was Roy Freeman's turn to recoil. An old man, very much older than he had appeared just a few hours earlier, looked back at him in astonishment. "My God," he muttered, "what the hell happened?" He reached up to touch his wrinkled face and realized that the malady had affected his hands as well. They were wrinkled, discolored and palsied. Slowly, he turned and looked at the woman. When he did, he was shocked by what he saw.

Linda Cavitt's symmetrical face with its firm, tight, flawless skin and haunting ice blue eyes had been twisted into a disfigured mask, lined with age, heavy with wrinkles and networked with a series of broken and prominent veins. Involuntarily, his hand reached out and brushed lightly across the coarse fabric of the woman's blotchy skin.

"What the hell's going on here?" he wheezed.

Linda, seeing her own image in the mirror,

staggered backward, holding her gnarled hands up to ward off the feeble, telltale light. She was crying.

Freeman began rummaging through the debris of the vigil, frantically searching for the flashlight. He located it, turned it on and ran across the room toward the still sleeping Gladys Ann. He shined the light in her face and realized that she wasn't sleeping; she was dead. Her sightless brown eyes were hauntingly fixed on some unseen thing in another time and place. Her bloodless, bleached white skin was stretched tautly over a skeletal face, laced with a chaotic pattern of tiny fissures and crowned with a tangled net of dull brown hair.

Instinctively, he reached down and tried to pick up her hand. It was rigid and clammy to the touch. Again instinctively, he released it, stepped back and felt his labored breathing coming in harsh gulps. He turned and looked helplessly at Linda, his face betraying the feeling of confusion and panic. Like him, she too had caught a brief glimpse of Gladys Ann, and the scream was still lodged in her throat.

Freeman staggered away from the old woman's lifeless body to the middle of the room.

"Is she dead?" Linda finally quaked, her voice thinly audible.

The harried doctor stood in the middle of

the room, the flashlight dangling from his hand, the beam dancing eerily off the walls of their darkened confines. "Moxie . . . where the hell is Moxie?" he gulped.

The searching beam found him. The little man was slouched in the far corner of the room, half-sitting, half-standing, propped against the wall. His emaciated, rotting body looked back at them with pleading, anxious eyes.

Linda's scream finally escaped as the little man's body slumped to the floor, his withered, once strong hands clawing desperately for something in life to hold onto.

Freeman plunged headlong across the room, banging into tables and bouncing off chairs in the darkness. He knelt beside the tiny man. "Moxie," his own withered voice rasped, "what happened?"

Moxie's hollow brown eyes stared emptily up at him, the pleading appeal giving way to an aura of nothingness stealing over them like a thin veil of fog.

The doctor bent over and laid his trembling hand on the stilled man's chest. There was nothing. He looked up at Linda with hopelessness mirrored in his eyes. "He's dead," he muttered.

"My God . . . what about Bart?"

Freeman scrambled to his feet and plunged back through the darkness, this time toward his patient. He brought the beam of light around and focused it on the deputy.

For a moment, Linda couldn't believe her own eyes.

A splattered trail of telltale blood traced its way across the floor and up the man's body. His shirt was saturated, and his hands lay limp at his sides. The deputy's face was fixed in a grotesque kind of knowing smile. His eyes were open, looking right at them.

Freeman played the beam of light back down the man's body and across the blood-stained floor to the place on the bar where Ruthie's grotesque present had once resided. It was as he expected—gone.

The young woman fell to her knees. "Bart," she shouted, "can you hear me?" Her voice betrayed her mounting hysteria.

Freeman stood behind her, motionless, his mouth agape.

Bartholomew Miller's eyes shifted mechanically in her direction. His mouth struggled to form the words. "Are . . . are you Ruthie?"

She looked nervously up at the doctor. "Ruthie?" she repeated.

Before Freeman could respond, Bartholomew's voice rasped through the darkness again. "I am that thing," he hissed. "We are one . . . it is willing me . . . and I it."

"What's he talking about, Doc?"

Freeman stepped forward unsteadily.

"Don't pay any attention; it's the narcotic. He's hallucinating. I gave him enough Mellaril to knock him out for days. There's no way he could be rational."

Bartholomew's head turned mechanically toward the old man. With each word, his voice was growing stronger. "Quite the contrary, Dr. Freeman. I am in complete control of my faculties. I am, as you so delicately put it, 'rational.' In fact, I think you can already see evidence of how completely in control I am. You saw them. I willed that to be done."

Linda Cavitt inched her way back, away from the man. "Bart, you're talking nonsense. What's the matter with you?"

A sinister smile slowly inched its way across the deputy's swollen face. "It is so simple. I have a mission."

"Don't pay any attention to him," Freeman admonished, "he's on overload. Doesn't know what he's saying."

"I have a mission," Bartholomew repeated. His voice was growing stronger and more direct.

"Mission," Linda cried. "What kind of a mission?"

Freeman stepped forward again, his fevered eyes fixed on the man.

"Which one of you is the one called Ruthie? Is it you . . . or the other old woman?"

Linda recoiled.

"The other woman is dead," Freeman shot back at him.

"Was that Ruthie?" the thing in Bartholomew questioned.

"The one called Ruthie is gone," Linda said evenly.

"If you will not tell me, then I will have to kill you all." The voice had become menacing, unrecognizable, sinister, something apart.

Linda struggled to her feet. She was frantically trying to get away from the man she had made love to only the night before. "Doc," she stammered, "what's wrong with him?"

Freeman fixed the unsteady beam of light on Bartholomew's changing face. His hand trembled as he studied the deputy's constantly evolving features. The once youthful, ruggedly handsome face was being transformed into a nightmarish mask of hate and revenge. He stepped forward and aimed the light directly into his patient's eyes.

"Where's Ruthie's present?" he choked out. He was sure now that he already knew, but the reality of it was too bizarre, too incomprehensible to acknowledge. It was preposterous, beyond logic.

Slowly, stiffly, Bartholomew raised his hand and pointed to his heavily bandaged head. "It's in here, Dr. Freeman, it's in here. I am that thing. It is me."

"Linda," Freeman ordered, "get back. Get away from him!"

"Do something," Linda pleaded as she stumbled away.

"It is pointless to run, Ruthie. You *are* Ruthie, aren't you?"

"I'm *not* Ruthie!" she screamed.

"I was sent here on a mission." Bartholomew's voice was no longer human. It was a thing—mechanical, menacing, maddening. "I am a present for the one called Ruthie."

Freeman continued to play the eerie yellow light over the man's contorted features. "Linda," he whispered, "listen to me. He's heavily drugged; I don't think he can get up. I'm not sure what's going on here, but you've got to get out of here."

"But he's sick," she whimpered.

"Yeah, Bartholomew's sick . . . but we're dealing with something else now," Freeman hissed. "I don't know why, I don't know how, but somehow that thing in the jar has possessed him. He thinks he's somebody else, somebody whose sole mission it is to destroy this person called Ruthie—and we can't stop him."

"But . . ."

"Damn it, Linda, do what I tell you. You've got to get out of here!"

"It is pointless, Ruthie," the voice intoned malevolently. There was a terrifying assuredness in his words.

"Run, dammit!" Freeman screamed. He lunged forward, arching the heavy metal flashlight down in a savage blow that smashed into Bartholomew's heavily bandaged head. The thing screamed as Freeman repeated the violent act again and again in a frenzied, desperate effort to still the awful voice.

Linda raced for the door.

Freeman felt the assaulted tissue and bone turn to a pulpy mass under his onslaught. Blood began seeping through the bandages and cascading down the deputy's twisted, hate-filled face. Within seconds they were both covered with the gory evidence of his furious attack.

Even then the voice managed to drone on. "It is . . . it is . . . it is . . . pointless . . . pointless . . ." Then the horrifying sound of the words began to trail off.

Freeman dropped the makeshift bludgeon and staggered backward, clawing at his aching chest. A stabbing pain ripped through his body, slamming into his brain, seering down again into his chest. His hands went numb; his throat constricted. His world was spinning, and he suddenly felt panic. The pain ripped through him again, and he clutched his exploding chest before slumping over on one of the tables.

Linda had one final, frenzied glimpse of the old man's face as he rolled over in his death throes. His withered and aged face looked like a grotesque mask from some ancient ritual.

Freeman's lifeless body tumbled to the floor, and Linda Cavitt ran screaming from the room, out the door and into the teeth of the howling storm.

Chapter Eight

Red Gleason's real name was Albert, but no one had actually called him that since he was a kid. He had a thinning crop of unruly reddish brown hair and a craggy flushed face that was splattered with freckles. He had been sheriff over a domain that included the tiny island resort for over 25 years, a period, he liked to say, that had enabled him to see it all. And now he had. The devastation of Ernestine would take a lifetime to describe, as well as rebuild.

He unwrapped another in what seemed like an endless chain of Cameroons, lit it, turned off his ignition and crawled wearily out of his patrol car. Carlos was squinting at him, and

Merle Chesterton, the only other deputy to find a way over from the mainland, was scraping the mud and silt off his boots.

It was hot, uncommonly hot for so late in the year. The south Texas sun had been hammering unmercifully down on them for three days now. It came at them out of a crystal clear, cloudless sky that failed to offer even an occasional if temporary reprieve from the scorching ball of orange that hovered high overhead. Red sagged against the side of his cruiser, inhaled deeply, his mind, for the moment, disengaged, taking a break from the chaos that had been his way of life since the storm.

South Padre was in shambles. It would take months to pick up the pieces and years to put it back together again. There wasn't much that had escaped the ravage of the storm. What hadn't been broken had been battered. What hadn't been battered had been bent. What hadn't been bent had been blown away.

Even now, there was no way of estimating the damage, no way of knowing how many had lost their lives. Scores of people, people Red knew well, still hadn't been accounted for. There was no way to keep count, no way to tally up the score. Perhaps they were only the folks who were reluctant to come back and face the devastation. Maybe they wouldn't come back at all. Maybe, just maybe, it would be easier to go somewhere and start over without having to clean up the mess first.

Red reached back in his car and put on his sweat-soaked Bailey in the hope it would afford him some protection against the sun. The stench was everywhere. There were dead animals, dead birds, and even, like they had discovered at Pasquel Morgan's place, dead people. Unaware that he had already started to do it again, he found himself mentally trudging back through the list. There was Morgan, the two security guards at the island end of the bridge, the dock boy who had volunteered to ride out the storm at the Marina—and the bodies of the two young Mexicans. The last two were hard to figure— one skinny, one fat. Their bloated bodies had been discovered wedged in the pilings along with the remains of their splintered skiff down by the public pier. What, Red wondered, could possibly have possessed the two young men to try to row across the inlet to the mainland in the teeth of an approaching hurricane?

The respite was over. The two men were walking toward him. He took a deep drag off his cigar and braced himself. It was only midmorning, but Red Gleason had already put in a full day. "What'cha got?" he asked. Merle was the one who had called him which in itself was unusual, because Merle was the kind who prided himself on being able to handle things without getting Red involved.

The heavyset deputy with his open, preposterously round face, stood in front of him, furrowing the toe of his boot back and forth in the sand. It was one of the few things Red Gleason didn't like about his long-time deputy; he had to pry the problem out of him. The alternative was simple enough; wait until Merle decided to talk about it. Then it was often too late. Carlos, on the other hand, was just the opposite of the hard-working Chesterton. Though gregarious to a fault and a big hit with the tourists, Gleason usually had to prod the youngster to do the bare essentials of his job.

Carlos slipped into what little shade Gleason's cruiser afforded the trio, took off his hat and mopped his forehead. Gleason knew the men were exhausted. All of them had been on duty around the clock since the waters had receded enough to allow the first search teams to begin the salvage operations. As soon as Bart Miller showed up, Red was planning to begin a rotation that would give his men some much needed relief.

"You been out to this part of the island?" Carlos asked lazily.

Gleason shook his head. "Naw, haven't had the chance. Didn't figure I'd have to. The Gull House always seems to make it through these things. That old shack's been hammered by the best of 'em over the years."

Merle shook his big, shaggy head. "That's why Carlos and me figured we'd better get you in on it," he said softly.

Red Gleason knew his role. He started back up between the sweep of the two dunes. The storm's winds had shifted the huge mounds to such an extent that the view of the old landmark tavern was blocked from the road. The original drive was now under several thousand tons of damp brown sand. He came at the building from the southeast and stopped in his tracks. Red Gleason wasn't prepared for what he saw. "Holy shit," he muttered.

Merle Chesterton had stopped several feet behind him. Carlos hung back even further, squatting down on his haunches to make the most of the shadow cast by the dune.

The Gull House had been reduced to little more than a pile of splinters, a tangle of twisted sticks and debris. Red felt a lump in his throat. The old watering hole had been a part of his life ever since he was old enough to crawl up on a bar stool. He surveyed the disaster for several minutes before he found the courage to start walking again.

The roof and the entire second floor of the building were destroyed, scattered out over the deserted, mocking beach. The old plank patio, where he had courted and won the hand of Lucy Johnson and asked her to be his wife, was gone. An empty, useless wooden stairway still anchored to the north wall of the lower level storage area was all that remained. The storeroom, where he, Bart, Ben Samuels, Merle Chesterton and a host of others had played their marathon poker games, had three walls standing.

Gleason circled the mountain of destruction once then paused next to the twisted wreckage of the old beer cooler. Idly he wondered how many times he had walked around the bar, listened to Gladys Ann's churlish reprimands for doing so and gotten his own beer. "Suppose someone would see the sheriff goin' back there and gettin' his own beer," the old woman would complain. "Pretty soon they'll all be a thinkin' they can do it."

Gleason took off his hat and used his index finger to wipe the sweat off of his sunburned forehead. He loosened his tie and began the trek back to his patrol car. There he flipped on the radio, waited for the channel to clear and began drawling out instructions. "Patch me through to Port Isabel and get me the latest availability report. I'm still lookin' for Doc Freeman and Bart Miller. If you see Miller, better tell him the Gull House got hit pretty hard. If he walks in cold out here, he'll get the shock of his life."

The dispatcher put him through to his

office, and Red repeated his request. When he finished, the small voice on the other end of the line informed him that the rescue team had just discovered a family of four in the basement of a small house. They had drowned.

Gleason sighed. He knew there would be more. It was just a matter of time until they uncovered them. "Any ident?" he probed.

"Negative."

"Keep lookin' for Freeman and Miller," Gleason reminded his contact. "I need both of them." He stood momentarily with the mike still in his hand, staring out at the shimmering heat rising off the baking sand. "That's it," he grumbled and tossed the defenseless piece of gear onto the seat of his car.

Chesterton stepped forward. "Red," he began hesitantly.

The sheriff nodded. Merle had apparently gotten himself ready.

"You smell it?"

Gleason stomped out his cigar in the damp sand and sniffed at the stagnant air. "Uh-huh," he admitted. "Been tryin' to ignore it."

Carlos watched the two men exchange knowing glances and started to laugh. "Okay, you two, let the new guy in on it. What is it I'm supposed to be smellin'?"

"The worst smell of all," Gleason said matter-of-factly. "Death. Ain't much doubt there being somethin' under that pile of rubble."

"Dead?" Carlos mumbled, "Who?"

Gleason shrugged his shoulders. "Well, it ain't a dog or a cat or a gull; they don't smell like that."

Carlos wrinkled his nose. "I can't tell the difference. The whole damn island smells bad."

The sheriff turned to Merle Chesterton. "You know what we gotta do," he said soberly. The deputy nodded.

The dozers and diggers were pulled off of their highway clearing assignment at the entrance to the park. Two dozers and seven men, already bone weary and sweat-soaked from their earlier task, arrived at the scene in the late afternoon. Gleason and Carlos had each been called out on other matters during the course of the day, each time leaving Chesterton with the grim, solitary sentinel over the remains of the Gull House.

Each time Gleason checked in with the disaster recovery unit and the civil defense people. Each time the answer was the same; no one had had any contact with either the doctor or the deputy since the day of the storm. With the second confirmation, Gleason's hopes had begun to sink. Both had had ample time to get back to the island, or, at the very least, let someone know where they were.

A little past six, Gleason found himself leaning back through the window to his police cruiser again, this time telling the dispatcher to tell Lucy he wouldn't be home for supper. He had just started back to the site of the cleanup when a long-legged young man in a pair of faded blue jeans fell into step beside him. He was carrying the classic black leather medical bag with him.

"Sheriff Gleason, you probably won't remember me, but I'm Jeff. Jeff Freeman. Roy's son."

The weary lawman stopped walking. It had been years, more years than he cared to think about, since the young Freeman boy had haunted his and Lucy's house on Cross Street on the pretense of looking for odd jobs. Even then Red realized it wasn't the boy's vocational ambitions but his daughter Julie's emerging bustline that was the real attraction. A rush of warm, all but forgotten memories flooded back on him, and he stuck out his hand in greeting.

"Love to talk to you, boy, but we got our hands full back here."

"I know," the young man drawled. "That's why I'm here."

"Don't tell me you're a doctor now?" Red Gleason shook his head. He had lost track of the lad. It was a fact of life for a man who had too many things to do and not enough hours in which to do them.

"Like father, like son," Jeff Freeman said. "I've been following the progress of the storm. The more I listened, the more I got to thinking I'd better come down and see if Dad needed some help; figured he'd have his hands full. Have you seen him?"

Gleason shook his head. "Not since the day the storm hit." He hoped the young man didn't detect the despair in his voice.

Jeff Freeman's mobile face easily slipped into a frown. "Well, when we're done here, I'll just have to see if I can scout him out."

They had just emerged from the twilight world between the dunes when Gleason spotted the hunched silhouette of Merle Chesterton hunkered down beside a pile of debris. A group of men had gathered around him. The deputy was motioning to him.

It didn't take him long to see what Merle wanted him to see. A bloated, discolored arm protruded from a pile of damp trash and broken boards.

Chesterton pointed down. Gleason peered back into the rubble and saw two legs intertwined and twisted through the heavy plank boards that constituted a portion of the old stairs leading up to the second level. Red felt his heart stutter a beat. It was exactly what he had feared. They had been right. "Better start digging," he said flatly.

The rescue crew began clearing away the area several feet around the body. They were joined by others, but there was now a sense of useless urgency about the effort.

In a matter of minutes the tortured and weathered face of an old woman glared stupidly up at the floodlights that now circled the site. Gleason shuddered. It was the face of agonized death, a face that knew death was inevitable. The eyes were hollow black sockets; sand crabs, glass worms and red ants had already performed their cannibalistic ritual, a probing autopsy that left little. For all practical purposes, they were looking down at a "thing," a thing drained of color, battered and shredded by the storm that had assaulted her.

Jeff Freeman muscled his way through the crowd of onlookers and bent over the body. "Skull's been crushed. Can't tell whether she got her legs tangled up in those stairs there and fell, or if something landed on her. Been dead a while, though; four, maybe five days."

Gleason's eyes darted around the rapidly darkening area. "Anybody recognize her?"

There was a collective kind of ominous silence, as though to know the woman was to admit to something dark and sinister. Finally, Merle Chesterton stooped and began probing the sand with his fingers. When he stood up, he was holding a small gold bracelet with the initials L.C. carved on the back.

"For a moment there I thought I recognized the bracelet," he muttered. "Guess there could be more than one bracelet like it though. The gal I remember wearing something like this was a lot younger."

When Carlos gave the signal, a group of men moved in to take the body away. The old woman's remains were zippered into a rubber sack and carried away. The rest of them stood waiting for Gleason's instructions.

"Better keep digging. Chances are when you find one, you'll find more. People don't usually decide to ride out a storm alone." Almost reluctantly, they began to disperse, trudging back to whatever it was they were doing when Chesterton discovered the old woman's body. Then he turned to Carlos. "Better call the disaster center and tell them we uncovered another body," he sighed. Then as an afterthought, he added, "Maybe you'd better tell them she's a Jane Doe, no ident." He looked up at Jeff Freeman and shook his head. "Worst part of it is, we'll probably never know."

It was 10:12. The additional floodlights that had been brought in to assist the rescue teams had been turned off and the men sent home for the night. There was still more digging to do, but Gleason was convinced that any hope of finding someone alive under the piles of rubble had long since passed. Slowly he led an entourage consisting of Merle Chesterton, Jeff Freeman and Carlos Avico back up between the dunes toward their cars.

"Tough one to explain," Gleason said wearily.

Carlos shook his head. "Weird," he muttered. "Sure makes a fella wonder what the hell went on in there."

"It must have been a nightmare," Freeman allowed. "What do you suppose happened to Bart Miller? He was all bandaged up, head all caved in. One of those collapsing roof beams must have scored a direct hit on him."

Merle Chesterton caught himself wistfully looking out at the tranquility of the gulf. "Yeah, but how do you suppose he got so banged up in the first place?"

Gleason slumped back against the door of his car and began peeling the cellophane off of another cigar. He bit a chunk off the end, spit it in the sand, lit it and inhaled. "It's a helluva way to put it," he drawled, "but did anybody keep score?"

Chesterton dug the spiral notepad out of his shirt pocket and began leafing through the damp pages. "There was the old woman we found near the steps. Another old woman that Doc here said looked a lot older than the first one we found. We found her in that pile of stuff Carlos said looked like it was furniture from the dining room. Then there was the two old men and Bart Miller."

"Couple of things about all this that bother me," young Freeman admitted. "The first is the advanced age of the four people we weren't able to identify. Are any of you aware of a place on the island where four people that old would have been housed?"

"Coulda been tourists," Carlos volunteered.

"What kind of fool would have four people that old and apparently immobile around when he knew a storm the size of Ernestine was coming ashore?" Freeman questioned.

There was no response from his companions.

"Then you have to ask yourself why Miller decided to ride out the storm with four old people like that? It's all the more curious when you stop to think he had his head all messed up and there wasn't any way they could be of assistance to him in an emergency."

"Maybe there's a real simple answer to all of this," Merle volunteered. "Maybe when Bart found them it was too late to get 'em off the island, and he figured the Gull House was the best place to ride out the storm. Red tells me it's survived more than one of these storms."

Gleason inhaled deeply and allowed the

look of puzzlement to unfurl. The grim set of his jaw seemed to relax. "Merle's probably close to the truth," he acknowledged. "Fact of the matter is, don't make much difference what the truth is. The outcome's the same."

"That explains everything but the body of the third woman," Carlos finalized. He looked at Gleason to see if his boss agreed.

The sheriff looked at Jeff Freeman, wondering if the hour was too late or if his men were too tired to dredge up the past. "You weren't around these parts a couple of years ago when Bart and Ruthie were doin' their public fussin'. Everybody around these parts knew Ruthie couldn't keep her pants on. Little blonde short thing, kinda foul-mouthed. I always figured she was just feelin' the pressure of the years. Anyway, one day she just came up missin'. She'd done it a couple of times before. Everybody around here just sorta figured she'd gotten another one of her wild hairs up her ass and took off with some guy. She gave everybody a hard time. In the end it was pretty hard to find anybody who had anything decent to say about her."

Young Freeman leaned up against the cruiser next to him. "Weird, isn't it? If it hadn't been for the storm, it's not likely her body would have been uncovered for a long, long time, what with it being stashed away under that old plank flooring like that."

Merle Chesterton started tracing the toe of his boot back and forth in the sand again. Finally he asked the question that was bothering him. "What do ya think, Red? Think Bart's the one what done it to her?"

Red Gleason shook his head. "Don't rightly figure we'll ever know, Merle. Lots of people didn't care much for Ruthie. Lots of people were happy to see her gone—Gladys Ann, Moxie, Bart, maybe all of them together. Who knows? Lots of people were loyal to Bart Miller."

Red Gleason stomped out what was left of his cigar and crawled into his patrol car. "See you fellas in the morning. I'll report in at the disaster center and tell 'em what we found. Six dead, four no idents, Bart and Ruthie Miller."

As he pulled out on the highway he breathed a sigh of relief. Now his secret was safe. Now no one would ever have any way of knowing. The night Ruthie told him she was going to tell Bart, he knew he had to do it.

PART FOUR

Chapter Nine

It was exactly the kind of setting Charlie Frazier would have expected. Theodore was so damned predictable. His brother had always had a penchant for the finer things of life, and this was no exception. The sign said it all—"CRESTVIEW ON THE HARBOR"—and it was straight ahead. Another smaller, far less pretentious sign directed deliveries to another entrance to the left.

The guard at the gate wore the conventional security force uniform—gray epauletted shirt with a yellow patch on the shoulder, meticulously creased blue gabardine trousers and black shoes. He was young, all of 20 perhaps, and it was obvious he took his job seriously.

He held up his hand in a halting motion, slightly more animated than necessary.

Charlie rolled down the window and the young man peered in. His assessment of Charlie was brief, but his assessment of Peggy took a little longer. The man's eyes boldly traced over every curve and angle of her long, well-proportioned legs.

"We're here to see Theodore Frazier," Charlie announced. He hadn't counted on this; it could be considered the first wrinkle in his plan. Now someone could tie him to this place on this particular weekend, and he had hoped to avoid that.

The guard poked a battered clipboard through the open window and instructed Charlie to write down his name and license number. "Did anybody ever tell you you look a lot like Mr. Frazier, sir?" He accomplished his duties without once allowing his bloodshot eyes to stray from Peggy's revealing hemline.

"You're not the first person to see the similarity," Charlie smiled and handed the clipboard back to the youth. In the same motion he turned to Peggy and hissed, "For Christ's sake, pull your skirt down or the damn kid's gonna crawl in the car with us."

Margaret "Peggy" Bowles was an acknowledged master at the fine art of bestowing intolerant looks at people, and she did so at Charlie. The reprisal was wrapped around a less than feminine sneer. "So what," she shot back at him. "Let the kid see what the big boys play with."

Reluctantly, the young man stepped back and motioned them on.

"You're a goddamn exhibitionist," Charlie snarled.

As usual, Peggy Bowles' response was preceded by an expression of indifference; she shrugged her shoulders and slumped back against the door on her side of the car. "Know something, Charlie Frazier? You're a snob. Some pimply-faced kid gets his kicks looking at my legs and you go off like a cheap rocket. Who the hell does it hurt?"

Like the setting, the weekend was starting out just like Charlie had figured it would. It was Friday, and already they were bickering at each other. Par for the course—Peggy the Mouth; Peggy the Acid Tongue; Peggy, the woman for whom no amount of male attention was enough. With Peggy Bowles there were admitted consistencies, things Charlie could count on, like too short skirts, see-through blouses and cheap jewelry. He had met her on a fast track, and the barrage of flippant answers that intrigued him at first had now grown tiresome.

"We're looking for unit twenty-eight," he sighed, ignoring the obvious and trying to hold things together. The weekend was too important. He had to do what he had come to do, and Peggy Bowles was a part of it. He was counting on her.

"There it is," she said. "I see the names on the mailbox. Ted and Betty Frazier."

Charlie edged the big Oldsmobile over to the curb and studied the exterior of the building. This was it, the place where it would finally happen. It was just like he had pictured it—the redwood siding, the lofted roof, the manicured lawns, the hooded walkway lamps that subtly illuminated the flagstone path leading up to the pretentious entrance.

Charlie sucked in his breath and held it for a moment. Ted, old buddy, old asshole brother of mine, this is going to be a weekend you'll never forget. One by one, he clicked off his preparations right down to the final touch, the roses he had sent ahead for Betty. Now it all revolved around the special present for Theodore, the one he had carted all the way from Newfoundland, the one that had been stashed on a shelf in his closet all these months just waiting for this weekend.

Peggy leaned toward him and peered out his window. "Nice," she cooed. "I like it. So tell me, just what is it this brother of yours does for a living?"

It was typical Peggy Bowles, straight to the heart of the issue. Paraphrased, she was asking just how much money Theodore Frazier actually had. Peggy's reaction to almost anyone was based on just how much money she thought they had.

"Third generation money," he hissed. "Old Theodore can't take the credit. He inherited it."

"So," Peggy asked, "what happened to you? I thought you were brothers."

"We are," Charlie admitted, "the difference being he played the game and I didn't."

Peggy gave him a quizzical look.

"My grandfather started a small loan company back in the twenties, and my father parlayed it into something big. He made a fortune during the second world war, loaning money to servicemen. Then, when my father died, I was in the service and Theodore stepped in and took over."

"Then half of this is yours, right?"

"Should have been," Charlie sighed, "but I never quite measured up to my old man's expectations. At the time of his death we weren't even speaking."

"Surely he didn't cut you out of his will entirely?" Peggy asked. Charlie was convinced he could already sense a shift in Peggy's loyalty.

"That's exactly what he did, but I think he had some help."

Peggy continued to study him. "I don't get it."

"I've always believed old lovable Teddy had a little too much influence over the old boy."

"You mean your brother talked your father into cutting you out of the will?"

"That's exactly what I think."

"So why are we here if there's bad blood between you two?"

Charlie knew his companion all too well. Peggy didn't need an explanation. She could take what little information he had already given her and figure out the rest. For all her obvious faults, Peggy was a pragmatist and a survivor. She understood things like this.

"What you're really saying is the name of the game is to be nice to brother Theodore, right?"

"Right," Charlie said. "The stakes are high. I've waited a long time for this. I don't intend to blow it now."

Peggy curled her long slender fingers around the upper part of his arm and inched her way toward him on the front seat. When she was satisfied that the momentary intoxication of her perfume had properly titillated his libido, she slid her other hand across his thigh and down to his crotch. "Tell me," she said huskily, "which excites you more, Charlie Frazier. The thought of what I can do with this, or the little scheme you've got planned for brother Theodore?"

Charlie laid his head back, closed his eyes

and allowed the encroaching smile to play with the corners of his mouth. "Peggy, my dear, even I have to admit that you are one of the best at what you do, but in this case even your considerable talents are still running a distant second to what I have planned for my dear brother."

She hissed the epithet. "Bastard!" Then she clamped her teeth into the soft flesh on the side of his neck just above the collar.

Charlie reacted exactly the way she knew he would. They were kindred souls, bonded in the sense that evil embraces evil. He shoved her away, still smiling and watching the late afternoon shadows fall across her hard smile. For the moment, Peggy fit very nicely into his long-planned scheme.

It had been ten years since the brothers had seen each other; there was much they remembered, but there was just as much that they had forgotten.

They were fraternal twins, a fact that Charlie had not mentioned and a reality Peggy was not aware of until she walked in the room and was stunned by the disturbing similarity between the two men. Both men were taller than average, standing approximately six feet two inches in height, and both possessed the same rusty, some would say ruddy, coloring. Between them they constituted the total offspring of Malcolm Frazier, a man who claimed three wives in his span of 67 years. A harsh man of enormous sexual appetites, he was forced to endure the anguish of impotency for the last 20 years of his life. He was known for venting his frustration with that condition on his two sons, Charlie more so than the favored Theodore.

The women were equally at odds with their place in space and time. Peggy was a blamer. Others were always at fault for her misfortunes. Life, in her view, was unfair; all men were bastards, secretive and users, so she in turn used them. Never had she owned up to her responsibility for the sorry state of her life.

Betty Frazier, or Betty Elizabeth, as she began insisting others call her following her marriage to Theodore, was herself an accomplished huntress. She had successfully tracked the heir to the Frazier fortune through a social jungle that reduced lesser women to the role of mere bystanders in the competition to claim half of all he had gained through his father's death.

She was a willowy brunette with willowy qualities. She bent, but she never broke. Her adversaries as well as her few friends knew this. Tall and attractive, she possessed a fatal kind of cultured elegance and a steel heart to go along with her killer instinct. She would, as Charlie already knew, present an even more formidable obstacle to Charlie's plan than Theodore himself.

The reunion was played out in a predictable scene of tension—half-hearted embraces, clumsy introductions and periods of strained silence. Peggy's irritating habit of clearing her throat betrayed her discomfort with the situation. It was only one of several chinks in the woman's social armor that she had never learned to control. Peggy cleared her throat when she was nervous and when she was lying. Both, Charlie had long ago learned, were frequent occurrences.

They retired to a conversation pit, an enormous circular sofa that embraced most of the intimate brick-walled room with massive windows that overlooked the harbor. The conversation was tenuous with meaningless exchanges of pleasantries over weak martinis, a drink that Theodore had never mastered at full strength. And, when the small talk ceased altogether, Betty Elizabeth escorted Peggy from the room on the pretense that she needed to know where to put her things. It was, in the final analysis, probably less uncomfortable for the women because they understood and accepted each other. The same anatomical phenomenon had gotten them both where they were now, and universal sisterhood, in that sense, bonded them.

The animosity between the two men had no

such common bond, and only the thinnest veil of social veneer kept them from open hostility. They remained in the brick room, sizing each other up after the passage of ten years, each jealous of their territorial prerogatives. Each realized that it was only a matter of time until that tension elevated to the next and perhaps uncontrollable level.

At that moment, it was Theodore who was convinced he held all the cards. After all, it was Charlie who had come to him. He looked at his brother and smiled.

Charlie understood the game his brother was playing, but that was of little concern to him. Charlie was fortified with his own surprise. After all these years, it was match point, and Charlie held the advantage.

"So, Charles," Theodore sneered, "just how long do you intend this little charade of brotherly interest to go on?" As he asked the question, he finished off his third martini and bent to pour himself another.

Charlie gave his brother a quizzical look. Theodore was right; "charade" was a good word for it, but he would never admit it. Besides, there was a certain amount of savoring to be done, an anticipation to be finally enjoyed, a scene to be staged; there was no need to plunge headlong into this. This was foreplay of the highest order.

"Charade?" Charlie repeated, seemingly perplexed.

Theodore slouched back into the protective folds of the pretentious piece of furniture and smiled over the rim of the stemmed crystal. This was, he told himself, something akin to setting his brother up for the kill. "Okay, long lost brother of mine, I'll play your silly little game. Tell me, why is it you finally show up now, after all these years?"

"Because I think it's time to put an end to all of this nonsense," Charlie said.

"Come off it. Ten years, Charlie, ten goddamn years. No cards. No letters. Not even a 'fuck you.' Ten years go by and all of a sudden here you are, with a contrite look on your face. Ask yourself, Charlie, don't you think I've got a pretty damn good reason for asking 'why now?'"

At that very moment there were two parallel lines of thought running through Charlie's mind. The first, of course, was the response; it had to be a reasonable response, something Theodore could buy, something that dovetailed nicely with his twisted sense of values. The second was simply to see if all the planning, scheming and effort were worth it. And that required little more than a simple test. Charlie had already decided he wouldn't go through with it if Theodore had fallen on hard times. That, in and of itself, would be enough, because then it would all be his anyway; he would see to that.

But neither seemed to be the case. There he was, gloating, still a pompous, posturing mannequin posing as something his father had wanted him to be. And that, in the end, would make it all the more rewarding. To Charlie's way of thinking, taking something from a man who had nothing requires little in the way of skills. Taking something from a man who seems to have everything requires a great deal of skill, because men who covet and possess are themselves people who take. It was Charlie's turn to lean back in his seat and smile.

"I figured we'd carried this silly feud on long enough," he finally answered.

Theodore continued to study him suspiciously. Despite the eloquence, he doubted him; Charlie would have to do more than show up to prove he had changed.

"I missed a lot," Charlie continued. "Dad's last days, the funeral, everything. When it happens like that, there isn't much opportunity to patch things up."

"There were a lot of opportunities, but you just didn't take them. The old man was sick for a long time." It was a flat statement, void of compassion, concession or understanding.

"I didn't even know he was sick."

"Of course you didn't, but then how the hell could you? You were always too damned busy to have time for anything except what you wanted. Everything else could go to hell, everything else be damned." Theodore's voice trailed off, disappearing in a sip of his drink.

Charlie felt a rush of heat flush up the back of his neck, and he took a deep breath. Let him do it, he thought to himself. Let the insufferable, pompous little ass pontificate. Let him inflate that goddamn insatiable ego of his.

"Can't we put all that behind us?" Charlie tried again.

Theodore pushed his way up and out of the confines of his overstuffed world and walked over to the window. He can't even do that like an ordinary man, Charlie thought. He has to pose, has to make a theatrical gesture out of everything.

"Why now?" Theodore asked.

Charlie's practiced grin came into play. "We're not getting any younger. Besides, what the hell are we accomplishing by dragging this thing out?"

"Know what I'm thinking, Charlie? I'm standing here thinking I've got it all. And you know why I've got it all, Charlie? I got it because I stayed here and fought for it. You know what our father left us, Charlie? I'll tell you what he left us—a pathetic pile of debts

and damn near worthless paper. If there was a
bad investment to be made, he made it.

"But I read—"

"I know what you read. But it was me,
Charlie, me. I did it. I'm the one who turned
his mess around. Have you got any idea what
I've been able to do with the miserable little
charter he called Frazier Securities?"

Charlie had done his homework. He knew
all too well. He knew a great deal more than
he was willing to let on at that point. But the
scene hadn't been played out yet, and there
were still things to do. It was too soon to rush
into the big climactic scene.

"No," he lied, "no, I don't." He was doing
his best to sound like the contrite family
member committed to correcting the wrongs
of the past.

Theodore turned away from the window
and glowered at him. For the first time, he
thought he could see his brother not as he was
when this all started, but for what he had
become. The desire to tell Charlie that he
didn't believe him was overwhelmed instead
by the gnawing need to pay homage to his own
successes. After all, Theodore reasoned, if you
have accomplished something, if you have
overcome adversity, why not? Is it not a victory to celebrate?

"Last month, Charlie, our asset base topped
two billion dollars! Think about that, Charlie

—two billion dollars. Is that a number your stilted military mind can even begin to grasp?"

"I've put my military career behind me," his brother said evenly.

Theodore began pacing back and forth in front of the bank of windows overlooking the harbor. His hands were locked behind his back, his head tilted slightly forward. "I suspected as much. So now, after all these years of me pouring blood and sweat into this thing, you show up. You show up, and it just happens to be two weeks after that article appeared in *Newsweek*. An article, I just may confirm, that quite accurately proclaims Frazier Securities to be one of the fastest growing firms of its type in the country. How very interesting. Quite a coincidence, Charlie, quite a coincidence. Think about it. No one hears from you for over ten years, the article appears, and suddenly you're here. My question still is why? Why the hell are you here?" He had stopped pacing; he was standing still, hands locked behind his back, glaring down at the man who claimed the only reason he was there was to right the wrongs of the past. "The fact of the matter is, Charlie, I don't believe you. I think you're here because you want your cut of something you turned your back on years ago."

"Look, Ted, I know how it looks. But tell

me, would it have been better if I had waited? Would you be any less suspicious of my motives if it were two years from now and Frazier had accumulated an even bigger asset base? Think about it. Just when would be a good time for me to show up? Tomorrow? Next year? Or was yesterday the only window in time?"

Theodore walked back down in the pit and stood in front of the man who looked so much like him, yet he hardly knew. In reality Charlie was little more than a vague memory. "All right, Charlie," he heard himself saying, "if it's not part of Frazier Securities, what the hell is it you want?"

"Do I have to want something?" Don't stray, he reminded himself, do it just like you rehearsed it. Be patient; don't deviate from the plan. He smiled at his brother, contrived but effective.

Theodore, still skeptical, continued to glower at him.

"This is the hard part," Charlie said. "This is the part we have to get past—the distrust, the suspicion!"

"And just how do you propose we do that?"

"I've given that a lot of thought, and maybe a good place to start is out where this all started to go wrong in the first place. I guess I'm saying I want to go see where my father is buried."

"Why?"

"It's hard for me to imagine what it's all like now. I wasn't here for the funeral. I didn't go through all that. I guess part of coming back is that I'm trying in some way to help you shoulder some of the pain."

"It's a little late for that. What's done is done. You haven't been a part—"

"Do you know a better place to start?" Charlie pushed.

Theodore was silent.

"Look, Ted, I'm trying. I'm desperate. I have to do this. I can't continue to let this go on. I even brought something for Father. It's something I brought back from overseas. Let me do this one thing. It's important to me."

The appeal was working. Charlie could see the doubt beginning to fade from his brother's face. The harsh gray eyes, even after all these years, were still out of concert with his ruddy complexion, but even as they spoke, the harshness softened. Slowly, word by word, the practiced contriteness, the contrived humility, the persistent pleas for forgiveness were beginning to erode the wall of his brother's suspicion and doubt. Peggy was right; he should have been an actor. He was a master at what he was doing. He was erasing time, ten years of doubt and distrust. I'm reeling you in, Teddy boy. I've got you right where I want you. You're buying it, Teddy boy. You're buying it hook, line and sinker.

"I know you buried Father close to here," Charlie said softly. "I remember how he loved this area, how he looked forward to coming here every summer."

Theodore sagged down on the seat next to his brother and nodded. "He died in Detroit. He was there on business. I was with him. He knew it was happening. We talked for hours the night he died. We talked about you and death and where he wanted to be buried. He asked me to find a spot in the old cemetery at Cold Springs. He wanted a place that overlooked the harbor."

"Will you take me there?"

Theodore's eyes were clouded. He nodded. Maybe, just maybe, after all these years, his brother had changed.

Harbor Hill Cemetery was all but abandoned. It sat high on a tree-sheltered bluff overlooking the harbor, three miles from the village of Cold Springs. Charlie had been there only once before, when his grandfather had died, but the images had emblazoned themselves on his mind for all eternity. Now, as his brother slowed to turn off the narrow ribbon of blacktop onto the overgrown gravel path guarded by two decaying and weathered cement lion sentinels, the hurt in those recollections rushed to the forefront of his thoughts. Even now it was painful; it was something he didn't want to remember.

The images materialized.

His father's strong, thick fingers were locked around his tiny wrist and dragging him out of the back seat of the old Packard. Theodore wasn't like that. Theodore walked ahead; he was brave and held his head high, like he was marching to the beat of some silent drummer. Theodore wasn't afraid, like he was.

Charlie looked up into his father's stern, grim face, and he could see just how much his father despised him for being what he was. He was trying desperately not to let the childish protest escape, but it did, and his small tremulous voice reverberated through the throng of mourners. "No," he pleaded, "please, Daddy, don't make me."

The outburst only served to make the coiled steel grip on his wrist grow tighter.

"What the hell's wrong with you, boy? Look at your brother! Look at Theodore! You don't see him hangin' back, whimpering like some damn beaten dog."

"Please, Daddy, don't . . ." Even now he could hear his childish plea. The whole thing was indelibly, permanently etched into the darkest recesses of his mind like acid eaten into stone.

"Charles, dammit," he remembered his father thundering, "either you face this thing like a man or I'll have to take you back to the house and lock you in the cellar again."

It was then, even as now, the most terrifying thing that anyone could have said to him. The threat of darkness and the even more consummate threat of aloneness conjured up for him the most terrifying specter of all. Being alone and the dark, after all these years, were still a threat without parallel.

"Didn't you love your grandfather, boy?" his father growled.

There was no way to tell his father the truth, because in truth, he hated the old man—the fat old man with the foul smell of his tobacco breath and the even stronger odor of the pungent liquid he drank out of the old jug in the basement.

Even now he remembered the gravesite, a tomb within a tomb. A wall of solemn men and women, indistinguishable in their black on black, formed a morbid curtain, a second tomb, a ring of curiosity. Even then he knew they were asking the same question he was asking himself. Could it be that Cleveland Jasper Frazier was really finally dead?

It was Charlie's first death, and he dared tell no one that he was responsible for it. That would truly make his father angry, if he knew that his cowardly son was the real reason the old man was dead. Oh, how he had wished for it. Was it possible that they already knew?

He spied Theodore again. His brother was standing beside his grandfather's coffin, erect, eyes down, dutifully paying homage. He saw his father smile at Charlie's brother, a smile of pride, a smile that to Charlie said, "See my manly son."

He remembered the women wailing, a symphony of long, loud, ugly sounds orchestrated with gasps for breath and interspersed with sobs of despair. He remembered wondering why they cared. Grandfather Cleveland was cruel and old, and he smelled bad. None of it made sense to an eight-year-old. It was dumb to cry.

An old woman began to sing. It was the same song Pastor Henry sang at the close of the Sunday morning service while Mrs. Locke played the old bellows organ and Mr. Carpenter took the offering. Charlie twisted his hand out of his father's grip and tried to melt back into the throng of people. It didn't work. His father's strong grip recaptured him. When the song concluded, the Pastor stiffly stepped forward, separating himself from the mourners. He laid his Bible on the lid of the coffin with one hand while his other worked on the starched celluloid collar. He cleared his throat and began to tell a lie. The words came out in fragmented chunks. The man was as uncomfortable with his eulogy as Charlie was with being there.

The words were empty, hollow, meaningless things, and those that were assembled stirred nervously. Charlie somehow understood what many of them didn't. Regardless of what the clergyman promised, life was over for Cleveland Frazier, and there was no choice but to acknowledge that fact.

His father let go of his hand and stepped around him to his grandfather's coffin. To Charlie's horror, the man reached down and lifted the lid. Charlie recoiled. There he was again, that despicable old man with his ugly face all shiny and puffed out, his eyes closed like he was merely sleeping. It wasn't at all like Theodore had told him it would be. Theodore had told him their grandfather's cheeks sunk in the moment he died, and that the eyes got brittle and fell apart like shattered pieces of glass, and that the teeth rotted instantly. None of those things had happened, and he wondered why his grandfather didn't look dead. Maybe he wasn't responsible for his death after all. Maybe, he decided, everyone was just as tired of the old man as he was, and they were going to bury him while he was sleeping. Wouldn't that be something?

When he saw his father bend down and kiss the man in the coffin, he shuddered.

Theodore followed, curling his young fingers over the edge of the coffin and pulling himself up until he could lean in and kiss the dead man. When he did that, all the old women cried.

Only then did Charlie realize that he was expected to do the same. His father turned to him and picked him up, swiftly propelling him down to the icy face. "Kiss your grandfather one last time before he begins his journey to heaven, Charles." His father's command was hissed more than spoken.

Terrified, he stiffened and felt his father's hand clasp the back of his head, shoving it down until he felt the cold, hard, unyielding feel of the old man's blood-drained lips against his young face.

Charlie's boyish scream shattered the gravesite stillness.

The car rolled to a gentle stop and he was suddenly catapulted back into the present. As his muddled recollections slowly began to fade, the emotional debris of the nightmare was swept aside again, but he knew it would return, just as it had thousands of time before.

"Any of this look familiar?" Theodore asked.

In truth, it didn't. It wasn't at all like he had remembered. His eyes darted nervously about the aging landscape of weathered and broken monuments. Where were the manicured expanses of grass between the stones? This wasn't it. This was a place of indescribable loneliness. He shuddered. There was the reminiscent chill, and he momentarily reestablished contact with his fear-filled past. He had refused to kiss his grandfather and had been relegated to the dank, foul-smelling confines of the basement for three whole days.

Charlie shook his head as though the gesture might help him clear the memory from his troubled mind. Unconsciously, his fingers curled around the door handle, and he had a sudden, overwhelming feel that he would suffocate if he didn't get out of the car. He stepped into the chill of the dying twilight and looked around him.

"Funny," he muttered, not caring whether his brother understood or not, "I've known that this day would happen. I've pictured it, played it out in my mind, and now that it's happening, it isn't anything like I thought it would be."

The shadows of the long autumn night had started to creep across the landscape. He searched for something familiar, something that would tie him to his past and yet free him from it. A raw wind stirred the nearly naked branches of the twisted oaks, whipping the dried leaves into a swirling pile at his feet. When he moved, he could hear them fragment into countless tortured pieces.

"Where is it?" he finally had the courage to ask.

Theodore had turned up his collar to ward off the chill. He pulled a hand out of his jacket pocket and pointed at a small tidy patch of mowed grass on the crest of the hill overlooking the harbor. "There," he said, "right next to Grandpa Cleveland."

Charlie had partially regained his equilibrium, and he forced himself to start up the small rise to where the swell of the land entombed the two men. The markers were plain, the epitaphs proclaiming only that they lived and not what they had been nor what they had done. The first and obviously older stone read simply, "Cleveland Jasper Frazier." The second was that of his son, Malcolm Cross Frazier. There were no flowers, no shrubs, no evidence that somehow had come to mourn their passing. Charlie decided that was appropriate.

He turned and looked at his brother, suddenly aware of how intently his sibling was watching him.

"You're a strange one, Charlie. Anybody ever tell you that?"

The question was a giveaway. He knew now he was winning his brother over. Theodore was lowering his defenses. Charlie decided it was time for a small challenge. "Why, Ted? Because I don't think like you? Or share your value system? Or because things that are important to you may not be important to me?"

Theodore shrugged and looked uneasily out over the water. "It's strange, real strange. We look so much alike, yet right now I could swear I don't even know you, that I've never known you. For that matter, I don't know why anything has turned out the way it has."

Inside, where small victories are won and cherished, Charlie felt the glow of his triumph. His scheme was working far better and far faster than he had ever dared hope. You're hooked, Theodore Frazier, he said to himself. You're stymied by the same archaic rationale that warped our grandfather's thinking and our father's as well. This family stuff is all a bunch of bullshit. Yesterday doesn't count; yesterday is the past, meaningless in the sense of what must be done. The only thing that matters is the present and what we do with it. Even tomorrow is not important, because you have no assurance that you will live to experience it.

Theodore turned away and walked slowly over to a straggly old pine, flanked by a monument that was tilted to one side by the tree's searching roots. He sat down on it and stared out at the last traces of orange-red in the distant western sky.

"When I look at you, Charlie, it's like I'm

looking in a mirror. I see the face and I hear the voice; it's familiar, and yet it isn't. There's nothing beyond the image." He paused. "It's like seeing me and not recognizing myself."

Charlie sat down beside him. "Being what we are gets in the way. When I was in the service I read a lot about how it is with twins. The resemblance stuff is all on the surface; inside it's all quite different. But that's just part of the problem. You were what Father wanted me to be, and I couldn't. Because I looked like you, he expected me to be like you. When I wasn't, he was disappointed, so disappointed that he didn't know how to react to me, how to accept me for what I was inside. I guess the only thing he ever really understood was that I wasn't you."

Theodore studied the man he called his brother, the man he had all but forgotten existed. Was it possible he was wrong? Was it possible that Charlie really did care, cared in a way he couldn't understand? If that were true, there was a great deal of catching up to do, secrets to probe, questions to ask. There were things about the man he needed to know.

They sat that way for a moment, each lost in his own thoughts, each looking at but not seeing the wellspring of their legacy.

Finally it was Charlie who shattered the uneasy tranquility when he stood up. "Well," he sighed, "I came here with a specific mission. Guess I'd better be about it."

"Be about what?"

"I came to Cold Springs with two very specific objectives in mind," Charlie lied. "The first was to begin mending the fences between you and me. It's time to put all the bitterness, the recriminations and the past behind us. The second is something a little different." He told his brother to wait there while he went back to the car. When he returned, he was carrying a nondescript cardboard box.

Theodore watched in silence as he unwrapped a bulky glass container from layers of torn terrycloth. "What is it?" he asked.

Charlie Frazier peeled away the last layer of fabric and held it up for his brother's inspection.

Theodore stared at the container. It was filled with a nearly opaque liquid that sloshed back and forth in Charlie's unsteady hand. "Okay, I give. What the hell is it?"

Charlie lowered his voice, mostly for effect. "A little something I've owed my father all these years," he answered.

"Yeah," Theodore shrugged, "maybe so, but you still haven't told me what it is."

Charlie forced a crooked smile. He had done his job, all right. Old Teddy boy didn't appear to be the least bit suspicious. He had actually woven a bit of the truth into his little scheme, and old conventional Theodore hadn't noticed the difference.

"Look, I wasn't with you when Father died, and I couldn't come home for the funeral. I never got a chance to even try to heal all those wounds. All that went past me, and I've lost something."

"Just a few minutes ago you were telling me the past wasn't important."

"In this particular case it is. If I'm ever going to make this up to him, I have to find a way to bridge the gap, fill in the space between the now and the then. You see, Theodore, I couldn't come back until I found a way to eliminate the chasm between life and death, because that empty space is the erosion of everything that I am and still have the potential to become."

Theodore looked at his brother in the failing light, too stunned to say anything. Charlie had truly changed, far more than he would have ever thought possible. The way he looked, the way he talked—it was their father reincarnated. He had to force himself to repeat the question. "You still haven't told me what's in the jar."

Charlie managed another practiced smile. "I'm not sure I can."

"Try me."

"Have you ever been to Newfoundland?"

Theodore shook his head.

"Ever hear of the Witch of Sixkill?"

His brother's face twisted into a look of disbelief. "Witch? You mean like spooks and goblins?"

Charlie set the container down beside him in the dried grass and resumed his seat on the gravestone next to his brother. The sky had yielded to darkness, and the chill was even more pronounced. The nearly empty boughs of the trees rattled like weary sabers.

"That's exactly the type of witch I'm talking about. I heard about one just before I rotated back to the States when I was finishing my tour in Saint Johns. She lived in a little village called Sixkill. A few of the people I knew had gone to her and believed in her; some of them claimed she could bridge time and space and death."

"You mean like bring the dead back to life?" his brother snickered.

"Exactly," Charlie admitted.

This time his brother laughed out loud. "Come on, Charlie, you don't actually believe in that stuff, do you?"

Charlie lowered his eyes and worked his foot back and forth in the dried leaves. "I know how it must sound, but desperate men do desperate things."

"So what's the big secret? What's the stuff in the jar supposed to do? Bring back the dead?"

Charlie tried to appear as though he was

hesitant to divulge the deal he had struck with the woman from the village of Sixkill. "I told her what had happened," he began, "told her about not being able to see my father before he died, told her there had been a lifelong rift between us. Then I told her I was desperate to reach across the years to try one last time to establish contact with him." He allowed his voice to fade to a whisper and in the darkness wiped away an imaginary tear. Very good, Charlie. He applauded himself. You're getting better at this all the time.

"And that's what this jar is supposed to do? Bring him back to life so you can talk to him?"

"Whatever is in it," Charlie lied, "and the witch didn't tell me, it will let Father know how I really felt and how much I cared."

Theodore shook his head. "I can't believe you're telling me this. You actually went to this witch and paid her for some potion that's supposed to . . ."

"I didn't pay her," Charlie protested. "She gave me one year to judge for myself how it worked, then she wants me to go back and settle up."

"Then she didn't try to sell you some cock-and-bull story about how this stuff is going to bring him back to life?"

Charlie was doing his best to look slightly wounded that his brother would think him a fool for believing in such potions. "I don't know what the stuff is supposed to do. She simply told me to take it to the gravesite, set it on the tombstone and walk away from it."

Theodore wrapped his arms around his knees and rocked backwards. He was laughing out loud now. "I can't believe I'm sitting here listening to this. More than that, I can't believe there are still people around who believe in potions and witches and the supernatural. Especially you, Charlie. I know you know this kind of shit ain't real. The only thing you've told me so far that doesn't fit is that she didn't charge you an arm and a leg for the stuff."

Charlie was well-rehearsed; he knew his role and how to play the scene. He looked forlornly down at the pile of leaves at his feet. "I told you I'm desperate. I've got to try. Somehow I have to get through to him." He pulled the collar of his windbreaker up, rubbed his hands together and made sure his brother saw him shiver.

"So what do you intend to do? Set that thing on the grave and sit here all night waiting for something to happen?"

"No," Charlie said softly, "I intend to leave it, just like the witch told me to. Whatever happens, happens. It has nothing to do with what I think or feel. The forces are already put in motion. The witch has promised me."

Again Theodore let go with a coarse laugh.

He stood up and walked slowly over to the tombstone where the jar and its obscure contents rested. He picked it up and held it so he could peer through the glass at the murky contents. The autumn moon yielded insufficient light and the identity of the thing housed within the jar remained hidden.

"And you really don't know what's in there?"

Charlie shook his head. It was getting easier by the minute.

Theodore walked back to his brother and did something he hadn't done in years. He put his arm around the trembling man's shoulders. "I can't believe I'm saying this," he began, "but if it makes you feel better to put that damn thing on Father's grave, if it makes you feel like you're doing something to right the wrongs of the past, then by all means, do it. What the hell can it hurt?"

Charlie shrugged. "I'm glad you understand," he whispered. He got up and put his arm around his brother's shoulders, and they walked together back down the darkened path toward the car.

The last thing the two brothers saw as they left the crest of the hill where their father was buried was the brooding glass jar sitting atop the weathered tombstone.

Chapter Ten

Dinner was a strained affair. They went to Theodore's club and were treated with candlelight and an expensive port imported from a small French village where Theodore and Betty Elizabeth had spent their honeymoon. Unfortunately, the subtlety of the evening was lost on Peggy, who, after a few drinks, insisted on recounting how she got pregnant in high school. The whole topic, complete with Peggy's liberal use of four letter words, alienated their pretentious hostess. So, instead of a protracted after-dinner conversation as Betty Elizabeth had planned, the foursome returned to the condo and retired for the evening.

It was only after Theodore had showered and returned to the bedroom that Betty Elizabeth had the opportunity to ask her husband about the episode at the cemetery. She tried to ask in a casual fashion, as she fluffed pillows and turned down covers. Because of her own involvement, it was a conversation she felt entitled to know about.

"So," she asked, "what happened out there today?"

Theodore was still sitting on the edge of the bed, removing his slippers. "Strange, real strange," he reflected. "Would you believe it? He actually had a present for Father."

Betty Elizabeth had long ago learned that it wasn't necessary to hang on every word her boring husband uttered. In fact, she had confided to one of her girlfriends that the poor quality of his conversation only was exceeded by his even clumsier attempts at lovemaking. Now, even though she was the one who had asked the question, she was only half-listening.

"Present?" she repeated idly.

"Uh-huh," Theodore muttered, "a jar of something."

"What do you mean, 'a jar of something'? Didn't he tell you what was in it?"

Another of his irritating little habits resurfaced. He didn't answer her. He scooted off the edge of the bed and lay on the floor, face down. The nightly ritual had begun—50 push-ups, 40 sit-ups and ten minutes of jogging in place. It was a regimen that would make him sweat profusely, after which he would crawl in bed and monitor his diminishing pulse until it hit precisely the level Doctor Whitehurst had told him was right and proper for a man his age, weight and build. Betty Elizabeth had tried, without success, to get him to alter his schedule and shower after his calisthenics, but Theodore had never quite grasped the implications of her timely suggestion.

"Actually, I don't know," he finally got around to answering. "Pretty weird though, don't you think?"

Betty Elizabeth laid down her book on her quilted lap and looked at her husband. It was his typically vague, ambiguous answer. "How was it strange, Theodore?" Her voice had that first tinge of impatience in it. "Be specific. You said your brother brought a gift for your father, then you tell me it's a strange gift, then you top it off with the statement that you don't know what it is. At the moment, I don't have the slightest idea what you're talking about."

Theodore batted his lazy eyes, propped his hands behind his head and stared lethargically up at the ceiling. "If you can believe it, he said he got it from someone who calls herself the 'Witch of Sixkill'. Said he brought it all the way home from Newfoundland."

"Witch of what?" Betty Elizabeth asked. Suddenly she was paying closer attention.

"Sixkill. How's that for a name?" He was indulging himself in one of his dull little laughs of ridicule.

"I think I've heard of her," Betty Elizabeth said, frowning.

This time Theodore laughed out loud. "Oh, for Christ's sake, Betty, not you, too."

She had already swung her long thin legs over the edge of the bed and was slipping into her robe. She knotted the cord around her slender waist and headed for the bedroom door. "Be back in a minute," she informed him.

When she returned, there was a look of triumph on her thin face. She was carrying one of her tattered collectibles. It was an antiquarian book, one of many she carted home from the used book stores she haunted. The difference between Betty Elizabeth and most folks who go around collecting similar stock was that she actually read them before they were buried on the shelf to collect dust.

"Listen to this," she said excitedly. "It's in the section entitled 'Actual Documentation of Known Witches'. It's on page one-hundred and eighty-seven, and it's a listing of certified witches. The third one on the list is a lady by the name of Jubell Caron, who was also known as the 'Witch of Sixkill'."

"Certified?" Theodore laughed. "Who the hell certifies witches?"

Betty Elizabeth looked up from the pages of the dusty book, her disdain apparent.

"Probably aren't all that many places called Sixkill with witches," Theodore yawned.

"Listen to this," she pushed on. "According to this, the Witch of Sixkill was the widow of one of six whalers who were lost in an ice storm in eighteen forty-three. The book claims she was a young bride who hadn't consummated her marriage, and when she heard what happened to her husband, she tried to kill herself by throwing her body off the jagged cliffs outside the village of Sixkill. Somehow she survived, but she was terribly disfigured, so much so that none of the villagers could stand to look at her. After that she became a recluse, and because she was crippled to the extent that she couldn't get around, she developed her psychic powers and became a priestess of the supernatural."

"Eighteen forty-three," Theodore repeated. "Sorta makes you wonder what a one hundred and twenty-two-year-old broad looks like." The remark was followed by his usual dull, derisive laugh.

Betty Elizabeth sighed impatiently and thumbed to the front of the book. "Come on, this book was published in eighteen eighty.

The woman would be dead by now. Charlie probably read about or heard the same story. The question is, why did he go to all the trouble to set you up?"

Theodore followed with one of his laconic shrugs. "Look, all I know is Charlie said he got it from her this spring just before he was rotated back to the States from Newfoundland."

"Impossible," she snorted. "This Caron woman would be dead by now."

"Don't forget, my Aunt Ethel lived to be a hundred and three," he reminded her.

It was exactly the kind of observation she would expect from her dullard husband. She already knew what was happening; for whatever reason, the conniving Charlie had set Theodore up for something. Or Charlie himself had been taken in by someone trying to capitalize on the Caron woman's legend.

Betty Elizabeth put down the book and glowered at her husband. "Describe the jar," she ordered.

"What's to describe? A jar's a jar."

"Damn it, Ted, what did it look like?"

He blinked and tried to get a clearer picture of the glass object in his mind. "Big," he began, "like a pickle jar. It was full of something like a cloudy substance, real thick. Not as thick as syrup, but real thick."

"Did the jar have any markings?"

"None that I remember." Theodore hesitated. He was somewhat taken aback by his wife's intense interrogation. All things being equal, Betty Elizabeth hadn't shown this much interest in anything he had said in years.

She moved around to his side of the bed. "Okay, where is it?" she demanded. "I want to see it. I want to see this so-called gift from the Witch of Sixkill."

This was just one of the many aspects of Betty Elizabeth that Theodore didn't care for. Every now and then, she became just a little too demanding, and when she did, he did his best to ignore her. With that in mind, he rolled over, turning his back to her, and pulled the quilt up over his shoulders. "I'm tired," he grunted. "We can talk about it tomorrow."

She jerked the covers down and bent over him. Her thin, pinched face was flushed. "Look, you fool," she growled, "just what did Charlie ask you for today?" Betty Elizabeth had a terrifying vision of her husband's long lost brother suddenly appearing on the scene and demanding his share of Malcolm Frazier's legacy.

"Nothing," Theodore sighed. "He never once asked for anything. He told me all he wants to do is to try to atone for some of the wrongs of the past, particularly the ones with our father. He claims that all those years haunt him, and he wants to get it all behind him."

"I'll bet it haunts him," she hissed. "It haunts him that he pissed away the opportunity to get his hands on some of the money." Her face clouded, and her voice was suddenly strident. "You didn't tell him what was really in that will, did you?"

"For God's sake, Betty Elizabeth, what do you take me for, a fool?"

"Damn it," she snarled, "if Charlie ever uncovers how you and one of your crooked lawyer friends doctored your father's will, we'll all end up in jail and lose everything we've worked for."

"Relax, there's no way for him to find out," Theodore said confidently. "Everything's been taken care of. The original was destroyed; we've been ultra-careful. Don't worry, our tracks are covered."

"Well, if he doesn't want his share of Frazier Securities, what does he want?"

"I told you," he sighed. "He told me he thinks this feud has gone on long enough. He wants to make things right. I'm telling you, Betty, if you had seen him at the cemetery today and seen how torn up he was when he set that stupid jar on Father's tomb, you'd believe what I'm telling you."

Betty Elizabeth sagged down on the edge of

the bed and glared at the man she had shepherded through the elaborate scheme. "I can't believe he's shown up after all these years and doesn't want something. You're missing something."

"What's to miss?" he asked. "It's a goddamn, stupid jar, nothing more."

"Tell me this," she insisted, "exactly what was it he thought this present was going to do when he put it there?"

Theodore was resigning himself to the fact that he wasn't likely to get any sleep until his wife's morbid curiosity was satisfied. He pushed himself into a sitting position with his hands folded behind his head and propped himself against the headboard. "That's what I've been trying to tell you all along. The whole thing is strange. Even more, it's downright weird." Then as an afterthought, he added, "Know what I really think? I think Charlie actually believes that jar has some kind of magical power that will bring old Malcolm back to life."

Betty Elizabeth's already white face somehow managed to turn even whiter. The frown was gone. She got up, walked over to her ornate dresser, opened the top drawer and rummaged around until she found her pack of cigarettes. That was the giveaway, the indication of how upset she actually was. Betty

Elizabeth only smoked when she was really upset. The blue-grey cloud of smoke enveloped her and drifted toward him. "Answer me this, Theodore Frazier," she hissed, "what do you think is going to happen if Charlie's gift actually works?"

He stared back at his wife in disbelief. "You can't be serious," he challenged.

"You bet your sweet ass I'm serious," she thundered. "Think about it. Think about what would happen if your father did come back."

His smile was beginning to fade. Theodore had always been short on patience, and what little he had was already starting to slip away. "Jesus Christ, Betty, go to bed. It's a goddamn joke. Some broad has found a way to milk the tourists by calling herself a witch and selling them jars full of dirty water. What's the big deal? It's my brother who ought to feel like a fool. He's the one who bought it."

"I can't buy it," his wife snapped back at him. "I've read about things like this. They work. I'm telling you, Theodore, they work. And if this one does, we've lost everything we've worked so hard to get."

Theodore had heard enough. He slid back down in the bed and started to roll over. Then he stopped. He had figured out a way to put the lid on his wife's concern. "Look," he said, his voice half-muffled by the pillow, "if it makes you feel any better, we'll get up in the morning and drive out there so you can see for yourself just how harmless the damn thing is."

He felt his wife's long fingernails dig into his fleshy underarm. He looked into her fearful eyes and realized that she was trembling. "No," she said emphatically, "we're going out there now."

Theodore raised himself up, propping his weight on his elbows. "Like hell," he snarled, "it's late. I'm tired. We'll go in the morning."

"No," she said emphatically, "we go *now!*"

Peggy watched Charlie from across the room. She had never seen him quite like this before. To her way of thinking, Charlie had acted just a little bit strange ever since she had known him, but this was bizarre behavior even for him. He had been prowling back and forth ever since they had retired to their room. From time to time he stopped just long enough to put his ear to the door and listen. Then, obviously not hearing what he wanted to hear, he continued his pacing.

"Charlie, honey, why don't you come to bed?" She did her best to make it sound like there was the slightest hint of an invitation in the suggestion. The truth of the matter was, she knew she couldn't go to sleep with him prowling back and forth like that.

He ignored her, paused again and put his ear to the door.

"What the hell's the matter with you?" she complained. "If I wasn't in the mood, you'd be pawing all over me." Peggy pulled the covers back to reveal her total lack of bedtime attire and blew him a kiss. "Come on over here," she whispered huskily. "Let little Peggy show you something that's a helluva lot more fun than listening to the couple in the next room."

Charlie held his index finger up to his lips and made a shushing sound. He had his ear pinned to the door again.

"Drop dead, you bastard," she hissed, jerking the covers back up and over her nakedness.

Charlie's face broke into a toothy grin, something it seldom did, and he whispered, "At last, I think they're leaving."

"Good riddance, I say," she shot back at him. "Can I tell you something, lover boy? Your brother and that frigid bitch he calls his wife are two of the most boring, fucking people I have ever spent an evening with. So they're gone. Big deal! Now, come to bed. Mama Peggy's got a little surprise for you."

Charlie walked across the room and, to Peggy's surprise, pulled his suitcase out of the closet. "Get up," he barked, "and get your clothes on."

"You're kidding! I just got comfortable."

"Like hell I'm kidding. You and I are gonna be long gone by the time they get back."

"But Charlie," she whined, "it's late. Where the hell are we going at this time of night?"

"We're driving into town. I've got reservations at the Holiday Inn."

"But what's wrong with staying right here?" she persisted.

"I've got this all planned out and I'm not deviating from my plan. Now, dammit, get out of that bed."

Peggy's mouth curled into a pout. She crawled out of the warm bed and began pulling on her underclothes. "Know somethin', Charlie Frazier, you're really acting weird. When are you gonna tell me what this is all about?"

"Later, I'll tell you later. Right now we've got to get our stuff together and get the hell out of here."

The gravel drive up the hill to the old cemetery seemed even longer in the darkness. Theodore's headlights reached out only to be soaked up in the blackness.

"Are you sure this is it?" Betty Elizabeth asked.

"Of course I'm sure," he shot back at her. "I was just out here this afternoon."

"This isn't the way I remembered it."

"Everything looks different in the dark." The words weren't even out of his mouth before he realized that it was the kind of statement that only proved what his wife said about him being boring. "Sorry," he muttered.

They reached the crest of the hill where the gravel drive ended and crawled out of the car into the damp chill of the night air. The moon was full, thinly veiled by a deck of high, thin cirrus clouds. It gave their surroundings a hazy, murky, almost brooding look.

"I don't like this," she chattered nervously.

"Dammit," he spit, "of course you don't like it. Sane people are supposed to be home in bed."

"Where is it? Where's the grave?"

Theodore pointed up into the darkness. "Up there, on the rise, overlooking the harbor, close to that big tree."

Betty Elizabeth switched on her flashlight and started defiantly up the rise, dancing the harsh yellow circle of light off the ground in front of her. The sound of dried leaves cracking under her feet betrayed the fact that she was moving with trepidation.

Theodore slumped back against the fender of the car and waited. It was just late enough and he was just tired enough not to care that he was destined to be berated for not going with her. It was the sound of his name that shattered the stillness.

"Theodore," she shouted, "come here!"

Dutifully, he trudged up the hill toward the gravesite.

"Is this it?" Betty Elizabeth played the beam of light down on Malcolm Frazier's headstone. In the middle of it sat the glass jar.

"That's it. Told you it wasn't anything to get excited about."

"But . . . but it's nothing more than an old . . ." she said in amazement. "It's a jar full of . . ."

"Precisely," he concluded for her, ". . . full of dirty water."

Betty Elizabeth bent over and put the flashlight up close to the jar to illuminate the contents. Then she studied it carefully. "I can tell you one thing," she announced. "There's more there than dirty water. I can see something in there."

"Like what?" Theodore yawned. He had had about all he wanted of his brother's mysterious jar.

She beckoned her husband down for a closer scrutiny of the cloudy vessel. A compliant Theodore bent over and peered into the murky contents.

"See right there?" she asked. She was pointing to a seemingly solid substance floating close to the bottom of the jar.

"Doesn't look like anything to me," he said.

"Dammit, Theodore, you're just being stubborn." She pointed to the cloudy substance again. "I say there's something there, and I say I saw it move."

It occurred to him that maybe logic would help. "Of course it's moving. It's suspended in liquid; the liquid is moving."

"Why?"

"Why what?"

"Why is the liquid moving, stupid? The jar is resting on a heavy stone monument. The jar is sealed which means the wind isn't doing it. The earth isn't shaking. So, why is it moving?"

Theodore looked first at the jar, then at his wife. He wanted to tell her that it was because of the constant wagging of her tongue, but his better judgment prevailed. Instead he admitted that she was right. It was a sealed container, and there wasn't any tremor in the ground. There was a breeze, but not enough to make the jar shudder. Finally he admitted that he didn't know. In the end he figured that was the only answer that would satisfy her.

"I don't like this the least little bit," she announced.

Had he been asked, Theodore would have admitted that he didn't like it either, but for entirely different reasons. He thought the whole jar thing was just so much nonsense, a waste of time that had already gotten far more attention than it deserved.

Betty Elizabeth was in one of her demanding moods. "I want you to pick that disgusting thing up, carry it over to the cliff and throw it over."

"But . . ." he protested.

"No buts about it," she snapped. "We're here, so we might as well get rid of the disgusting thing once and for all."

Theodore's second protest was aborted before the words even got out of his mouth.

"Just do it," Betty Elizabeth said icily. "I don't like it, and if your father were here, he wouldn't want that disgusting thing sitting on his headstone either."

"Well, he isn't here, and the truth of the matter is that I doubt if he'd give a damn whether the jar was sitting there or not."

Betty Elizabeth hauled out her ultimate weapon. "Either you move that jar, or I move out of the bedroom," she threatened.

"I don't see how the two are connected," Theodore sputtered. He followed his feeble attempt at logic with a surrendering shrug. What the hell, he thought to himself, if it's so damned important to her, why not do it? Besides, it was the path of least resistance. He bent over and picked up the jar, surprised at how much heavier it felt now than it had earlier in the day. It was heavy enough that he actually struggled with it.

"Oh, for Pete's sake," Betty Elizabeth grumbled, "you're such a wimp, Theodore. Give it to me." She reached out to take the cumbersome object from him, felt it start to slip through her hands and watched helplessly as it plummeted to the ground. It hit with a dull thud. She shined the beam of light down on it and saw the crack in the glass that zigzagged the length of the container.

"Now look what you've done," she hissed. Then they watched as the cloudy liquid began to seep from the jar, staining the ground around the base of the tombstone.

Their eyes were still locked when it happened. Betty Elizabeth reacted first. A second later, Theodore took note of the fact. There was a distinct movement in the ground at their feet. There was actually a shudder in the cold earth.

"Did you feel that?" she whispered.

Theodore looked at his wife's flushed face, then down at the ground where they stood. He snatched the flashlight from her, shined it first on the tombstone, then down at the broken jar slowly spilling its murky contents onto the clutter of dried leaves. "Feel what?" he asked. The tremor in his voice was a dead giveaway.

Before Betty Elizabeth could respond, there was a second occurrence, more pronounced, stronger, and lasting longer than the first. Her eyes began darting nervously from one dark spot to the next, her brain frantically searching for a plausible explanation. "Teddy," she cooed, her voice suddenly free of stridency, "Teddy . . . what was that?"

Theodore had seen it all before. She was acquiescing. If she couldn't be in complete control, she didn't want any part of it. Now she was looking to him for answers, even willing to settle for one of his dumb, monotonous explanations.

But Theodore was pressing for his own sense of order, for any fragment of reality he could hold onto. He was still computing, still mulling it over when they heard the grating sound—the coarse, grinding, shifting sound of a great mass.

Betty Elizabeth screamed. It was the shrillest scream he had ever heard. It echoed through the old cemetery and seemed to hang in the nearly naked trees.

Theodore stumbled backward.

Betty Elizabeth was frozen where she stood.

The monument had shifted, moved to the right. There was now a space between the great stone itself and the cast concrete base.

Almost imperceptibly at first, something appeared. A thing, tiny and inconspicuous, curled its way up and over the coarse edge of the piece of stone, snaking its way out of the dirt and dried leaves.

Theodore was transfixed.

Betty's mouth moved, but now the words didn't come out. Her lips were trembling, her whole body shaking violently.

Theodore fared no better. The flashlight dangled from his hand, the beam dancing eerily in space, betraying his mounting terror.

What was at first something unidentifiable had become a single finger, slowly transforming, as more of it was revealed, into a clutching, clawing, desperate hand.

Finally it was all too apparent. What was under the earth—the dank, foul-smelling, black earth—was trying to escape its confinement.

"My God," Theodore muttered. The words stumbled out, tumbling over each other.

The grisly phenomenon continued, metamorphosing into hideous reality right before their terrified eyes.

Clumps of earth began to heave, and the ground began to tremble. The stone teetered and toppled over. The heavy base shifted still further, grinding against the protesting stone. The thin layer of high clouds that had thoughtfully masked the sordidness of their surroundings was gone, and the full empty face of the moon cast down a somber, revealing light.

The yawning pit at their feet belched out stagnant, foul air—and he was there, staring up at them, assessing them through dried, long dead hollow sockets in a mask composed of shards of flesh and rotting teeth.

It wasn't until the grotesque specter began to move again that Betty Elizabeth felt the first stabbing sensation of unfettered panic slam into her chest. She was frozen in horror, unable to move, mouth agape, eyes fixed on the decaying remains in the bottom of the yawning hole.

"Oh, my God," she muttered. Her knees had already given way from under her. She was dizzy and nauseous.

Theodore wasn't faring much better. His legs were like stone, and the horror of the moment had all but overwhelmed him.

The ravages of time had rendered what they knew to be in the tomb into something wholly unrecognizable. If they hadn't been there to validate each other's experience, neither would have been able to describe what they were witnessing. There, transfixed, they saw the thing move again, one hand reaching up and out of the abyss, fingers symbolically locked on the edge of the earth as it tried to reenter the realm of the living.

The dirt shifted and crumbled.

Betty Elizabeth staggered clumsily backward, trying to extricate herself from the horror of the moment.

What was left of the earthly remains of one Malcolm Frazier actually moved. Theodore felt his mouth go dry and the acids in his churning stomach revolt. His eyes clouded with tears of fear, and it was impossible for him to breathe. Betty Elizabeth had somehow found the courage to bolt. She was running back down the hill toward the car. She fell, screamed out, regained her footing and started running blindly down the path again.

Theodore was no longer thinking, operating solely on instinct. Now he too ran, gaining on her.

Betty Elizabeth was already behind the wheel by the time Theodore reached the car.

"Gimme the keys!" she shouted.

Theodore frantically slapped at his pockets. He couldn't find them. Where were they? How could anyone misplace a cumbersome ring of keys? Betty Elizabeth was slapping at the unoffending dashboard, screaming at him. He repeatedly groped for the keys—pants pockets, front and back, shirt, jacket—nothing. Then he glanced down and saw them lying on the passenger seat. They were mocking him in the pale, eerie light cast by the full moon.

He was hammering on the window, pointing to them. "On the seat, beside you!"

Betty Elizabeth snatched them up, feverishly jamming them in the ignition and instantly grinding the reluctant engine to life. Theodore was clawing at the door handle, but it was locked and his wife seemed oblivious to his plight.

"Betty, for Christ's sake, let me in!" he screamed.

She had turned on the headlights and was racing the engine, revving it higher and higher. He watched her thin body slam back against the seat as the car rocketed forward, the lights penetrating the blackness and illuminating the thing that was now freed.

It stood erect, directly in the path of the car. He knew now what she was doing. He watched in stunned silence. There was a sickening collision as the car plowed into it and continued on up and over the crest of the hill, spiraling out over the edge into the blackness and plunging out of sight.

The sickening inevitability of Theodore's world of logic returned. The sequence of events suddenly became wholly predictable. He knew exactly what would follow—the sounds of tearing metal and shattering glass, repeated violent collisions with the jagged rocks at the base of the cliff, and finally the explosion, violent and final.

That was followed by the conflagration, a ball of flame in the nightmarish sky.

Theodore, numbed and terrified, staggered up the hill, seemingly oblivious to the threat of a confrontation with the specter. He peered over the edge of the precipice and down into the consuming inferno. For a terrible instant he thought he heard the sound of a woman's screams. There was a second explosion—the gas tank, he thought logically—and then even more odious silence.

Reality gave way to hysteria, and he sank to his knees. He fell face first in the dirt. The earth itself muffled his desperate, unbridled anguish.

Chapter Eleven

"Are you Charles Frazier?"

Charlie looked up from his morning paper into the tired eyes of a tall man with a hawk nose. The man was gaunt, accentuated by the fact that he hadn't shaved. The stubble was gray and splotchy. His raincoat was damp and smelled musty. Across the table, Peggy was looking up at the newcomer and eyeing him suspiciously.

"Can't deny it. I'm Charlie Frazier," he admitted. "What can I do for you?"

The intruder looked relieved. "Detective Sergeant Mason Seacraft," he said. "May I sit down?"

"By all means, Sergeant, pull up a chair."

Charlie gestured across the table. "This is my friend, Peggy Bowles."

They exchanged nods without words. "The desk clerk said you had already checked out but that I might still find you in the dining room."

"Is there something wrong, Sergeant?" Peggy asked.

Seacraft was still settling in his chair. "There isn't any easy way to break the news on something like this. So I usually follow the manual and say something like there's been an accident."

Charlie set his cup down and stared at the man. "What kind of an accident?"

"It's Mrs. Frazier, your brother's wife. She was killed last night in an automobile accident."

Charlie was momentarily stunned. Mrs. Frazier? The man had distinctly said *Mrs*. Frazier. It wasn't what he had expected him to say. But even though he was caught off guard, he was too well-prepared, too well-rehearsed. "How? When?" he asked.

It was obvious the gaunt man was exhausted. He leaned forward with his forearms on the table and stared at the remains of their breakfast for a moment. "I know this is all going to sound strange," he explained, "but from what little we've been able to piece together so far, your brother and his wife, for some strange reason, went out to Cold Springs Cemetery last night. And even though we can't explain it now, it appears Mrs. Frazier drove right on up the hill. Instead of hitting the brakes she must have hit the accelerator. From the tracks, it appears she was going at a high rate of speed and drove right on out over the edge. It's an eighty foot drop, straight down. I don't guess I have to tell you what happened."

As was his habit, Mason Seacraft gave his account of the accident without looking at the faces of his audience. It was a game he played. When he was finished, he would look up, already knowing what he would find. The recipients of such news always looked the same. They would be too stunned to speak, their faces etched with an expression of disbelief and their eyes glazed. Somewhere he had read that it was called the mask of incredulity. It was no different this time. They looked exactly like he expected them to look.

"You said Mrs. Frazier was driving?" Charlie repeated. "What about my brother?"

Seacraft's weary face furrowed into a puzzled frown, and he shrugged. "That's what we don't know," he admitted. "We haven't found him yet. All we know for sure is that he was with her when they left the complex last night. The security guard at the main gate confirmed that. That's how we knew you were in the area. When you checked in yesterday, you told him you were weekend guests of the Fraziers."

Charlie was hoping the nervous smile playing with the corners of his mouth didn't give him away. He was stunned. Betty Elizabeth was dead which was fine with him. But what about Theodore? Without one very obviously dead Theodore Frazier, his whole scheme meant absolutely nothing.

"Poor Theodore," Charlie muttered. It was a line he had rehearsed but was now using in an entirely different way than he had rehearsed it. "Betty Elizabeth meant everything to him."

Seacraft sighed. "We know he was up there with her. We found footprints, but other than that, nothing. I've had a crew searching around down in the rocks at the base of the hill on the theory that one of the car doors might have come open and thrown him out. So far, we haven't found anything. The only way we could identify Mrs. Frazier was that one arm was torn off on impact. It didn't burn. Her jewelry was how we identified her." He said it before he thought, looked at Peggy and apologized. "Sorry, Miss Bowles, I wasn't thinking. Sometimes my wife tells me I get a little too graphic."

Charlie's mind was racing. Betty Elizabeth was dead, but what about his brother? As soon as Seacraft departed, he had to find a way to get out to the cemetery and find out what happened. Something had happened, he knew that much, but based on what Seacraft had told him, it happened to the wrong person. The so-called gift he had brought home from Newfoundland had apparently worked —or had it? For that matter, he wasn't certain any of the jars he had obtained from the woman who called herself a witch had actually worked. He had no way of knowing, and it made him feel a little foolish. Now he found himself talking to a man named Seacraft and wondering just exactly how he would end up fitting in the picture.

"Well, is there anything I can do, Sergeant?"

Seacraft shoved himself away from the table and unfolded his long, angular frame into what must have passed for his version of erect. His arms were long enough that he idly trailed his bony fingers back and forth across the tablecloth as he looked at Charlie. "Guess I should be askin' you how long you intend to be around?"

"We were planning to drive back down to the city tonight," Charlie conceded.

The officer began to fish absent-mindedly through his pockets. Finally he located a small plastic packet of business cards. "I'd appreciate it if you'd stop by my office before you and the little lady decide to leave town. The address is on the card; it's a little brick building across the street from the post office. That way if I've learned anything during the course of the day, I can bring you up to speed."

"What about my brother?"

Seacraft sighed and shoved his hands in his pockets. "We'll just have to keep looking for him. I'm not rightly sure where to look. The lake got pretty stirred up this morning when that squall line moved through. I told my men we'd have to search those rocks at the base of the cliff a second time. If he was in the car when it went over the edge, he could have been thrown out on impact. If that's the case, he could be wedged down there in those rocks someplace. I've already made up my mind that if we haven't located him by late afternoon, I'm gonna put out an APB on him."

Charlie glanced across the table at Peggy. She was watching him intently. He knew she suspected something. He could tell by the look on her face.

Seacraft tipped his hat, revealing for the first time the long, ugly purple scar that had traversed its way up from behind his right ear to the top of his head. For the most part, the officer was bald and there was no way to hide it other than the hat. He started to walk away from the table, stopped and pursed his thin lips. "Mind if I ask you a question, Mr. Frazier?"

"Of course not."

"Can't say as I knew your brother and his wife all that well, but I do know that him bein' the head of a big company and all that they used their place to do a lot of entertaining. Stories I heard had 'em entertainin' six, eight, maybe more people on any given weekend. I was lucky enough to get invited out there a time or two, and I couldn't help but notice that that place of theirs was big enough to sleep lots of people—"

Charlie cut him off. "And you're wondering why his own brother didn't stay at the condo last night, right?"

"Somethin' like that," Seacraft admitted.

Charlie leaned back in his chair and gave the officer one of his carefully rehearsed smiles. "That's easy enough. You see, Sergeant, my brother and I haven't seen each other in years. You might say the situation was a little bit strained."

Peggy slipped her hand across the table and patted his. "I think you should tell the Sergeant the real reason, dear," she cooed.

Seacraft turned his attention to the woman. "Better yet, why don't you tell me?"

Peggy had her cup of coffee poised halfway between her mouth and the saucer. "I heard

283

you mention you were married, Sergeant. So I just might turn the tables and ask you if you'd want anybody around if you and your wife were having a little disagreement?"

The expression on Seacraft's gaunt face changed from weary hopelessness to curiosity. "The folks around these parts aren't long on polite talk, Miss Bowles. Is that a polite way of lettin' me know Ted and Betty Frazier were havin' a fight last night?"

Peggy took a long sip of coffee and set her cup down. "You can draw your own conclusions, Sergeant," she said icily.

Charlie could have kissed her. She had jumped in at just the right time. "Miss Bowles is right. When we saw how things were going, we thought it would be better if we stayed at the motel last night."

Seacraft studied them for a moment, started to ask another question and thought better of it, tipped his hat, nodded and left.

Peggy waited until she was sure the man wasn't going to stop again and reached back across the table to recapture Charlie's hand. "Did I do good?" she asked, smiling.

Charlie nodded. "You did good," he confirmed. "Very, very good."

"Okay, my pet, if that's the case, suppose you drop the big damn mystery and tell little Peggy what the hell's going on. You're up to something. It's written all over your face."

Charlie's sometimes handsome face broke into a toothy grin. "Can't," he said emphatically. "But I can tell you that my plan is unfolding quite nicely."

Three times they went out and drove around. Three times they drove slowly by the entrance of the cemetery, and three times they returned to the motel to wait for another interval to pass before they tried again. Charlie's mood deteriorated as the day wore on. By late afternoon, Peggy was bored, and Charlie's mood had turned sullen and morose.

Peggy had tried repeatedly to find out what was on his mind. But the more she probed, the more determined he seemed to withdraw into himself.

After the third such aborted venture he told her to wait at the motel while he went out on his own. He returned 30 minutes later, saying nothing about his brief journey.

Peggy, unsuccessful at prying any further information out of him, had retreated into her own world. She didn't even look up when he returned, contenting herself instead by casually thumbing through stacks of old magazines she had retrieved from the motel lobby.

It was late afternoon when Charlie convinced himself that it was time to try again. "It's now or never," he grumbled. "Let's risk it."

"Risk what?"

"We've got a little chore to take care of."

"Charlie," she whined, "it's getting late. When are we heading back for the city?"

"Not till we're done here," he growled.

They took the same route they had taken previously, heading north on the two-lane highway out of the village, past the chain of fast food restaurants, over the railroad tracks, past the old brewery and finally dropping down on Shore View Road past the condo complex where his brother lived. It was the only way Charlie knew how to get to the cemetery on the outskirts of Cold Water Springs. By the time they passed the old abandoned airport, it was spitting snow.

At the entrance to the cemetery, he stopped. Peggy knew better than to complain at this point.

"We'll just have to chance it," he announced.

Peggy had had enough. "For Christ's sake, Charlie, chance what?"

"We're going up there."

"What the hell for? You were just there yesterday."

"I've got to know."

"Got to know what?"

This time there was no response. He shoved the car in gear, headed through the gate of the cemetery and on up to the gravel drive leading up the hill. By the time they reached the crest, Peggy had slipped into a pouting silence. He stopped the car, crawled out and headed directly for the site of his father's grave. Peggy was right behind him.

"They've been here, all right," he muttered. He was studying the telltale car tracks and footprints that crisscrossed the area. "The question is, did they find it?"

Peggy watched him in disgust. She had asked a string of questions, none of which had been answered. At this point, she was reluctant to ask any more.

Slowly he circled his father's tomb and then his grandfather's. "They could have picked it up," he muttered. "They could have picked it up, thinking it was just an old jug that somebody left behind. They couldn't have known what it was."

Finally she grabbed him by the arm and spun him around to face her. "Damnit, Charlie, this has gone on long enough. What the hell's going on? How can I help you if I don't know what we're looking for?"

"A jar," he said simply, "a big glass jar. I left it here yesterday. I left it sitting right here on my father's tombstone."

Peggy's face twisted into a frown. "A jar?"

she repeated. "What kind of jar? A jar full of what?"

"I don't know what was in it," he admitted. Suddenly he felt a little foolish trying to explain the bizarre object he had so carefully concealed all these months.

Peggy shook her head, all the while scanning the somber surroundings. She didn't understand, and at this point she didn't want to understand what was going on in his mind. All she really wanted to do now was get away from this place, and if Charlie would ask her, she was ready to admit that she wanted to get away from him as well.

Instead, while he continued to search their surroundings, she walked up to the crest of the hill and looked out over the edge into the craggy rocks below. It was easy to reconstruct the terrible scene of Betty Elizabeth's death, fortified as she was by Seacraft's all too vivid description. To her surprise, the car was still there, a charred chunk of metal that just yesterday had been shiny and new. She hadn't known the woman very long, but in the short space of time she did know her, she knew her well enough to know that the words "expensive" and "new" described the only kind of car they would be seen in. Idly she wondered how they would ever get the car out of its resting place in the jagged rocks.

While she was still occupied with her

thoughts, she heard a car door slam. She turned to see Charlie trudging back up the hill carrying a pick, shovel and lantern. He was headed back to his father's tomb.

"What the hell's all that for?" she demanded.

"I've got to know what happened."

She stopped him again, this time by moving in between him and the gravesite. "Damn it, Charlie, this has gone far enough. If you don't tell me what this is all about, I'm leaving. So help me, I'll take the car and leave you stranded out here."

Charlie's brows furrowed into a tight knot over his squinted eyes. "You don't understand. I've got to know. My father hated me. It's all mixed up. He died and gave everything to my brother. In his eyes, Theodore was everything. I was nothing. Theodore got everything. I got nothing. You don't understand. Nobody does."

"But your father's dead. I don't see what this proves."

It was obvious now that Charlie was becoming more and more disturbed. Reluctantly, Peggy withdrew. She stepped aside, and he lit the lantern and buried the nose of the spade in the soft earth. She could hear him muttering as he went about his grisly chore. "I've got to know if it worked."

"This whole damn thing is obscene," Peggy

complained. "None of it makes any sense. What could have caused them to be up here in the first place? And what in the world would make anyone drive their car over the edge of a cliff like that?"

The shovel repeatedly gorged its way into the tortured earth around the base of the monument. Charlie's frantic efforts had already carved out a sizable hole. The pale orange shimmer of the lantern gave the whole scene a bizarre dimension of unreality that made Peggy shudder. Within a matter of minutes, he had managed to tunnel his way into the surprisingly yielding earth beneath the base. Despite the raw chill of the wind blowing in off the water, Charlie had to stop from time to time to wipe the sweat off his forehead.

Now even Peggy's mood was beginning to change. The threats were forgotten. She watched him with her own growing morbid curiosity.

The blade of the shovel hit something hard. She heard him mutter and watched as he laid down the shovel, braced his foot against the edge of the hole and put his shoulder to the cold marble of his father's monument. "Help me," he grunted. She was surprised that he thought her strength would make a difference, but it did and the stone shifted, grating along on the base until it toppled to one side, over and onto the mound of freshly dug dirt.

Suddenly Charlie was a man possessed. He grabbed the pick, gouging it into the soft earth near the partially recessed base. After three such efforts, it moved. Then with the same frantic zeal, he began scooping away the layers of earth under the base.

Within minutes they were standing at the edge of the grave, staring down at the partially revealed lid of his father's coffin. The air was suddenly heavy with the musty smell of things very old and a long time dead.

Charlie slumped to his knees, and his fingers groped along the side of the metal shell, looking for the release lever.

"My God, Charlie, you're not going to try to open that damn thing, are you?" Her question mirrored her repulsion at the idea.

His fingers found the triggering mechanism, and he pulled it out. There was a momentary hissing sound, and the nauseous smell of foul air permeated the darkness.

"Help me," he insisted.

But Peggy was unable to move. It was wrong. It was too terrible to watch, to even think about. She began to cry.

The lid yielded, and he struggled to pull it open. More dirt had to be cleared away. That accomplished, the cumbersome piece of steel slowly hinged up and revealed a scene that sent a wave of horror racing through Peggy. Even then she knew it was a sight that would haunt her till the day she died.

Slowly, deliberately, Charlie lifted the lantern and cast the pale yellow glow down into the yawning blackness of his father's tomb. Theodore was there all right, and in death he had managed to get even closer to his father than he had in life. His brother, in death, was desperately embracing the rotted remains of Malcolm Frazier. A large, broken glass jar lay beside them in the recesses of the decaying coffin.

Peggy felt her stomach revolt at the gruesome sight. She spun away, her senses reeling. A bone-chilling numbness had gripped her in its icy fingers.

Theodore's face, frozen in a bloated and discolored smile of triumph, was a grotesque testimony to his eternal achievement.

The lid mercifully slid from Charlie's trembling hands and slammed shut. The unforgettable specter had been cast back into the darkness. Numbly he turned to look at Peggy and felt his breath lock in his constricted throat as the image emerged from the shadows behind her.

"You know, Mr. Frazier, ever since I met you this morning I've been asking myself how you fit into all this." His voice was the same tired monotone it had been earlier in the day. Now, as he materialized from the shadows, Charlie realized that the Sergeant had been watching them from the very beginning. Charlie also knew that he was trapped in the immediacy of the moment. This time there were no prepared or rehearsed answers.

"Do . . . do you know what's in there, Sergeant?" he stammered.

Seacraft nodded. "Uh-huh, but I didn't know if you knew. And that, Mr. Frazier, was the key to all this."

"How could I have known?" Charlie protested.

The officer sighed and rammed his hands down in the pockets of his baggy raincoat. It was soiled, and the pockets were torn. In the flickering, too dim light of the lantern, it occurred to Charlie that his adversary looked as though he was a fugitive from a garage sale.

"Easy enough," Seacraft said. "Men in my line of work are naturally suspicious, Mr. Frazier. If they aren't, they don't make very good cops. We think the worst and expect the worst. The worst thing about being a cop is that we're usually right."

Charlie stared back at the man, unwilling for the moment to commit himself one way or the other.

"Think about it, Mr. Frazier. Your brother there has managed to amass himself a right tidy little fortune. All of a sudden his long lost brother shows up, a brother none of us have ever even heard about. And the same day that brother shows up, Betty Elizabeth drives her car over the edge of a cliff and old Theodore comes up missing. Now ask yourself, if you was me, wouldn't you think that was all kind of strange?"

Still Charlie knew better than to answer. He stared back defiantly at the hawk-nosed man, waiting for his next move.

"Well, like I said, me bein' the suspectin' type, long before I showed up at that motel this mornin' to see you and the little lady, I did some checkin'. I got ahold of the folks at Frazier Securities and found out the name of the law firm that handled your brother's legal affairs. I only had one question to ask them, Mr. Frazier. Know what that question was?"

Charlie shook his head and continued to force the smile. This was no time to blow it.

"Well, sir, I wanted to know what would happen to all that money if both Betty Elizabeth and Theodore was out of the picture. I mean, what with them not havin' any children, I got to wonderin' who would inherit all that money."

Charlie folded his arms and allowed the weight of his body to sag against his father's tilted tombstone. "So tell me, Sergeant, what did you learn?"

Mason Seacraft shuffled his boot back and forth in the dried leaves, looking up and appraising the black starless sky overhead. "I learned that a fellow by the name of Charles Frazier would suddenly become a very wealthy man."

Charlie was stunned. It was a turn of events he hadn't anticipated. He had long believed that if the day was ever to dawn when he got his hands on a portion of the Frazier inheritance, it would come only after a long protracted court battle. He glanced over at Peggy. She was already grinning in anticipation. Now he looked at Seacraft. He wasn't quite sure how to play it. Did the Sergeant really think he had something to do with his brother's death? There was only one way to find out. He decided to chance it.

"So tell me, Sergeant, are you standing there thinking I had something to do with my brother's death?"

Seacraft was the kind who was slow to let his emotions show. Eventually the frown faded, and he relaxed. "Gotta admit that at first I did," he admitted, "but I don't guess I think that now. You see, the way I figure it, if you was the one who caused all of this up here last night, you'd have hightailed it out of town by now, 'cause you'd be figuring we was still out lookin' for your brother. And, I oughta add, you'd be hopin' we never found him. But then I got to thinkin', if that really was the case and old Ted's body didn't show up, you'd be spendin' the rest of your life in the courts tryin' to get your hands on the money. So when you kept drivin' by the cemetery all day, I knew you wanted to get up here for some reason. I figured I'd just let that happen, let you come up here and find out what you knew. What I found out was that you didn't really know where the body was. It took you too long to decide to dig. If you'd have known, you'd have gone straight for it."

"But how did you know Theodore's body was in there?" Charlie asked.

"One of my men thought this whole site looked a little strange this morning when we discovered all this. We was up here investigating Betty Elizabeth's accident. He dug up your daddy's grave on pure hunch."

"That still doesn't tell us who killed Theodore."

The Sergeant shrugged his sloping shoulders. "All in due time," he said confidently, "we'll get it figured out. Only thing we know for sure at this point is that they're both dead. And," he added, "we know one other thing. Somebody went to a whole lot of trouble to put your brother's body in there with your daddy's."

Under the veil of darkness, Charlie's face began to slip back into the greedy half-smile. The damn thing worked, actually worked, and the best part about it, it was starting to look like it was going to turn out even better than he had ever hoped for.

Chapter Twelve

The lawyer's name was Robert Lamont Shurley. He was a full partner in the law firm of Merrick, Hampton, Cross and Shurley. He sat across from Charlie, leafing through a ream of papers that looked as though they hadn't been out of the files in years. His featureless face was fixed in a noncommittal blank expression that gave no indication of how he felt about the matter. He was dressed in a dark, pin stripe, three-piece suit with an expensive gold watch chain stretched ceremoniously from one vest pocket to the other.

"My father, Robert Senior, handled your father's personal affairs, Mr. Frazier. As a consequence, I had to spend several days verifying certain matters with which I was unfamiliar.''

Charlie was skeptical. He sat across the long, excessively ornate, black walnut table from the man, certain that the jousting had just begun. His brother and Betty Elizabeth had controlled a sizable majority of the Frazier Securities stock. And, by a twist of fate, the time of death for Betty Elizabeth had been officially determined to be almost an hour before her husband's, which meant that technically her stock had reverted to him and his will took precedence.

"Actually, Mr. Frazier, it's rather unusual for matters of this nature to be handled in this fashion, but the estate of your late brother, Theodore, is being handled as an extension of your late father's will."

Charlie studied the man suspiciously. "Tell me what that means in plain English."

Robert Shurley had a puffy little face that looked like it could have been made of latex. At the moment he had it contorted into his best "momentous occasion" look. "It simply means that your brother chose to leave your father's will intact. That was the way your father wanted it to be handled. Theodore simply added one small codicil."

"Plainer English," Charlie insisted.

"It means, Mr. Frazier, that you are the sole

heir. It's that simple. Except, of course, for the codicil."

"Codicil? What codicil?"

"At the time of your death, your entire estate and all that remains of the assets of Frazier Securities revert to the control of and ownership by the Portland Foundation."

"Like hell it goes to the Portland Foundation," Charlie shot back at the man. "It's mine. If and when I decide to check out, I'll do with it as I damn well please."

Shurley shook his head disapprovingly. "I'm afraid that's not possible. Malcolm Frazier's will is very explicit. Your brother's estate at the time of his death is to be turned over to you only if his wife and any heirs resulting from their union have all preceded him in death. Betty Elizabeth is dead; since they had no children, you, so to speak, Mr. Frazier, are the benefactor of their untimely demise. Frazier Securities is yours the moment you agree to the stipulation set forth in the codicil."

Slowly, as Shurley knew it would, the first traces of a smile began to inch its way onto Charlie's face. "Sure I'll sign it. For that kind of money, I'd sign my own death warrant." He reached across the table and snatched the document out of Shurley's hands. He scrawled his signature across the bottom of the yellowed sheet of paper and allowed himself the luxury of a full and hearty laugh. "Now, Mr. Shurley, stand back and watch me. What you're going to see is a man with a lot of money take this stupid piece of paper to court and have Teddy boy's codicil overturned. There ain't a man alive or dead that can tell me what I can and can't do with my own money."

Shurley studied the scrawled signature and smiled. "As you wish, Mr. Frazier. As they love to say, it's a free country. But I have to ask . . . you don't really believe that one either, do you?"

Charlie was equal to the challenge. "Tell me, Mr. Shurley, in round numbers, what am I now worth?"

The sober-faced lawyer cocked his head to one side. "Only an updated audit could pin down the exact number, Mr. Frazier, but I'd say that your net worth is somewhere in the neighborhood of between one point six and one point seven billion."

Charlie sagged back in his chair, smiling. "That's a very exclusive neighborhood. Can I tell you I'm already becoming accustomed to living there?" Then he leaned forward and placed his elbows on the table. His brain was spinning. The lawyer's casual estimate of a sum of money so large had sent his thoughts into a euphoric turmoil. He was experiencing an exhilaration unlike anything he had ever experienced before. "Tell me, Mr. Lawyer, how soon can I get my hands on some of that money?"

Charlie was oblivious to the man's look of disdain. "There is a procedure, of course," he said primly. "I will have to notify the Board of Directors of Frazier that the will of their late chairman so stipulates that you are the legal heir to your brother's assets."

"Tell me again about this Portland Foundation," Charlie suddenly blurted.

"The Portland Foundation should really be of no concern to you, Mr. Frazier. The Foundation gets nothing as long as you are alive."

"Maybe they get it, maybe they don't. I don't know who the hell they even are, but you can tell them I have every intention of hauling their ass to court to get that codicil overturned."

"That would be a long and arduous undertaking," the lawyer said. "But, of course, that's entirely within your rights. It could be in the courts for years."

"But who the hell are they?"

"Quite simply, Mr. Frazier, they were your late father's favorite charity. He was involved with them his entire life. When he passed on, the Foundation lost a true friend."

"Doesn't sound to me like anybody would mourn too long if they knew they were getting that kind of money."

The lawyer continued to glare at him. "Like I said, Mr. Frazier, it's a function of time and money."

Charlie appraised the straight-laced little man coldly. "Both of which I have plenty of. Actually, Mr. Shurley, the more I think about it, the more determined I am to keep Daddy Malcolm's favorite charity out of my knickers."

"That's your prerogative, Mr. Frazier, but I feel that it's my duty to warn you that . . ."

"Save it," Charlie shot back at the little man. He pushed himself away from the table and stood up. "When you get it figured up, send me a bill." He turned, started for the door and paused. "One last thing, lawyer man. Better call those yokels on the Board of Frazier and give them a little advance warning. Tell 'em old Charlie is coming." He waited for a moment and laughed. "Oh yeah, better tell them to start counting me out some money."

The three men sat in the last booth, their faces concealed from the rest of the patronage by the room's poor lighting. One was short, impeccably attired and obviously successful.

The second was a much taller man with a used look about him. The third was coarse and squat with a ruddy complexion and the constant look of anxiety etched into his aging face. It was their weekly meeting and the only time they met. By agreement, there was no contract, business or social, outside of these hushed, clandestine gatherings in the last booth of Carson's diner each Monday morning during the breakfast hour.

"And he never even asked what the Portland Foundation was?" Seacraft asked in amazement.

Shurley shook his head. "Hey, we're not exactly dealing with a mental giant, Mason. All this character was interested in was how soon and how much money he was going to get his hands on."

The Sergeant chuckled in amazement. "Unbelievable!" He laughed bitterly. "If someone had just told me that when I died everything I owned was going to be handed over to some outfit called the Portland Foundation, I'd damn sure want to know everything I could about it."

"It's a question he'll eventually get around to askin'," the third man in the trio opined. The words had to work their way out and around the stub of a cigar he had wedged in the corner of his crooked mouth.

Collectively, the three men were satisfied. The long unsolved riddle finally had a solution, and the end was in sight. It wasn't exactly the one they had hoped for, but it was a tolerable one. True, the distribution was going to be delayed a while longer, but the end was clearly in sight. After all, one problem was easier to solve than two.

Seacraft's eyes casually scanned the other tables in the diner. He was the unofficial sergeant-at-arms of the group and was certain that no one was close enough to overhear them. He leaned closer to the table and lowered his voice. "Okay, Henry, what the hell happened up there?"

The one with the ruddy complexion also leaned forward in an exaggerated air of confidentiality. He cleared his throat. He was facing Seacraft, but his eyes darted back and forth to Shurley's face as well. "I went out to the Frazier condo Saturday night just before ten o'clock, just like we planned. The security guard was right on schedule. He crawled in his car and slipped up the street to Wendy's, just like he always does. Well, just about the time I'm ready to slip through the gate, here comes Teddy Frazier and that skinny wife of his drivin' out. For a minute or so I didn't know what to do, but finally I decided to follow them. You can imagine what kind of weird stuff was goin' through my mind when I seen 'em pull into the old cemetery."

Henry's dissertation was interrupted while the waitress refilled their cups. He waited until she had moved toward the front of the restaurant before he continued.

"I could see them up on the top of the hill. They had a flashlight, and even though I couldn't get close enough to hear what they was sayin' to each other, I could tell by the sound of their voices they was both upset. Well, all of a sudden Betty Elizabeth starts runnin' down the hill and gets in the car. She starts the thing up, and old Ted is real upset by now and yellin' at her. Damned if she don't drop the thing in gear and drive right up the hill and over the edge of the cliff. I hear a helluva explosion, and the sky lights up like a Christmas tree. Ole Teddy runs up to the edge and watches everything. The rest was easy. By the time I got up there he was layin' on the ground blubberin' like a baby. I just walked up there and did what I said I'd do. It was easy. I could feel his back snap. He knew it was me, all right. He was screamin' and yellin' just like a little kid."

Robert Shurley still had a puzzled look on his face. "But I still haven't figured out why you dug up that grave and put him in the coffin with old Malcolm."

A corrupted smile played with the corners of Henry Lor's mouth. "Like that little touch, lawyer man?"

Shurley looked at Seacraft in a brief exchange of knowing glances.

Henry dislodged the stub of the cigar from his brown teeth and examined it. "Probably wouldn't have thought of it," he admitted, "but I guess old Betty knocked the damned tombstone off Malcolm's grave when she drove over the edge. So there I was with old Teddy layin' on the ground whimperin' and that big black hole yawnin' up at me. Honest to God, I could actually look down there and see the casket . . . and then it hit me. I figured I'd just drag old Teddy over to the hole, pry the casket open and dump him in there with his daddy. You know how he was always braggin' about how him and his daddy was so close. Just for the hell of it, I got down in there and wrapped them brittle old bones around Teddy just like they was a huggin' each other. You shoulda heard Teddy boy screamin' when I slammed that lid shut. Fact is, I could still hear him right up to the time I slid the base of that old tombstone back over the hole."

Robert Shurley felt a chill race down his back.

"Well," Seacraft sighed, "it's done. Two down and one to go."

"We won't have to wait too long," Shurley

said confidently. "I get the distinct impression Mr. Charles Frazier is one of those people that walks around with their fingers on their self-destruct button. The guy's pure toxic, filled with hate and greed. People like him don't last long."

Seacraft slid out of the booth, pulled on his raincoat and studied the clutter on the table. "Who's gonna pick up the check?" he asked idly.

"Well, this bein' a business meetin' and all, I figure you oughta," Henry said, grinning.

Robert Shurley laughed as he disengaged himself from the clutter as well. "Yeah, what the hell, Mason. Why not? After all, you're the President of the Portland Foundation. You pay the bill."

PART FIVE

Chapter Thirteen

Charlie Frazier reached out, nestled the receiver back in its cradle and leaned back in his chair. The weather forecasters had missed again. The predicted "two to four-inch accumulation by late afternoon" had failed to materialize. At the moment there was little more than an occasional spit from a cotton dry February sky hanging ominously over the Manhattan skyline. Snow or no snow, he had a great weekend planned. He glanced at his watch and smiled. There was less than an hour to go.

He sighed, locked his hands comfortably behind his head and took note of the ream of pink telephone messages Hazel had stacked neatly next to the phone. He thumbed through them idly, wondering why people even bothered to call late on a Friday afternoon. It was get-away time, time to forget about Frazier Securities and time to get away from the city. He rifled through the collection a second time—names he hadn't heard, people he didn't know, except one. Peggy Bowles. For a fleeting moment he toyed with the thought of calling her. Then he discarded the idea and flipped through the stack again. It was nothing more than a game with dumb Peggy. He knew why she was calling. He laughed. He had confided to Bertram Hollister only yesterday at lunch that he had one helluva idea for Bertram's rapidly growing toy company—a Peggy doll! Peggy dolls stood up and uttered four-letter words, a veritable string of obscenities that would make a teamster blush. Then, if you poured a little alcohol on it, the doll laid down on its back and spread its legs.

Hollister had laughed. He had laughed because Frazier Securities was holding the purse strings on his overextended toy empire and the chairman of Frazier had made the joke in passing. Bertram Hollister had no way of knowing that Charlie knew the 60-year-old toy czar had Peggy ensconced in a tidy little play pad on East Short Drive, and so he laughed. There was a bitter betraying irony in the old man's laugh, and Charlie knew why. It was make-believe imitating life; the fool plays the fool plays the fool.

Charlie knew what Peggy wanted. Charlie hadn't seen her in months and hadn't returned her calls over the holidays. Why, he wondered, did she expect him to call now?

The phone rang. Charlie glanced at his watch again. Right on schedule. Thoughts of Peggy quickly faded as he waited for the discreet little buzz that would be Hazel, dutifully telling him Kristen was on the line. Good old, ever-screening Hazel; nobody got through to the big man without first walking her gauntlet. When the buzz came, he snapped up the receiver.

The aging brunette's voice purred through the line like a cat in heat. "Mr. Frazier, there's a Mr. Raymond Armond calling."

"Raymond Armond," Charlie repeated. "Did he say who he's with?"

"No sir. The gentleman seemed quite confident you would recognize the name."

"Kiss him off," Charlie barked. He hit the disconnect button and immediately began stabbing out the sequence of numbers that would put him through to the only person he did want to talk to.

"Well," the voice informed him cooly, "you almost waited too long. I was just on my way out the door."

"I thought you were going to call me," Charlie protested.

"Why, you're a big boy. You know the schedule."

"All systems go?"

"Eastern terminal, six-forty-two. Think about it," the woman teased. "We have dinner reservations at Mama JoJo's at nine. You, me, and the moon-bathed gulf. I even checked the weather. Nothing but stars and seventy-six beautiful degrees. Think you can handle all that plus one slightly love-starved and you-know-what deprived female in the same evening?"

Charles Frazier felt that old familiar sensation. Kristen Masters was setting the stage. And classy Kristen Masters was a long way up the ladder from the Ruthies, the Cappy Salems and the Peggy Bowles of the world.

"Do I need to bring anything?"

"You know what you're going to need," she continued. "I've got all the tickets. All you have to do is show up and brace yourself for a fun-packed, sun-filled four days and three action-packed nights in glorious Florida." She paused and then giggled. "How am I doing? Like the commercial?"

This time Charlie nestled the receiver back in the cradle and hit the button on the intercom. "Hazel," he barked, "call off the dogs. I'm outta here."

"Have a nice weekend, Mr. Frazier," the sultry voice purred automatically.

Charlie released the button, picked up his briefcase and stopped just long enough to take one last fleeting look at the rapidly darkening skyline. It had started to snow. He turned off the lights and left by the side door.

In a distorted, bigger than life sense, Kristen Irene Masters represented everything that had become Charlie's way of life since he had taken over at Frazier Securities. She was a well-connected, eastern-educated slice of the big apple way of living; she was cool, hip, liberated and monied. If there was anything about the lady that Charlie Frazier would have liked to change, it was the excessive notoriety she carried around with her everywhere they went. Kristen Masters was pure front page tabloid; every woman in America was reading about her protracted, name-calling, scandal-ridden divorce from the President's top security advisor, Martin Masters. Still, it was Papa's money and her own largely private condo on Port Belle that provided them with their getaway for the weekend.

She was, for Charlie's tastes, a trifle too tall, a trifle too thin and, in the final analysis, had a trifle too much control. What Kristen Masters wanted, Kristen Masters got. She was olive-skinned with a perfectly symmetrical face, passionate green eyes and ebony black hair. She was, in every sense of the word, a user. And, at the moment, she was using Charlie.

She lifted her glass in a toast. "To Port Belle."

Charlie reciprocated and watched her slender hand snake across the table to ensnare his.

"So tell me, money man," she teased, "how goes the world of big bucks? Talk to Mama Masters about money; it's a turn-on."

"I like your world better than mine. The people that come to you come to spend money. The people that come to me come to borrow it. I always have to wonder whether I'll ever see mine again. On balance, I think you've got the better of the two deals."

Kristen smiled. "It's not my fault God made women vain. Nor is it my fault that men have this thing about their women being beautiful. When most men I know undress their little playmates, they like to feel nice things between their fingers, things like silk and lace and mink. And, my darling, just in case you haven't noticed, silk, lace and mink aren't the kind of things men bargain hunt for."

It was Charlie's turn to smile. Kristen was sending him a message, and it was coming through loud and clear.

The lady's hand pulled away and picked up the menu. "How about it? What looks good to you?"

Charlie reluctantly turned his attention to the menu and out of the corner of his eye caught the long shadow of an intruder spreading over the table. A tall, angular, somewhat disjointed looking man of advanced years was standing at a respectful distance from the table staring at them. Kristen had noticed him first.

"I think we've got company," she whispered over the rim of her glass.

Kristen was used to interruptions, used to people gawking at her in restaurants, whispering from behind upheld menus, seeing her picture in the tabloids and catching the sideways glances in elevators. But she sensed something different about this one. Charlie could see her draw back as he turned to confront the intruder.

"Is there something I can do for you?" he asked brusquely.

The man was old, much older than Charlie had at first realized. Yet despite his age, he had taken a surprisingly defiant posture. He held a decidedly outdated hat directly in front of him and, oblivious to the semitropical temperature and clear sky, he wore a tattered raincoat.

"You are Charles Everett Frazier?" The old man mouthed the words so that they came out sounding more like a pronouncement than a question, as though he was verifying something he already knew as fact.

"So what if I am?" Charlie hissed.

"I must talk to you," the man insisted.

"Look, if your business relates to Frazier Securities, I'll have to insist you make an appointment through my secretary. If it doesn't, then let me go on record as saying that your manners are really quite rude. Can't you see the lady and I are having dinner?"

The old man appeared to be completely unfazed by Frazier's initial volley. There was no effort to move. His placid expression remained unchanged. Diners at surrounding tables were turning to stare at them.

"Get rid of him, Charlie," Kristen hissed. "You're causing a scene, and we don't need that. Half the gossip columnists in Florida will know we're here within a matter of minutes."

The words had no more than escaped Kristen's mouth when Charlie's hand shot in the air as a signal to a nearby waiter. Mama JoJo's people were quick to the rescue.

"This gentleman is bothering the lady."

The old man stepped forward. "Please, Mr. Frazier, I must talk to you." His voice was raspy and warped with a sense of exhaustion.

"Get him out of here," Charlie said. "If you can't guarantee your better patrons a . . ." There was no need to finish the tirade; one waiter already had the old man by one arm and another was moving to assist him. They were hustling him toward the lobby.

"Let's get out of here," Kristen insisted.

They were already on their feet and headed for the rear entrance when a young woman stood up and thrust a piece of paper in Kristen's face. "May I have your autograph, Miss Masters?" the woman pleaded.

"I think you've mistaken the lady for some-one else," Charlie lied, elbowing his way past the young woman.

Kristen had already made it to the door, but it was obvious now that others had recognized her. The thwarted autograph seeker with her empty piece of paper looked up at Charlie and gave him an impish smile, shrugged her shoulders and sat back down at her table. "Geez," she muttered, "you'd think I'd said something to piss her off." The girl's escort tried to console her. At the same time he was glowering at Charlie. That bothered Charlie only because the young man was built like a bulldozer and appeared to have about the same amount of reasoning power.

"Better tell your skinny girlfriend to be nicer to people," he grunted, "otherwise I just might have to put a couple of dents in that shit-eatin' smirk of hers."

Charlie ignored the young man and fol-lowed Kristen. When he got to their car she was leaning against it with her arms folded.

"Why the hell didn't you quietly find out

what the old man wanted, instead of making a big goddamn deal out of the fact that you were being inconvenienced."

"I don't like being—"

"Who cares what you like?" she fumed. "All you would have had to do was listen—"

It was his turn to cut her off. "Look, can I help it if your picture has been plastered all over the front page of every goddamn supermarket rag in the country in the last two months?"

That was all it took, and Charlie knew it. Kristen wasn't built for this kind of fighting. She had her own way of handling conflict. A shout, a threat of violence, a heated exchange was all it took. The former wife of Martin Masters handled the situation the only way she knew how. For her the battle was over. The ice thawed, and the heat cycle began. She reached out and pulled him to her, encircling her arms around his neck, pressing her long slender body against him in the way all women understand all men want them to respond. She pressed her lips against his while one arm disengaged itself, slipped between them and began unbuttoning her blouse. It didn't stop until she had opened the blouse and pressed the fullness of her nakedness against him.

"Touch me," she demanded. "Touch me . . . now!"

Charlie started to comply, because that was

part of the game. He had learned it was what she wanted. But the seering pain as her even white teeth savagely sliced into the fullness of his lower lip stopped him. Then she began laughing and pushed him away. She was still laughing as he stood there staring stupidly at the inviting fullness of her exposed breasts. He could feel the sensation of the warm blood trickle out of the tear in his flesh.

"Get in the car," she hissed. "I'm not through with you."

Charlie responded like an obedient child. He walked blindly around the big Lincoln and slumped into the seat on the passenger's side. Kristen was already behind the wheel, starting the engine.

They drove through the nearly deserted streets in silence. It had been like this before. He was only partially aware of the parade of lonely streetlights, of the occasional traffic, of the young people standing on street corners, of neon lights and the relentless sound of the surf.

The woman parked the car and walked silently beside him across the parking lot. He could hear the staccato click of her heels on the pavement, and he kept on enduring the silence as they walked through the deserted lobby. In the elevator she continued to display the sullen yet provocative smile. He understood it all; it was an invitation, a promise, a threat. He was like an animal being led into a surrealistic arena. It would be barbarian and ritualistic, and yet he was anticipating it hungrily.

In her apartment, she stripped herself, then undressed him, and they consummated her uncontrolled passion time and time again until she finally rolled over on her back and huskily described in dehumanizing detail how inadequate his attempts at fulfilling her needs had been. Then she cried.

Through it all Charlie was aware that even the emotional heights and physical depths they had already explored would not be enough. Kristen was not finished with him.

When the crying stopped, she got up and walked naked through the darkened apartment into the bathroom. She would return, as she had before, with a warm, damp cloth, and she would bathe him, tenderly entreating him to forgive her and to love her. And that's how it would continue until the passion flared again and the whole scene was repeated. That's how it would be throughout the long night.

Charlie was aware of the first dim evidence of a new dawn when it was finally over. She lay beside him, her tousled head nestled in the protection of his arm. She moaned quietly in her troubled sleep. He ran the tip of his tongue over his tortured lips and tasted the bitter, salty taste of his own crusted blood.

Finally, in exhaustion, he gave in and his own eyes drifted involuntarily shut.

When he finally awoke, she was gone. And that too was as he knew it would be. He was alone in the bed, covered by a pastel yellow sheet. Somewhere, in an indescribable other world, he could hear the reassuring sounds of the surf and feel the warmth of the sun bathing the furthest reaches of the spacious room. The doors to the balcony were open, and a warm, gentle breeze caressed him.

He opened his eyes cautiously and carefully felt his puffy face and lips. He was sore and stiff and still exhausted. There was a haunting sense of emptiness in the world surrounding him. Then slowly, in a gesture tinged with trepidation, he inched his feet out over the edge of the bed and walked to the balcony overlooking the expanse of surf and sand. There were people, sunbathers all, worshipping the great burning ball in a cloudless sky. He spotted Kristen apart from the others, her long slender legs extended in front of her, a towel draped over her shoulders, sipping a drink through a straw. A beach boy hovered expectantly over her, anticipating her next need, anticipating one of Kristen's smiles and, just maybe, in his wildest fantasy, a generous tip. He laughed when he thought about how disappointed Kristen would be if she realized the devoted young man periodically averted his squinting eyes to appraise the attributes of a shapely, younger bikini-clad blonde some 30 yards further up the beach.

Charlie studied the scene for a moment, stretched his aching body and retired to the soft shadows of the living room and Kristen's well-stocked liquor cabinet. He poured a glass half full of grapefruit juice, added a small amount of ice and filled the rest with vodka. The first sip trickled its way down his parched throat and fiendishly curled its way like some evil thing into dark recesses deep inside him. The second followed the first, and there was a new awareness of all the parts of his tortured body. He was on his way back to the balcony when the doorbell rang.

He took just enough time to ferret out the robe Kristen had bought him, went to the door and opened it. Staring back at him was the same gaunt old man they had encountered in the restaurant the night before. His appearance hadn't changed; the haunted, empty look of the ages was still mirrored in his eyes.

It took Charlie several seconds to regain his equilibrium, then his face flushed with anger. "Who the hell are you?" he challenged.

There was no change in the intruder's expression. It was as if Charlie was looking into a countenance without definition, a mask without a beginning or an end. Everything was there, all the parts of another being, yet nothing was there. He felt an unexplained chill and took an involuntary step backward.

"Look, fella, I don't know who the hell you are, but you're getting to be a pain in the ass. Let me give you a little advice, old man. You're bugging me, and you're bothering my lady. If you're not long gone by the time I walk across this room, pick up the phone and call security, you'll have your skinny butt hauled off to the local police station."

The old man walked stiffly into the room and closed the door behind him. "I wouldn't do that if I were you, Mr. Frazier."

Halfway across the room, Charlie stopped. "Who the hell are you and what makes you think you can come marching into someone's house and . . ." His strident voice began to trail off as the old man reached into his pocket.

For one terrifying moment, Charlie was inundated with a blur of ill-defined amorphous images. Who was this old man? What did he want? Why was he here? What was it that was spurring on the old man's determination? Ruthie? Was all this somehow related to Ruthie? Or was it Cappy? Had Bertram Hollister sent the man to shut him up about Peggy Bowles? If the man's hand emerged with a gun, what would he do? His mind was racing. He knew Kristen kept a gun in the apartment, but he had no idea where.

As the old man's hand cleared his pocket, Charlie saw that he held an envelope. The hand that held it out to him was gnarled and palsied by the ravages of time.

He stepped forward reluctantly, as if something or someone was compelling him to do it. He reached out and snatched the paper from the man's hand, ripped it open, unfolded the single piece of paper and stumbled over the excessively ornate penmanship.

"My beloved Charles,
The time has come. A year has passed. All that you sought has been granted. It is time for the settling.
Your lover,
Jubell."

Charlie Frazier reread the document a second time and then a third. Slowly the piece of paper slipped out of his fingers and fluttered to the floor. He looked up into the face of the hollow-eyed messenger and felt a cold chill engulf him. "What," he stammered, "is this all about?"

"I am Raymond Armond," the old man whispered. "Do you not remember me?"

The images were still blurry, but the recollection of the man stepping silently out of the shadows of Jubell Caron's ornate sitting room began to crystalize. Involuntarily, Charlie nodded. He picked up the paper and read it again.

"What the hell does she want from me?" he whispered.

"Did you not agree to a time of settlement?" the old man asked.

A sinister, twisted, half-smile began to play with the corners of Charlie's mouth. "She said it, but I never agreed to it," he argued. "But I'll tell you what I'm willing to do. You prove to me that the old girl actually made good on her promises, and I'll see that you and the lady get one of the biggest goddamned checks you've ever seen. So big, in fact, that you and she can give up this bullshit routine and retire someplace where it's warm."

Raymond Armond was not a man to show his emotions. He stared back at Charlie with eyes void of color and depth and compassion. "Would you mind if I sat down, Mr. Frazier? I'm a very old man, and it has been a long and exhausting journey."

"Why not? Fact of the matter is, you can sit anywhere you like. But there'll be no day of settling till you or your lady friend can prove she's delivered what she promised."

Armond moved stiffly into the room and

lowered his angular body into one of Kristen's antique rocking chairs. He placed his hands on his knees and momentarily closed his eyes. "I am very tired," he whispered.

Charlie continued to appraise the man. His movements were incredibly stiff and mechanical. It was almost as if he had been constructed with dissimilar parts. In the final analysis, Charlie decided he looked like a man on the threshold of the longest journey of all.

Now it was Charlie's turn. He followed him into the room and settled his weight on the arm of the long sofa. "Look," he complained, "I haven't got all day. If your lady friend sent you all the way down here to give me an accounting, get on with it. Let's get this thing over with so I can get out of here and get on with more important matters."

The old man slowly opened his eyes, and when he did they appeared to be little more than empty glass orbs, tiny windows reflecting the images that he conjoured up from the recesses of his mind.

"I believe it would be best to start with the fate of one Harry Driver," Raymond droned in a monotone.

Charlie sagged back against the back of the sofa, propping himself up on one arm. "Yeah, Harry Driver. Why not? How is the pompous old prick? Still bangin' that fat little housekeeper of his?"

"Haven't you heard? Colonel Driver is quite dead!"

"Dead? Driver is dead? When? How?"

"It was," Raymond said patiently, "an affair of the heart."

"Explain," Charlie insisted. "Are you telling me that pontificating, moralistic bastard suffered a heart attack?"

"You could say that," Raymond replied.

"I hope the old bastard suffered."

"It was your revenge, Mr. Frazier. Would you have it any other way?"

The thought pleased Charlie. He forced himself out of his languid position, walked over to the bar and freshened his drink. He took a sip, savored it for a moment and drifted back across the room to stand in front of the Caron woman's messenger. "I suppose you can prove all that?"

Raymond nodded.

"Okay, so much for Driver. What about the others?"

The old man seemed to slip into a momentary trance. It was as if he were reviewing the scene before he informed the man of the details. "Are you at all interested in the details surrounding the untimely demise of the young woman known as Cappy Salem?"

"Cappy is dead?" Charlie asked numbly.

"You act surprised, Mr. Frazier."

"Sure I'm surprised," Charlie sputtered. "I

wanted something to happen to her, something that hurt, hurt bad. But not . . . not to kill her."

"I'm afraid it's a little late for that, Mr. Frazier. Miss Salem and another friend of hers died in her apartment. They were—how shall I put it?—handed over to their fate."

Charlie was stunned. He sank down into the protective folds of the couch, staring into his half-empty glass. "Funny," he muttered. "Getting even with that little slut was almost an obsession at the time, but now, when you tell me she's dead, it all seems kind of pointless."

"At the time?" Raymond repeated.

"Yeah, at the time it seemed important. Now it doesn't even seem to matter. Know something? I can't even remember what she looked like."

Armond continued to watch him. Everything about the man seemed to be detached from the reality of the moment. Finally, after a lengthy pause, he began again. "Then there was the matter of the one called Ruthie. In this case, Mr. Frazier, there was really very little that Mistress Caron could do for you."

"I don't understand." Charlie shook his head. "Why not? Getting even with that bitch was a helluva lot more important than the other two."

"I quite realize that, Mr. Frazier, but it was

apparent that your former wife had any number of acquaintances whose feelings about her were even more hostile than your own. You see, Mr. Frazier, someone murdered your ex-wife many years ago."

Charlie was speechless.

Raymond Armond hadn't finished his report. "But since you had made the arrangements, it only seemed prudent not to waste the power. Mistress Caron saw fit to dispose of all who knew and loved the one called Ruthie." The old man managed to twist the word "loved" into something sinister and hollow sounding.

Charlie was trying to catalog his emotions. He felt something akin to elation, but at the same time he felt cheated. "Ruthie is actually dead," he repeated. His victory, his moment of triumph was unexpectedly void of pleasure. He finished his drink and set the empty glass on the coffee table. "That's three of the four," he said flatly. "What about my brother?"

"Ah yes," Raymond plodded on in his toneless voice. "There is the matter of Theodore to discuss, isn't there? And as you well know, Mr. Frazier, that matter was dispatched in the most timely of fashions."

"And that, old man, is where I've got you," Charlie crowed. "You can't take credit for that one. I was there. I know what happened. You and your lady friend had nothing to do with it. He was murdered and dumped into my father's grave."

"In view of everything I have told you, how can you be so certain?" Armond asked.

"I told you, I was there."

The old man continued to sit in the chair, hands poised on his knees, seemingly oblivious to his surroundings. Only his eyes continued to move. The images that he described seemed to be in his eyes. It was as if Charlie could verify everything the man said simply by looking into those bottomless pools. Again it was a protracted interval before he spoke. "Rest assured, Mr. Frazier, the hand of Jubell Caron can be found in all these incidents, no matter how bizarre or detached they may appear to you now."

There was a hollow bravado in Charlie's voice when he insisted that the old man give him some proof of his claims. "Coincidence," he shot back at the man. "We Americans have a saying: 'Prove it'."

"That isn't necessary, Mr. Frazier. I believe you already know these things of which I speak."

To emphasize his point, Charlie let go with a big, hearty but wholly contrived laugh. "Hey, old man, you're in over your head. We're right back where we started. Anyone could sit where you are and spin some hard to swallow fairy tales about how the old witch delivered the goods and made good on her promise. You say it's time to settle up for services rendered. I like my version better. Prove what you say is true, and the lady gets her money. No proof, no payment. It's that simple. How's that for getting straight to the point?"

Armond's eyes drifted shut. He continued to sit, motionless and silent. "Very well," he finally whispered in his flat, measured, lifeless voice. "You shall have your proof."

Raymond Armond stood up and headed for the door where he paused. "Within the span of the sunset and the dawn of the new day, you shall have what you seek. Then you will know."

After the door closed, Charlie refilled his drink and walked back out on the balcony. He was laughing. He had called their bluff. He looked down and saw Kristen still sitting on the warm white sand. Like Raymond, the attentive young man had moved on. He was nowhere in sight. Only then was Charlie aware that, despite the superficial laugh, there was a growing feeling of uneasiness stirring inside him.

They had worked hard at having fun. They spent most of the early part of the afternoon exploring a near deserted stretch of beach near Calling Point. They shared a cup of bisque in an out-of-the-way seafood shanty called Musty's late in the afternoon and spent the evening on board Kristen's father's yacht at the Windmore Yacht Club watching the old man make a fool of himself over a hard-looking, too plump blonde who had only recently been endowed with the pompous title of Mrs. Geoffrey Hampton. Kristen had followed him into the galley and giggled that she couldn't remember whether the woman was wife number five or six in her father's arsenal of bimbos. Daddy Geoffrey, Kristen reflected, was likely to marry anyone who was willing to crawl between the sheets with him. It was his way of avoiding guilt feelings about his decidedly non-Catholic behavior. Besides, in Geoffrey's mind, it was, at best, a short-term arrangement. Life, he believed, was to be lived to the fullest, and no man could live to the fullest if he had to settle down with just one woman. Bottom line, Geoffrey Hampton was always looking for greener pastures.

They returned to the complex close to midnight and discovered that the doorman had tucked a hastily scribbled message in the slats of her mailbox. After the flowery salutation, the man had boiled it down to a terse one-liner. "Package from Florida Services placed just inside your door."

Inside the confines of the condo, Kristen

picked up the bulky box and studied it curiously.

"Who's it from?" Charlie asked idly.

"Don't know." She shrugged, carrying it across the room and setting it on a small table near the telephone.

"Open it," Charlie urged.

"Not right now. I'm going to get into something more comfortable first. Be a darling and fix us a drink."

Tonight there would be no ritual. The passions were still spent from the previous night. Tonight Kristen would be reflective. Tonight the topic was more likely to bend toward the philosophical—what they were doing with their lives, or what was left of their dreams. The most likely subject after the reflections would be the outcome of the long and bitter court battle with Martin. She had told him once that it was difficult simply because the man took up all the air in the room and there was nothing left for her. Charlie had been intrigued by the way she described her relationship with a man so rich and powerful that most of the women in America would have been willing to let him put his shoes under their bed.

Charlie realized that it was probably Kristen herself who was the real enigma in the toxic relationship between herself and her politically powerful husband. Kristen had money, lots of it; Daddy Geoffrey had seen to that. She had a string of upscale boutiques in major cities all across Europe as well as the U.S., and she was the kind of woman who delighted in telling, once the divorce proceedings had gotten nasty, that high-rolling Martin, despite his political connections, was a real clinker in the bedroom. Reputations were smeared, and the public had a ringside seat to the entire proceedings.

Now she came back into the room wearing a pink cashmere leisure suit bedecked with enough gold to give the semidarkened room an occasional glitter. She scooped up her martini and curled up beside him on the sofa. "Nicely done," she purred, as she took a second long sip.

Charlie was more than willing to slip into the reflective mood with her. He settled back, propped his feet up and stared out the open balcony doors at the darkened gulf. In the distance he could hear the mournful wail of a passing freighter and the occasional ominous and dire warning signal of a buoy.

For the moment, Kristen was content to sit by him and stare reflectively into the colorless contents of her glass. It was several minutes, in fact, before she disengaged herself from him, stood up and walked back over to the plain package. It was almost as if she was reluctant to open it, as though she was going to be disappointed with whatever it contained.

"You'll never know what's in it until you open it," Charlie chided.

She furrowed her brow and read the label aloud. "All it says is Kristen Masters. No address, no return address. Curious, huh?" She gave the package a gentle shake, and Charlie watched while a smile snaked its way over her sensuous mouth. "Whatever it is, it sloshes." She giggled.

Charlie folded his hands behind his head. "Surely you have some idea . . ."

"None whatsoever. I guess there's only one way to find out."

Kristen was the kind of woman that, no matter what she was doing, there was a dimension of almost catlike grace to every task. Unwrapping a package was no different. She was making it a sensual experience. Charlie leaned back and watched her supple, sensual body through the thin, clinging cashmere.

The wrapping paper fell to the floor to reveal a used, nondescript cardboard box. She was quick to tear it open and extract a large, somewhat cumbersome glass jar. She walked across the room with the object and set it on the coffee table in front of him.

Charlie had already bolted upright in his

chair. The container, the box, everything was identical to the package he had received from the Caron woman. "Stop right there," he ordered.

Kristen looked at the jar and then at her lover. Her eyebrows were arched in a questioning expression of disappointment. "Why?" she challenged. "What is it?"

"Leave it alone," Charlie hissed.

"You're serious, aren't you?"

He moved quickly from the sofa and was down on his knees staring into the contents of the jar. It was identical to the one he had mailed to Ruthie's last known address in Texas. The cloudy gray-green fluid, something not quite distinguishable seemingly suspended within, and the warm, almost alive feel of the container itself were all there.

"Whatever you do, Kristen, don't open it," he warned.

"Why? What could be so terrible about a ridiculous glass jar full of dirty water? What is this, Charlie, some kind of joke?"

"Call it anything you want, Kristen. I know something about this. It's a joke all right, but a sick joke."

Kristen continued to study the glass jar, now more curious than ever. "Well, if you're not going to let me open it, what are we going to do with it?"

"We're going to get rid of it!"

"How?"

"I don't know yet. Maybe I'll take it somewhere down on the beach and bury it in the sand."

Kristen straightened up. She was no longer amused with the situation. "I've never seen you like this."

"Trust me," Charlie pleaded.

"That's just exactly what I'm not going to do." She turned away from him, picked up the unpretentious jar and started for the kitchen. "I'll show you . . ." Her tirade gave way to a scream as the container slipped out of her hands and plummeted to the floor. It shattered as it hit, splintering in an explosion of flying glass.

Instantly, the room filled with a choking, noxious gas of fiery vapors burning their nostrils and eyes. Charlie reeled backward toward the balcony, gasping for breath, desperately seeking an escape from the foul air. He slumped to his knees, coughing, retching and feeling his lungs revolt against the onslaught.

Kristen was staggering toward him. She pitched forward, the weight of her body sagging against his. He grabbed her by the wrists and pulled her convulsing body out onto the coarse concrete floor of the tiny balcony. The skin on her wrists peeled off sickeningly in his hands to reveal a tortured network of corrupted blood vessels and mutilated muscle. His hands recoiled. He could see now that her face was little more than a mask of ruptured tissue, blistered with open lesions and gaping fissures. The skin around her once passionate eyes had been completely eaten away by the acidic action of the deadly fumes.

Charlie slumped away in a fit of coughing, rolled over and slammed his body against the steel barrier that shielded him from the three-story plunge to the beach below. His own senses were locked tight against the terrible reality of the moment.

There was a sudden and terrible silence with only the droning sound of the surf to remind him that he was still locked into this horrifying moment in time and space.

Slowly, uncertainly, he opened his eyes. The dome of darkness that spread over him was needlepointed with a complex puzzle of tiny white and blue specks of light. Mocking stars were laughing down at him from the otherwise emptiness of the black sky.

The deadly fumes were gone, gone as quickly as they had come. He sucked in the air and felt the pain of his effort slam into his lungs. Reluctantly he opened his mouth a second time. He heard the tortured sound of her name stumble out of his own blistered mouth. "Kristen!" It was both a question and a plea. He could feel the weight of her body pressing against his. He wanted to look at her, touch her, establish contact with her, but his movements were sluggish and phlegmatic.

There was a baleful moan, then a gurgling sound like a pathetic plea.

Her eyes were open, haunted things, bleached white and unseeing, darting nervously from hollowed, pointless sockets. They looked like orbs of white ivory, crazed and useless decorations in a surrealistic painting.

A scream welled up in his constricted throat.

Kristen's once symmetrical face was twisted into something unrecognizable— distorted, bloated, discolored. The flesh was gone.

Charlie recoiled and rolled over, his own body again slamming against the ornate steel bars of the railing. There was the unmistakable sound of screws ripping out of concrete, and suddenly he felt himself plunge into the terrible blackness and inevitable collision with the sandy earth.

His body made a slapping sound when it hit, and he felt enormous pain shudder through his body. Dazed and shattered, he slipped from one nightmare world into the folds of the next. Only now was there the blessing of darkness and anonymity.

They were like recorded questioning voices, different pitches, garbled, uneven, fragmented. He tried to concentrate on what they were saying.

In the background, he could hear screeching gulls and unrelenting surf. Somewhere, in the hazy distance, two children were laughing, and he could hear the wind carry away their frantic, playful words.

The other voices were clearer now. The words were strung together in whole thoughts, things he could identify.

"What do you think happened?" a woman's small, anxious voice asked.

Another voice, further away but more authoritative, speculated. "See that broken railing up there on the third floor? Looks like he fell from there."

"Damn, that's three floors," a duller voice exclaimed.

The children were laughing again. They were closer now. Maybe they were coming to join with the other voices to see what the fuss was about.

"Well," still another voice droned, "at least he's alive. We can tell that much. Only question now, I guess, is how bad is he hurt?"

Another voice, one he hadn't recorded before, offered an opinion. "Must have been one hell of a party."

"That's probably what happened, all right," the authoritative voice speculated. "The poor bastard probably got blitzed, staggered out on the balcony, leaned over it and the damn thing collapsed on him. Zingo! A three story fall."

"Thank heaven for the sand," the woman said.

It was time for Charlie to try. He had heard enough. He forced his eyes open. They encircled him, open, questioning and sunburned.

"Hey, fella, you all right?"

"You took yourself one helluva fall," another said.

Charlie raised his hand up and brought it into focus. He tried to move his fingers, flexing, stretching and making his hand into a fist.

"How bad you hurt, fella?"

Charlie gave the impromptu recovery effort the consummate test; he tried to move his body. To his surprise, everything worked. To his even greater surprise, nothing seemed to be broken. Parts responded. There was a great deal of stiffness, but there was no pain.

"Maybe you ought to have a doctor look at you before you get up and try to move around," the woman suggested.

"Hell, he's all right," another groused. "You ever see a drunk get hurt when he falls down?"

"Yeah, but he fell three stories . . ."

"Please," a new voice interceded. It was raspy and somehow seemed familiar to Charlie. "Let me handle this."

"You know this guy?" someone in the background questioned.

"Yes," the man said patiently, "and I know what happened here."

Charlie opened his eyes again. The ring of faces was little more than masks and heads silhouetted against the morning sun. He squinted into the unforgiving glare. The stoic face of Raymond Armond was staring passively down at him.

It was time to try. Charlie began to groggily work his way up, first propping his weight on his elbows, then managing to get into a sitting position. The onlookers, no longer curious about the outcome and apparently dismayed that he was going to live, began to wander off.

"It is all right to get up, Mr. Frazier. You are not injured," Raymond informed him.

Charlie looked at the gaunt old man. "How the hell would you know? You aren't the one that fell."

The old man bent over and extended his hand. "I will assist you."

The first attempt was still somewhat wobbly, but on the second, Charlie managed to regain his equilibrium. The old man's surprisingly long fingers locked around his upper arm and began steering him toward the long wooden ramp that led up and away from the beach. Within a matter of minutes he was guiding Charlie through the lobby into the elevator and back to the third floor. When they entered the condo there was no sign of the tragedy that had transpired the previous night.

Charlie, steadier now, headed straight for the balcony then back into the dining area where Kristen had dropped the container. There was no sign of Kristen or the shattered glass jar. When he returned to the room to confront Raymond, his face betrayed his confusion.

"Where is she?"

"Where is who, Mr. Frazier?"

"You know damn well who I'm talking about. Where is Miss Masters?"

Raymond Armond, in his peculiar, detached, disjointed and mechanical manner, walked wearily across the room and stood staring out at the azure blue tranquility of the placid gulf. "I'm afraid I don't know what you're talking about, Mr. Frazier."

"Damn it! The Masters woman, the woman at the restaurant, the woman that owns this condo, the woman you left the container for last night."

It was Armond's turn to confront him. He turned back to Frazier, his face void of expression. "Miss Masters?" he repeated.

"Don't play games with me, old man," Charlie shouted, "you know damn well what I'm talking about. Kristen Masters, where is she? What did you do with the body?"

"I'm afraid, Mr. Frazier, that the woman you speak of does not exist."

"What do you mean, doesn't exist? Of course she exists. She owns this place. Her picture has been on the front page of every damn newspaper in this country for the last few months."

Raymond's raspy voice had somehow taken on the tone of someone tolerating the impertinence of an unruly child. "Believe me, Mr. Frazier, there is no one called Kristen Masters."

Charlie began searching the room, opening doors and closing them, looking behind furniture and then finally back at the old man. "What the hell did you do with the body?"

Raymond Armond turned his attention back to the water. "You wanted proof, Mr. Frazier. You wanted proof of the Caron power. Now you have it."

For the next several minutes, Charlie stood stupified in the middle of Kristen's apartment, struggling with the schizophrenic kaleidoscope of his nightmare. Was any of this possible? Was this some kind of feeble-minded psychotic apprehension? What was happening to him? Was it the fall? Sure, that was it, the fall; no man could fall three stories without being disoriented. It's a wonder, he thought to himself, that my brains weren't scrambled a helluva lot more than they are. No wonder I'm confused. But I'm not confused enough to let that old man snow me about Kristen. It's a trick of some kind. You know she's dead. Make him tell you what he did with the body; then his whole story crumbles. This clown hid Kristen's body and he's trying to scare you into believing you have to go back and settle up with that Newfie bitch. No way!

Charlie wheeled around and confronted Armond. "You haven't proved a goddamn thing, old man, except that you can hide a body and clean up an apartment. What's she paying you? Whatever it is, I'll double it, triple it—whatever it takes."

Armond sighed. "I'm afraid you still don't understand, Mr. Frazier. This has nothing to do with money. There simply is no longer a Kristen Masters. My mistress sends you this sign. If she chooses, something simply ceases to exist. Such is her power."

Charlie stared at Armond in bewilderment, then was confronted with the most terrifying realization of all; it had nothing to do with the fall, it had nothing to do with logic. The bargain he had struck with the witch—the woman intended to hold him to it!

He wandered aimlessly about the apartment looking for something, anything that might allow him to hold onto his rapidly eroding hope for a reprieve. The closets were empty, the cupboards scrubbed and cleaned, even the cosmetics were removed from the vanity in the bathroom. It was exactly as Armond had said. Kristen Masters, for all practical purposes, had ceased to exist, and Charlie knew in his heart that he would never be able to prove that she ever had existed. He walked back into the room and confronted the old man again.

"Look," he said, "money talks. I've got money—lots of it. Maybe money isn't your thing, old man, but I'll guarantee you one thing—money will talk to your mistress. You call her and tell her I'll pay her a walk away price. Tell her I'll hand it over to you in cash, cold, hard cash, with a bow wrapped around it."

Raymond Armond shook his head. "I'm afraid not, Mr. Frazier. You must return to Sixkill for the day of settlement."

Small crystals of sweat began to appear on Charlie's flushed temples. His voice had lost much of the tinny overtones of bravado and confidence. "Every deal has a bottom line," he said nervously. "What happens? What happens if I don't go back?"

"You have seen the power of Jubell Caron, Mr. Frazier. Would you risk offending her?"

"Damn it, old man, what does she want?"

"Time, Mr. Frazier. Jubell Caron simply wants some of your time."

Chapter Fourteen

It was different, yet it was the same. Everything about the provincial little village looked exactly as he had remembered it. Perhaps it was the house that was different. As before, the fresh snowfall had been meticulously shoveled away from the flagstone path leading up to the house, and the wind-whipped last vestiges of winter had been shaped into lonely gray mounds that decried the hope of an early thaw.

Charlie could hear the distant rumble of the angry North Atlantic as the wind drove it mercilessly against the jagged shoreline. Out of habit, he listened hopefully for the mournful cry of the gulls that followed each surge of the unrelenting tide.

Each step he took became more tentative. The mock bravado, so evident when he had boarded the Air Canada flight at Kennedy, was gone now, giving way to agonizing uncertainty. The prospect of confronting the Caron woman left him with a sense of maddening foreboding. He took a deep breath and began to climb the steps to the sprawling porch.

Unlike his previous sojourn to the isolated place, this day was without storm. It had dawned gray and stayed gray, threatening but failing to live up to that threat. Now it was late afternoon.

Just as he had 13 months ago, he knocked. Unlike that time, he knew what to expect.

The door opened and she stood there, just as lovely, exciting, provocative, and beautiful as any woman he had ever seen. Her smile radiated. Her eyes invited. She was seduction personified. "Ah, Mr. Frazier," she said dreamily, "I have been expecting you."

Charlie again stepped into the Caron woman's world of elusive shadows created by countless shimmering candles. They were the only illumination in the room. This, too, was exactly as he remembered it—ornate, intoxicating, beguiling.

His first fumbling efforts at speaking were aborted by the sudden rush of those recollections. His words choked off, leaving him standing foolishly, staring at the woman like a stunned schoolboy awed by enchanting beauty.

"You look quite different, Mr. Frazier." The Caron woman's appraisal was cool and measured, almost mocking in its confidence.

"Some things have changed," Charlie finally managed.

Jubell Caron glided toward him and around him, assisting him with his coat, taking it from him and laying it aside. She moved with an effortless grace, making no sound, accomplishing her task with an unnerving ease.

He followed her, just as he had the first time, into the great room with its crackling fire and the somber, shadowed corners that concealed things. She offered him a seat beside her on the plush velvet love seat. It was, he realized now, part of the ritual. He felt stilted and uncomfortable. Despite the draft, the subtle movement in the heavy drapes, the room seemed uncommonly warm.

She turned to him. There was an expectancy in her voice. "I thought perhaps you had considered not returning."

"I saw no reason to," he replied.

A small frown played with the corners of her cool, gray-green eyes. "Why, Mr. Frazier? Is it because you thought I had not acted upon your request?"

"That's exactly what I thought," he said candidly.

Jubell's frown intensified. "Is it true that you are as skeptical now even as you were then?"

It was Charlie's turn to smile. He was more sure of himself now, and he leaned back indolently in the folds of the massive piece of furniture. "Skeptical isn't the word for it. One year ago I made a nebulous request, and you made a nebulous response. I hardly consider four oversized jars of muddy-looking water to constitute the fulfillment of a contract. Then when you had your friend Raymond chase me down for this ridiculous thing called a day of settlement, I got a little angry."

"Angry?" the woman repeated.

"Hell, yes. This little den of candles and wiffle dust isn't exactly on my way to the office. I'm too busy to play games."

"I have fulfilled your request," she said evenly.

"Oh really, Madam Caron, can you prove that? Your man Armond couldn't prove it."

"Let me ask you a question, Mr. Frazier." Jubell Caron, despite her beauty, managed to convey a cold and chillingly calculating aura. "It is a very logical one. If you did not believe in my powers, why did you seek me out to inform me of your desires?"

"Call it a lark. Call it boredom. Call it anything you want."

The Caron woman stood up, both exquisite and elegant in her long, flowing velvet robe, and slowly traversed the room until she was standing by the row of candles burning on the mantle. She removed one from its holder and turned back around to face him. She held it so that the flickering flame cast a shimmering pale yellow light on the shadows concealing her features.

Charlie gasped. He realized that he was looking into the mutilated and haunted face of a dying Cappy Salem.

"Why did you do this to me, Charlie?" the young woman pleaded through her grotesquely twisted mouth.

"My God," he muttered.

"Was what I did so terrible that you had to do this to me?" she sobbed.

Charlie's hand flew to his face in an abortive effort to fend off the terrible sight of the young woman's agony. He recoiled because it looked as though the specter was coming toward him. Charlie turned away, choking on his own revulsion. Then, as if some dark and sinister force was compelling him to do so, he turned back to face her again. The terrible vision had vanished, and Jubell Caron was staring passively back at him.

"You recoil, Mr. Frazier," she said calmly. "It is rather frightening to live with the reality of our most darkly harbored desires, is it not?"

"What . . . what happened to her?" Charlie stammered.

The Caron woman somberly studied the wavering flame of the candle, waiting before she answered. When she looked up, her voice was husky and muted. "I will say only this. The young woman's fate was decreed by you—and you alone."

"But, I didn't say anything about mutilating her or killing her," Charlie protested.

Jubell sighed. "It was the lesser of evils," she said dreamily. "The mutilation without death would have been a terrible injustice for a young woman with her needs. She would have been deprived of everything she desired in this life. For that, even I have compassion."

Charlie didn't know why, but he got up and slowly began walking toward the woman. He was trembling; his heart was pounding.

Harry Driver was standing before him, no longer arrogant, no longer the officer and gentleman personified. There was a gaping hole in his chest, and the front of his ravaged pale blue military shirt was discolored by crusted blood. He stood dejectedly, his mouth hanging open as though it had been unhinged by the trauma. His face was drained of color.

The words fell out of Charlie's mouth. "My God, Harry, what happened?"

The ghostly white face contorted as the man struggled to mouth a response. The effort produced only a series of incoherent and vile guttural sounds as the half-formed words hissed out of the terrible hole in the man's chest.

It was the consummate revenge. Harry Driver was stripped of his power, his authority and his dignity; standing stupidly in front of Charlie, Driver was unable to communicate, unable to defend himself against the man who had willed this thing upon him.

Impulsively, Charlie's hand reached out to touch the tortured image, testing his senses against the horrible reality of what he saw. Instead, his trembling fingers made contact with the silky smooth skin of the woman who had been his most passionate lover.

"Are you now convinced, Mr. Frazier?" the woman asked evenly. She had made the transformation to Harry Driver and returned again right before his unbelieving eyes.

"Then Driver is dead, too?" he muttered dejectedly.

"Driver, too!" the woman confirmed.

Charlie stared back at the woman, trying to comprehend the terrible images she had conjured up for him.

She moved in closer to him and he could

feel the warmth of her body. "I wanted to please you," she said huskily.

Charlie turned away from the woman and walked stiffly back into the center of the room. Then, still in a daze, he walked soberly over to the heavily draped windows to stare out at the fading grayness of the day. There was a twisted kind of half-smile on his otherwise stunned face. When he spoke, his voice was muted by his strained emotions. "Should . . . should I assume that my beloved ex-wife suffered the same fate?"

Jubell Caron sighed. "Not all things are as we see them. She was once your lover and she pleased you, but in the end there were others whom she displeased as much as you. But the powers of Jubell are strong, Mr. Frazier. The circle is round, the cycle is complete. She, too, has joined those who face the consuming fires of hatred in a life without life."

"You'll have to be a helluva lot more specific than that. I have to know. Is she dead?"

The woman got up and approached him again, this time encircling him with her long graceful arms and drawing him to her. "Are you not pleased?" she whispered.

Charlie pushed her away. "Answer my question, damn it. What about Ruthie? Is she dead, too?"

Jubell nodded. "Your anger is wasted. She has been dead a long time."

The sensation was one of enormous relief. Pleased, suddenly freed from his hatred, he felt the initial stirrings of his passions. He pulled the woman to him and covered her mouth with his, his hands hungrily searching the firmness of her warm body. She clung to him, then pushed him away.

"I must resist until you know everything. Only then will I know if I have pleased you."

"What do you mean?"

"There can be no settlement until you know everything. Are you not curious about your brother?"

"I was there. I know what happened. He was murdered, and someone put his body in my father's grave. In this case, I know for certain that all this supernatural mumbo jumbo of yours had nothing to do with it."

Jubell's lovely face softened. "Are you so certain, my lover?"

Charlie studied the woman at length before answering. "No," he finally admitted, "I'm not certain. I'm no longer certain about anything."

Jubell stepped forward again, this time reaching out for his hand. She entwined her fingers in his and tenderly led him down the long, shadowed hall into the bedroom. With one hand she caressed his aching body, with the other she easily manipulated his clothing. She was breathing heavily in anticipation. But

Charlie's passions were momentarily numbed, muted by his fears. He began to whimper, cringing as horrifying images danced eerily around him, mocking his nakedness, laughing at his humaness. Jubell Caron's lovely face was rapidly transforming from one ghostly image to another, creating a kaleidoscoping nightmare of hate and anger and revenge.

She covered him as though she would devour him. He could hear words, but he could not understand them.

"This is the day of settlement," she breathed. "I have pleased you, and now, you will stay with me always."

He was imprisoned in her lust, and Jubell cried out in her passions.

The word was ringing in his head like a distant, mind-numbing echo; always . . . always . . . always.

Then it happened. There was one fleeting, terrible moment when everything crystalized. They were all there, intertwined in one maddening montage—Ruthie, Cappy, Kristen, Betty Elizabeth—laughing at him, becoming one with the woman called Jubell.

He knew it was too late. Charlie Frazier had forfeited his right to escape, and to live.

When she plunged the blade into his still heaving chest, he made no sound. The day of settlement had come.

Epilogue

Her radiance was reflected in the dark crimson burgundy in her glass. She was smiling. She was, Raymond Armond thought, even more lovely than he had ever seen her.

The ornate silver tray displayed it all in front of him.

On it lay the heart, the hand, the brain and the small silver vial that he had only heard about.

"They are yours," she smiled, "my gift to you. You are whole again, Raymond Armond. You have paid your settlement, and you have served me well."

The old man surveyed the items spread out before him and tried to cope with his disturbing uneasiness. He turned his no longer haunted eyes toward the woman. "I must ask," he inquired uncertainly, "since it has been a very long time. Is there much to fear in the world I venture back into?"

Jubell Caron intensified her radiance. "Would I give you less than you have given me?"

"I am afraid I do not understand, Madam."

"Charles Frazier was a shallow man, my trusted friend, a shallow man with an intense but short-lived hatred. He was not strong, nor brave, nor particularly clever. He was a user. And now, we will use him. He had neither the capacity for true love nor the capacity for sustaining his hatred. Even in his desire for revenge, he was without commitment. You, my friend, must use what he did not use."

"Then I am free?"

"You are free!"

The old man walked stiffly over to the table and picked up the tray. He nodded his gratitude to the woman and left the room.

Jubell Caron smiled, took a sip of the burgundy and fixed her languid pale green eyes on the softly pirouetting flames in her fireplace.

The doorbell rang.

"Please answer the door," she called out softly. "I believe we have a visitor."

A gaunt man with the vacant and hollowed

expression of the living dead stepped mechanically from the room's brooding shadows and started for the door. He opened it, admitted the guest, and ushered the youthful caller in from the cold.

"Do come in," Jubell smiled, "I am Madam Caron."

The young man stared back at her in amazement. The woman didn't look anything at all like he expected.

Jubell knew what the young man was thinking. She walked gracefully across the room and took his coat. She ushered him over to the fireplace. "It's a rather nasty day for such a long journey," she said.

"How . . . how do you know how far I've come?" the young man stuttered.

"A mere parlor trick," she admitted. Then she turned to the man with the haunted face and hollow eyes who had let the young man in. "Our guest looks weary from his journey. Why don't you get him something to drink, Charles?"